PEOPLE DON'T JUST DISAPPEAR

CLAIRE ALLAN

Boldwood

First published in Great Britain in 2025 by Boldwood Books Ltd.

Copyright © Claire Allan, 2025

Cover Design by Lisa Horton

Cover Images: Shutterstock and [Miguel Sobreira] Arcangel

A CIP catalogue record for this book is available from the British Library.

Paperback ISBN 978-1-83533-441-6

Large Print ISBN 978-1-83533-440-9

Hardback ISBN 978-1-83533-439-3

Trade Paperback ISBN 978-1-80656-096-7

Ebook ISBN 978-1-83533-442-3

Kindle ISBN 978-1-83533-443-0

Audio CD ISBN 978-1-83533-434-8

MP3 CD ISBN 978-1-83533-435-5

Digital audio download ISBN 978-1-83533-437-9

This book is printed on certified sustainable paper. Boldwood Books is dedicated to putting sustainability at the heart of our business. For more information please visit https://www.boldwoodbooks.com/about-us/sustainability/

Boldwood Books Ltd, 23 Bowerdean Street, London, SW6 3TN

www.boldwoodbooks.com

For
Joe & Luka
Always

PROLOGUE

The crying is shrill. Persistent. And nothing seems to be able to stop it. There are no words that seem able to bring comfort. No way to end the constant whining and pleading for something that can never happen.

Threats haven't worked. If anything, they have increased the lamenting and the wailing that makes his body react as if he were listening to fingernails being scraped down a blackboard.

He just wants it to stop. He can't think while this is happening. There are times when he doesn't feel able to breathe. There are times when he can feel anger seize him and start to squeeze every molecule of his body so tightly that he swears he will explode.

It should be easier by now. It's not that hard to get the message that life has changed and that it's not going back to how it was and that of course it's not fair, but life is not fair.

If it were fair, he would not be listening to the whining, and the crying, and the begging.

If it were fair, he would not be the person having to deal

with this. He didn't ask for it. So why is he the one picking up the pieces? Why is he the one trying to fix it?

Meanwhile everyone else, all those people who should carry the blame and the burden, are getting on with their lives as if nothing had ever happened.

He didn't do anything wrong.

And all he is trying to do is the very best he can to get through it.

He feels deep in his soul that he is doing the right thing. His intentions are pure. He doesn't know why she can't see that. He's a reasonable man. It's not like he has kept his rules from her. She knows exactly what is expected of her... and why.

But how is he supposed to think when she just won't stop with the noise? His temper rises further, his muscles tensing.

'I warned her,' he says to the boy who is sitting, wide-eyed, under the table. The boy doesn't respond; instead he just holds tighter his toy car, crashing it into the overturned toy truck. 'She won't listen. She won't obey the rules and we know what happens when people don't obey the rules...' He is pacing back and forth, ranting, muttering under his breath while the boy's eyes focus on him, following him as he paces across the kitchen again and again.

The man's mind is racing. What to do? What next? This should never have been up to him. None of this should have been his responsibility, but people had let him down. She had let him down. Let *them* down, he thinks as he glances at the boy. More trouble than he is worth. But it's not his fault either. He's not the one who needs to be punished, he thinks, as he lifts the keys to the cellar gate from the table.

1

BRONAGH

She doesn't know she is being watched, and that it's not the first time. She has no reason at all to suspect that something is about to happen that will forever change her.

She is existing entirely in the moment. A moment where rain falls fat and heavy, bouncing off the pavement and the bare skin of her feet. She'd known that today was not a day for wearing sandals, but what else was she supposed to wear when going to get a pedicure? Fumbling in her bag for her keys, she tries to distract herself from the slimy sensory hell of her wet feet sliding against the insoles of her Birkenstocks, reminding herself that in two short days she will be lying by a pool in Alicante drinking in the sunshine.

The rain starts getting harder, falling from the sky in merciless sheets. She can hear the rattle of it off the window to her right, the frantic rhythm of it beating against the ground, drowning out all other noise. Cursing herself for not bringing her small bag where keys have no hiding place, she digs around blindly amid tissues, lipsticks, opened letters and loose change, sure her hand will find what she is looking for any second.

She glances down to try and spot them, allowing the rain to hit the back of her neck before rolling in icy rivulets down her back. She shudders, swears under her breath and then feels her entire self sag with relief as her fingers meet the cool metal of her front door key. Already she is mentally calculating how long it will take for her to get inside, switch the heating on for a quick blast, grab a towel, run the shower and get under the steaming hot water so that she can get some warmth into her chilled bones.

Stepping inside, she kicks off her Birkenstocks – shoes definitely designed for summer wear and not for rainy days in October. The raspberry pink of her polished toenails does give her cause to smile though. They scream of the promise of warm sand and cold drinks. Of walking along the edge of the water, her feet being tickled by the incoming waves.

Having clicked on the thermostat and delighted in hearing the boiler come to life, she grabs a fresh fluffy towel from the tumble dryer and heads for the stairs and the highly anticipated shower. Already she has planned that she will wear her fleece-lined joggers and oversized hoodie when she is done. A pair of fluffy bed socks too. She might even allow herself the treat of watching TV from the comfort of her bed, under the warmth of her duvet. Maybe with a mug of milky tea and a chocolate biscuit for a treat. It counts as self-care, surely?

Climbing the stairs, she is scrolling the Spotify app on her phone, looking for the perfect soundtrack for her shower. Today, she decides, feels like a day for singing at the top of her lungs along to her favourite tunes from musicals. No one else is home. She can harmonise as loud as she wants and indulge in her fantasy of being a star of the West End. It's a dream that will never come true – her singing leaves a lot to be desired – but still, she enjoys daydreaming about stepping onto the stage, and about the hushed anticipation of the watching audience.

Having set the shower running to heat the bathroom a little, she is laying out her clean clothes on top of her bed when an almighty pounding at the front door startles her.

'Jesus Christ!' she gasps, her hand automatically clasping her chest and her now-hammering heart. There are a few tension-laden seconds of silence before another knock, even more frantic, rattles the door.

Looking around her, as if the right thing to do will make itself known in front of her eyes, she wonders if she should just ignore whoever it is. If it is someone belonging to her, they can always call her if they need her this urgently. Her friends and family are all at work, or on the other side of the country. Mal, her boyfriend, is most definitely in London on business. Hadn't she FaceTimed with him not half an hour ago? He was between sessions at a conference on funding and accessibility in the arts. When they had spoken, he had been his usual brand of passionate about his job and angry about increased cuts coming down the pipeline. As a programmer for a non-profit community theatre, he has been fighting an increasingly difficult battle for the last few years. This forthcoming holiday will do him the power of good and give him the chance to recharge.

It's probably just kids playing 'Knock', she surmises.

But as the door rattles a third time, she decides she can't ignore it. Whoever is pounding on her door clearly wants her attention and isn't prepared to wait.

She leaves her towel on the bed, plugs her phone in for a quick charge and pads down the stairs in her bare feet. It's only as she gets closer to the door that she hears the sound of crying. If she's not mistaken, it sounds like a woman, or maybe even a child. Strange as it sounds, the crying reassures her a little. She doesn't feel quite so unnerved opening the door to a woman or a child. In fact, if it means she can help them, then she actually feels quite good about it. A little smug even.

She isn't expecting the sight that greets her. A boy, perhaps five or six – she never has been very good at estimating the ages of children. She's not had too much experience of them apart from her best friend Shelley's three-year-old twins. He definitely looks older than them, but not all that much. There are still hints of baby face in his features – all wide eyes and messy hair. His eyes are red-rimmed, his face wet with tears – tears that have carved their way through the grime of unwashed cheeks. His hair is more than just messy; it is unkempt. Dirty blonde with an emphasis on the dirty. His little hands are curled into fists, either bruised or also in need of a wash – she can't quite tell – and he looks at her with a mixture of fear and hope.

'Mumma!' he says, his voice toddler-like, but hoarse.

'Hello,' she says, crouching down to look him in the eyes. 'Have you lost your mummy?'

He shakes his head, before calling out again, more urgently this time: 'Mumma!'

'Your mummy isn't here, pet,' she says. 'What's your name?'

'MUMMA!' he calls again, his distress increasing further.

'Why don't you come in out of the rain and we'll see what we can do to find your mummy?' she says, unsure if she's doing the right thing or not. Ordinarily she wouldn't allow a strange child into her home, but the boy appears to be alone and is very distressed. She peeks her head out of the front door, looking up and down the quiet street for any trace of his mother. She doesn't think he's from here. She's sure she's not seen him before – but how much attention has she really paid her neighbours anyway?

She feels a small hand grab hers, trying to pull her out of the door. 'Mumma!' he cries again, impatiently, as if he can't understand why she isn't automatically clear on what it is he wants.

'Is your mummy out there?' she asks and he nods enthusiastically, tugging at her hand to follow him. Maybe, she thinks, maybe his mother is out there and is hurt and the poor mite has run for help?

'Hang on!' she says. 'Let me get some shoes.'

The child is becoming more agitated again, but he lets her go as far as the bottom of the stairs where she slips her feet into the discarded Birkenstocks, cringing at the unwelcome feel of the wet insoles. Momentarily she wonders if she has time to grab her trainers but the little boy is now almost hysterical, wailing 'Mumma!' over and over again, until she nods and follows him down her garden path, leaving her front door ajar.

He picks up pace, running on skinny legs clad in well-worn joggers, which are at least an inch too short and as sopping wet as her feet. Keeping ahold of her hand, he runs to the end of the street, turning left towards the greenway that runs behind the houses. It's then she spots a car – one that has clearly seen better days – half spun around on the grass, its wheels having cut deep troughs in the mud. Both the driver's door and the passenger door are wide open but there is no one nearby outside.

'Is your mummy in the car?' she asks, trying to prepare herself for what she might see. It doesn't look like there has been a collision but it's clear that something is wrong. Something is definitely not as it should be.

The little boy simply tugs more on her hand and speeds up, running towards the car. From about twenty metres away, she can see a figure slumped in the passenger seat. A pale face, a mass of dark curly hair, head lolling to the side. Her heart rate quickens. If this is the little boy's mummy, then who was driving? Where are they? Surely no one would have left a person unwell or injured and run off? Not with a child in the car too. She glances around again, but can't see any sign of another person.

Reaching the passenger side, she stalls as she sees the way the wheels of the car have churned up the grass and how the rain has done a great job of creating a muddy mess. Knowing her slip-on sandals will be no match for the mud, she runs back to the driver's side, climbing onto the seat and reaching across to the woman.

'Hello!' she calls. 'Hello! Can you hear me?'

There is no response.

'Are you okay? My name is Bronagh. I'm going to get you some help.' Her hand reaches to her pocket for her phone and only then does she remember it is not here. It is on her bedside table, ready for her shower performance.

'Fuck,' she swears under her breath.

'Mumma,' the little boy says, his voice more mournful now as Bronagh climbs into the driver's seat and reaches for the unconscious figure. There's no obvious sign of injury. No blood. No broken bones. But the figure is pale, silent. A sickening grey colour. Cold dread trickles down Bronagh's spine as she steels herself to reach across and place two fingers on the pulse point of the little boy's mum. Willing a reassuring pulse to make itself known, she knows she is fighting to hear anything over the thumping of her own heart.

She feels nothing. Hears nothing but the little boy's crying. She reaches across farther, lifts the woman's eyelids, hoping for a reaction. She's just about to move backwards out of the car and run back home for her phone when she feels the deadening thud of something heavy crash into the back of her head.

Gasping, she wills herself to fight the blackness that is coming over her, but she knows it is pointless. She can't stop it. As the pain settles into her skull, her neck and her very teeth, she realises she doesn't want to stop it either. She just wants this searing agony to end. Which it does as the world around her fades out and the call of 'Mumma' is silenced.

2

MAL

Bronagh has not answered her phone, nor messaged him, in more than twenty-four hours. *This must be a new world record* he types into his phone before sending her yet another message, wondering if it – like the two he has already sent this morning – will also sit unread in her inbox.

This is completely out of character for the woman who normally has sent a reply before he has even had a chance to slip his phone back into his pocket but, he supposes, there must be a first time for everything.

She has promised that she will keep her phone in her bag, and on silent, while they are on their imminent holiday – save for when she wants to take a few pictures – and he has agreed to do the same. Maybe she's just getting in some pre-holiday practice.

They've both been working flat out and deserve to totally switch off. He knows it's likely that she is only too aware of how hard he finds it to switch off from work mode and if his phone were at his side constantly, he wouldn't be able to resist the urge to check his emails or pop off a few ideas to his team. That is the nature of his work – he always has to be chasing funding streams, or exhibitions, acts and facilitators to keep the centre open and thriving.

If he has felt the telltale signs of burnout creeping in, he has pushed them to the side and done his best to just keep going, but he knows he is on borrowed time. Bronagh is right about that. They need to put themselves first – as a couple and individually – for a while.

He smiles when he thinks of how excited she has been about this trip. She has revelled in all the details that he finds boring – arranging travel insurance, booking a hire car, packing their cases and planning an albeit fluid itinerary so they do more than lie by the pool all day.

Not that Mal would mind lying by the pool all day, if he were being honest. Especially if Bronagh is there beside him in one of the bikinis she has bought for the trip. Just the thought of her soft skin exposed and browning under the glare of the Spanish sun is enough to make him weak in the knees. Their sex life has become one of those things that they have also neglected, and which they have promised to prioritise once they get away from it all.

It might be low-level cheesy, but he has arranged for the bed in their hotel room to be scattered with rose petals and for a bottle of champagne on ice to await them on arrival. He absolutely is going to start as he means to go on. It has been a tough year and he wants this to be a trip where they reconnect fully. He knows they have it in them to make this work and he knows they *have to* make it work. He doesn't like to think of the holiday as a 'make it or break it' kind of affair, but deep down that's how he feels. And he doesn't want to lose her.

So he doesn't like that Bronagh hasn't read – never mind replied to – his messages. Not in a controlling way. He's not like that. He's always prided himself on being fairly laid-back. In fact, Bronagh has teased him on more than one occasion that he is so laid-back that he is practically horizontal. Mal sees it differently though. Why sweat the small stuff? He trusts Bronagh implicitly. He has no reason to jump to the worst possible conclusion if she doesn't reply to his messages straight away. It will simply be the case that she is busy with something. Or at least that's how he used to think. He has to acknowledge that he does perhaps sweat the small – and even the tiny – stuff these days.

This doesn't feel particularly small though. It's not her normal pattern of behaviour. Normally they wouldn't go this long without being in touch with each other. And especially not when a holiday is only a day away. Bronagh would normally be bombarding him with holiday-themed memes or fantasising about what cocktails they can drink. She'd be sending him cheeky little messages with pictures of the afore-mentioned bikinis, reminding him she's just been waxed from head to toe and spray-tanned to within an inch of her life so she doesn't stick out like a big white thumb on the sunbeds. Maybe her heart isn't in it as much as he'd thought, or maybe – he thinks as his stomach sinks – she has already checked out of their relationship. Maybe her earlier excitement was just an act – a case of 'fake it 'til you make it'.

Pushing down the uneasy feeling, he reminds himself he'll be home soon and he'll see her then. It will all be grand. His nerves are just getting to him. Twenty minutes will have him from City of Derry airport back to her. She's probably just misplaced her phone or something. Although he has never known his girlfriend to let it out of her sight, often joking that she loves it more than him – even though he knows, doesn't he, that she loves the very bones of him.

Still, as the taxi pulls out of the airport and heads back towards the city itself, he does another scan of her social media, hoping he will see some post or comment that will reassure him that all is well. Before they know it, they'll be drinking Aperol Spritz on the warm sand – a bright blue sky replacing the dull great clouds above him. It will be fine. It will all be fine.

* * *

Stepping out of the taxi, Mal sees the curtains twitch in the house next door to his and Bronagh's.

Bronagh's right when she says you can get away with nothing on this street, he thinks wryly. Someone is always watching. And that someone is usually Mrs Cosgrove. A woman in her eighties, she's relatively harmless. They could do worse when it comes to neighbours. Her hearing problems at least mean they can listen to their music as loud as they want on a Saturday night without annoying anyone, and she never complains about taking in parcels for them – which is a good thing since Bronagh is never done ordering online. He's long learned to stop asking questions.

The only problem, as such, with Mrs Cosgrove is that she likes to engage Mal in long conversations, which he doesn't have the heart to bring to an end too quickly. Clearly the old woman is lonely and it's no wonder she wants someone to chat with; he just wishes it weren't always with him. Bronagh jokingly refers to their neighbour as a cougar and Mal as her prey. Most of the time, he laughs it off but sometimes there is something about the way the older woman looks at him that gives him the distinct impression Bronagh is not far off the mark.

He is certainly not in the mood for one of her chats. He just wants to get inside, see Bronagh and celebrate the fact he doesn't have to worry about work for a whole two weeks.

Relief had washed over him when the taxi had pulled up and he had seen Bronagh's car parked in the driveway. That meant she was home and he could get down to teasing her about not taking his calls straight away – before chasing her up the stairs for some reunion sex of course. Thinking about the time they would spend together on holiday has put him in the mood, despite him being tired and a little hungover if truth be told. He might only have been away for three days, but it's a few weeks since they've had sex and he wants to rectify that as quickly as possible.

If he's quick enough, he can get into the house before Mrs Cosgrove reaches her front door. She's not half as nimble on her feet she used to be. He does keep meaning to ask her if she has thought about arranging some sort of home help. Surely there has to be some support available for an octogenarian living on her own? He'll wait until after his holiday to have that conversation though. He doesn't want anything to stall him.

Having grabbed his bag from the cabbie, he has raced up the path and is almost, tantalisingly, close to the front door when he hears her soft, reedy voice.

'Ah, there you are, Mal. I've been wondering where you've been!'

Swearing internally, he turns around and smiles at her. If he's not mistaken, she colours a little. 'Away with work for a couple of days, Mrs C. Nothing too exciting. But Bronagh and I are off on holiday tomorrow.'

A look of confusion passes over his neighbour's face and she takes a few steps closer to him. 'Oh, are you meeting her out there? Only, she's not been here this past day and a half.

Don't be getting mad at her, but she even left the front door open when she left. I spotted it on my way back from the shops and closed it for you. I thought she'd be back before now so I could mention it to her but—'

'What do you mean she's not been here?' he asks, failing to keep the alarm from his voice.

'Well, I've knocked on the door a few times and no one has come to answer it. And there have been no lights on in the evenings. You really should get one of those timer things, you know. Make people think there's someone at home. You'd never know who'd be watching your house these days.'

A deeply uneasy feeling settles in Mal's chest. Bronagh not there, and the car still in the drive? Coupled with her not reading his messages?

'Did she tell you she was going somewhere?' he asks, desperately trying to fit the puzzle pieces together even though nothing seems to be making any sense.

'No. No, as I said, I went to the shops and when I came back, I noticed your front door was open to the world. God knows who and his mother could have been in your house and away with all your belongings, so I went up and rapped on the door to let Bronagh know. Well, either she was out and left the door swinging behind her, or she was hiding from me again...' Mrs Cosgrove gives a wry little smile that makes Mal feel well and truly caught out. Yes, they have been known to hide from their neighbour from time to time. No harm meant to her, of course. They just didn't always have the time for mammoth conversations about the weather, or the bins, or dog fouling for that matter.

'Ah now, she wouldn't do that...' Mal says, but he knows it sounds weak.

'Well, whatever the reason, there was no answer. And I

shouted up the stairs and everything. So I figured she must've just nipped out and the door hadn't caught on the latch or something. Easy done when you're rushing, I suppose. Anyway, I pulled the door closed and went on home.'

'Thanks for that,' Mal says.

'It's not a bother. Sure isn't it what neighbours are all about? I was going to come over and tell Bronagh she'd left the door open when I next saw her, but as I said, there's not been a hint of movement since. Not her car, nothing. I started to wonder if maybe you too had had a falling-out or something? But then I said to myself, sure the wee girl would've taken her car, surely.'

Agitation nips at Mal. He knows his neighbour is fishing for gossip, when really all he wants to do is get inside and see for himself if Bronagh is there. It's not possible that she's left him, is it? I mean, to give the old woman her dues, she has it right. If Bronagh had gone, she'd have taken her car with her. Wouldn't she?

No sign of her. Her car untouched. Their front door left swinging open. Messages unread and unanswered. He doesn't know how long he can go on trying to fool himself that everything is as it should be. Starting to feel on edge, he has to put his mind at rest as quickly as possible, so he thanks Mrs Cosgrove for her concern, tells her he is absolutely sure there is nothing to worry about and that he will let her know Bronagh is okay once he speaks with her.

The older woman nods and for a split second, Mal thinks he hasn't got his message through and that she is going to stand there, on the front path, and wait for immediate confirmation of proof of life.

'You better get back inside,' he says, nodding to her house. 'Looks like rain is coming in again.'

'Aye, maybe,' she says and starts to shuffle away reluctantly while Mal puts his key in the lock and turns it. He is winding himself up for nothing, he tells himself. His gorgeous Bronagh will be up to her eyes in packing, Airpods in her ears and bopping around the bedroom, oblivious to any noise around her. The lights will have been off last night because she was round at Shelley's or something. They'd have sunk a bottle of wine, and she'd have slept over. That will be why her car never left the drive. And an open door? Sure, it's easy to do...

But as he walks into the house, he immediately knows something isn't right. It's cold – the kind of cold that comes with being unoccupied for a day or two. He almost slips on the day's post, which is still lying behind the door. Even if she had stayed over with Shelley, surely she'd have been home before now?

'Bronagh?' he calls. 'I'm home. Are you here?'

As his question is met with silence, his heart rate starts to rise, just as his stomach sinks further. *Jesus, Mal,* he thinks. *You're letting the old woman get to you. Everything will be fine. Trust yourself. Trust her. She wouldn't just leave.*

That's when he hears it. The sound of the water running – the shower! That's where she will be. Standing under the full force of the power shower he had insisted on getting fitted, and hosting her own private disco. Smiling at the thought, he drops his case and heads straight for the stairs, convincing himself the cold in the house will be a result of the home heating oil having run out. They've been caught before, not getting a top-up in time. Bronagh will have decided to wait until they are back from Spain before ordering more. He's such an eejit for getting himself wound up over it. Relief floods his veins.

The bathroom door is open. He feels a swell of desire thinking of her standing under the hot streams of water, soaping herself down. God... he just wants to get naked with this woman as soon as possible and start their holiday off with a bang. *No pun intended*, he smiles to himself as he reaches the top of the stairs.

'Okay, baby. You're in trouble,' he calls as he takes off his jacket and pulls his T-shirt up over his head. But when he steps into the bathroom, he immediately notices the lack of steam from the empty shower.

'Bro?' he calls. 'Is the shower on the blink?' It doesn't take long for the unease to return and settle in the pit of his stomach, yet he still half expects to hear her call back from the bedroom, or to walk out into the landing, maybe stripped to her underwear, and immediately get stressed about the broken shower and another unexpected repair bill. It's only been a couple of weeks since they had to pay to fix the clutch on her car.

But she doesn't call back. Not even when he calls her name a second time. No, the house remains much too quiet.

3

MAL

Mal walks to their room having absolutely no idea of what he may find. Please God he won't find empty wardrobes, doors hanging open, hangers stripped and bare. The dresser devoid of her make-up and skincare. All the things he sometimes thinks of as clutter but never wants to have to miss.

Catch yourself on, lad, he tells himself as he sees everything just as it should be, but that calm doesn't last for long when he realises no matter what *is* in the room, she is not.

Her handbag is there though, on the bed, spilling its collection of lip balms, receipts, coins and keys onto the duvet. Would she have gone out without her keys? Not on purpose anyway. He can't imagine her going out without her bag, while leaving the shower running and the front door lying open either though – but she's definitely not here.

And he knows she has received his messages thanks to the power of the two ticks in WhatsApp – even if she hasn't read them. Is she avoiding him? Has his being away these few days given her time, and space, to think and come to the conclusion that she doesn't need him after all? She might think she has had enough. That *he* isn't enough. He might have been fooling himself that they had come out the other side of things.

He knows he has tried to prove himself to her. Prove he's the good man she thought he was. He has never cheated. He doesn't drink any more. He has worked on himself. Gone to therapy. Faced his demons.

He treats her well. He always has, or at least he has always tried to. He's generous. He helps around the house – more than some of his friends do if their braying and bragging in the pub is anything to go by. He and Bronagh aren't perfect, but no relationship is. They work at it though. They love each other.

So right now he needs Bronagh to be here. 'Where the fuck are you?' he mutters, breaking the silence of the much too quiet house. Maybe she's left him a note downstairs on the kitchen table, or pinned to the fridge? Something that explains her disappearance as perfectly innocent, hopefully. There has to be something he just hasn't thought of yet.

As he makes to leave the room, a flash of light catches his eye and he turns his head. There it is. On the bedside table. Her phone, attached to its charger cable. The lit screen indicating a new notification. Without thinking Mal grabs it, sits on the bed, and taps in her passcode. They don't keep secrets from each other. Not even their passcodes. He has never had cause to doubt her, nor she him.

So why should he be doubting her now?

Her phone screen is littered with notifications – messages from her boss, her mum... From him. Each message he has sent her in the last day and a half is there on her screen. Nothing is read. Missed calls are stacked up on top of one another. If she's annoyed with him, she must be annoyed with everyone else too.

He taps into her WhatsApp. There are messages from

people, including Shelley, asking if she is okay, or why she is not responding. His heart is hammering in his chest, a sickening thud thud thud which reminds him with every beat that she is getting farther away from him. Away from their life.

Where is she?

Phone in hand, he runs down the stairs and goes straight to the kitchen looking for the note he hopes is there. He can handle anything, he thinks, as long as he knows that she is okay. If she's angry with him... if she has left... it will be okay. It won't be a forever thing. He can talk to her. They can get her back on track. As long as she is okay.

He repeats that over and over in his head as he scans the kitchen table, the fridge door, the worktops. He keeps thinking it as he goes back into the hall and checks the console where they usually leave their post. There is nothing.

As long as she is okay, he thinks again as he goes into the living room and spots her jacket hung over the arm of the sofa. A mug rests on the coffee table – a film of God knows what floating on top of a half-drunk cup of tea. It's cold, of course. At this stage he doesn't really expect to find anything different.

There is no note. Not on the table. Not on the fireplace. Not on the bookshelves. If he's being honest with himself, he didn't really expect to find one in here. The reality of the situation is starting to kick in.

Her car, her keys, her phone – all here. Her jacket too. The shower running icy cold as if she had been getting ready to step in but had been distracted by something. The door lying open. No lights. No sign of her.

He should start calling her friends and family, shouldn't he? Isn't that the done thing? Call them and see if they know where she is. Except he has seen the messages from her nearest and dearest and everyone is expressing the same concern that they've not heard from her. Bronagh is one of those people who lives life 'chronically online' – people notice when that's not the case.

Or should he phone the police first? Let them know she is missing? It's that serious, isn't it? Serious enough that he needs to report it. The thought nauseates him and he tries to focus on his breathing. He checks his phone to see the exact time he last heard from her. It was yesterday. Shortly after she had sent him a picture of her feet with her toenails painted a raspberry pink. He had joked he was going to set up an Only Fans account in her name and sell the pictures to foot fetishists. *We can throw a few extra quid in the holiday fund,* he'd written, and she'd replied with a laughing-face emoji.

Then silence. Nothing.

Scrolling through her phone, it seemed that emoji was the last message she had sent anyone. *Shit,* he thinks. *This is real.* Something is definitely not right. His beautiful, brilliant girl-friend is missing. And he hasn't the first clue what he is supposed to do about it.

4

MAL

His phone in his hand, he thinks of how easy it would be to tap those three nines onto the screen that will connect him directly with the police. Something he can't quite put his finger on is holding him back. Perhaps it's the fear that calling the police makes it real. Saying the words 'my girlfriend is missing' means it's true.

Every part of him that wants this to be nothing more than a bad dream whispers in his ear that maybe he is overreacting. Maybe he just needs to chill out. Maybe Mrs Cosgrove and her scandal-seeking ways are getting to him.

His finger hovers a moment more before he decides to call the one person more likely than anybody else in the world to know where Bronagh is.

Shelley is, after all, the reason he and Bronagh exist as a couple in the first place. Her best friend and his cousin, she had introduced them on a night out and had orchestrated the blossoming of their romance in a way that would've made Cilla Black proud. There is nothing that has happened in either woman's life that they have not shared almost immediately with each other. He'll call her and she'll tell him Bronagh is crashing on her sofa after they had too many glasses of prosecco at a quick pre-holiday brunch, and everything will start to make sense.

'Oh, I see Lazarus has arisen from the grave! Where the hell have you been, lady?' Shelley's tone is jovial, her voice dripping with the kind of banter only the very best of friends can get away with.

'It's me,' he says, his heart plummeting to his boots at further evidence something is very wrong.

'Mal? Why do you have Bro's phone? Is something wrong?' Shelley's concern is immediate. 'She hasn't been in touch since yesterday morning but I assumed she'd done a Bronagh and lost her phone, or dropped it in the sink or—'

'Her phone's here, at home,' Mal says. 'But Bronagh's not. And it's clear she's not with you either?' He knows he is clutching desperately at straws, but what else can he do?

'No. No, she's not. Do you not know where she is?' He tries not to take anything accusatory from her words, even though a part of him – probably the part of him that still retains the caveman-like desire to protect his woman – thinks he should, of course, know where she is. How could he have let it get to this point and only now be raising his concerns? It's been a day and a half.

'No. I don't. I was really hoping you did,' he says, the sense of dread in the pit of his stomach growing by the minute.

'Sorry,' Shelley says. 'Have you spoken to her work? Maybe she's grabbing some overtime before you head off and just left her phone at home. She did tell me the other day they were up to their eyes in it at the moment. Some Instagrammer or TikTok influencer gave them a shout-out and as a result, everyone is looking to get their lips done, or their brows done, or their wrinkles sorted...'

That is a plausible enough explanation, he thinks. As the practice manager for an upmarket aesthetics clinic, Bronagh is often subject to the whims of social media 'celebrities' and their followers.

Except he knows that she isn't at work. Hadn't he spotted messages on her phone from some of her colleagues asking questions and wishing her a lovely holiday?

'No. No, she's not there. It seems everyone is looking for her. Mrs C from next door greeted me on the doorstep to tell me the front door was left lying open yesterday, and it was her who closed it. She thought Bronagh must've been in the shower but—'

'What are you saying, Mal?' It isn't accusatory. Shelley's words are just mirroring his own confusion back to him.

'I don't know. I mean... the door was left open yesterday afternoon. I looked at her phone, and the last time she was in touch with anyone was very early afternoon. After that, it's all just a series of unread messages and missed calls.'

'It doesn't mean there's anything wrong though, does it? There will be some explanation we've not thought of.' Shelley's tone belies her fears. 'People don't just disappear. She has to be somewhere.'

'The shower was still running cold when I got home,' he says, remembering the icy hit of the water in the chilled room. 'Her bag is here, Shelley. Her keys. Her towels ready for the shower on top of the bed along with her half-packed case ready for our holiday. Her cup of tea was half drunk and on the coffee table...' His voice cracks as panic threatens to take over. 'I think something bad has happened,' he says, no longer caring if he sounds overly dramatic. He knows his girlfriend. He knows how her mind works and he feels it in his soul that she would never leave him like this. She would not just disappear and cause worry to her friends and her family – not unless she had no choice in the matter. 'I was going to call the police but then I thought maybe I was just being dramatic, but... I need to call them, don't I?'

There's a pause and a slow intake of breath down the line. 'Yeah,' she says. 'You do. I'll be right over.' She ends the call before he has the time to say goodbye himself, and – not giving himself the chance to overthink it any more – he immediately dials 999.

* * *

'And this woman – your girlfriend? What's her name?' the monotoned dispatcher asks.

'Bronagh Murray,' he says.

'And how does she spell Bronagh?'

Mal's frustration grows. The spelling of her name is hardly important right now.

'B.R.O.N.A.G.H.,' he says.

'What age is she?'

'Thirty-two.'

'And your address?'

He tells her.

'And you say she is missing?'

'I don't just *say* she is missing. She *is* actually missing. She hasn't answered her phone in over twenty-four hours. She's not at home, but her things are.' He's aware he sounds terse, but he can't cope with this woman's lack of urgency.

'Would your girlfriend be considered a vulnerable person? For example, does she have a physical or learning disability?'

'No. No disability. But that doesn't mean she doesn't require your help!'

'And you have spoken to her closest friends or family?'

Mal has to remind himself that it is the dispatcher's job to ask these questions. That she is, hopefully, not trying to wind him up with her responses.

'Well, no. But I have her phone. I've seen the messages from her friends asking her to reply to them. All the friends I would think to call. She hasn't read anything since yesterday lunchtime, as I told you. I was away on business – I got home to find the shower running, the house looking lived in, but there's no sign of her at all. And our neighbour found the door open yesterday, and said there were no lights on last night...'

'Are there any signs of a struggle? Perhaps items were disturbed, or glass broken? Anything like that?' The dispatcher sounds marginally more interested but only marginally.

'No. No. And nothing appears to be missing. Her things – her car, and purse and phone – they are still here. That's what I'm telling you.'

'And you didn't perhaps have a disagreement? Was there an argument between you two?'

With the worst timing imaginable, he can feel his temper flaring, but he can't show it. He can't display even a hint of anger or aggression because he knows how this will go if he does. He'll be written off as an angry man who has probably scared his girl away and... No. He won't let that happen.

'No. We didn't have a disagreement. As I said, I was away with work. In London. We're due to go on holiday the day after tomorrow. We were both looking forward to it.' He can feel a headache starting to build.

He wants to get through to the dour-sounding woman that Bronagh is important. She is his entire world, but he gets the feeling she wouldn't be interested. Not on *her* pay scale. She'll just be concerned with taking the details, making sure Bronagh is spelled correctly, and filing them away for someone else to look at.

'Sir, we will send a response team to you as soon as one becomes available. I must advise you that we are particularly busy tonight due to a public order disturbance in the city centre, but we will be with you as soon as we possibly can.'

'How long is "soon" likely to be?' he asks. 'We need people to be looking for her now.'

'Sir, we will get someone to you as soon as we can.' The response sounds rote, as if she is reading it off a screen.

'But she could be anywhere!' he thunders, well aware that raising his voice isn't likely to help, but finding it impossible to keep his cool all the same. 'Anything could've happened to her! It's over twenty-four hours since anyone has heard from her. Don't they say the first couple of days are the most important?'

'Sir, I appreciate that this is a stressful time for you, but if you could please refrain from raising your voice that would be helpful.'

Adrenaline coursing through his veins, he kicks the table in front of him, sending the slimy, mouldering tea flying all over the carpet. Bronagh will be raging, he thinks before he remembers Bronagh isn't here, and he'd give anything for her to walk in through the front door right now and give him a mouthful over ruining her good rug.

'Sorry,' he says. 'Sorry, I didn't mean to lose my cool. I'm just worried about her.'

'I'm sure, sir,' the woman replies, her voice a little softer. 'And we will get an officer to you as soon as we can. It might help to know that the majority of missing people cases are resolved very quickly and without the need for police intervention.'

'But this isn't like that. The house...' he says. 'The door was open. The shower was running. She's left her keys, bag... her car. For God's sake. Who leaves without all of those things? It's not like her.'

'I understand that and I've made a note of it and will pass that information on to the officer who will call you...'

In a fit of temper he ends the call and throws his phone across the room, where it lands in a puddle of the cold tea. This can't be right. Reporting a missing woman and getting a wishy-washy 'we'll get to it when we get to it' response. It's not good enough. How can an emergency – and this surely is an emergency – just be put on a 'we'll get there when we get there' basis? If this was a break-in, or a murder, would he have been told to wait it out? He doesn't care what might be happening elsewhere. That's not his concern. Bronagh is his concern.

Maybe he should get in his car and go down to the police station himself, demand to speak to an officer face to face. Threaten to cause his own public order disturbance. That might do it. He doesn't care if he ends up in the cells.

But at the same time, he wants to hope that the dispatcher is right and that Bronagh really might show up. He wants to make sure he is here when she does so he can tell her how she has given him such a fright. How he never wants to feel these feelings again for as long as he lives.

But as much as he wants to be here when she walks back in through the door, he can't fight the sinking and terrifying feeling that that isn't going to happen.

5

BRONAGH

The room is darkened, but it's more than just the dark of night. It has a pervasive nature all of its own, as if darkness were seeping from the very walls. Fear starts to tighten her throat. As she tries to call out, unsure if it is even safe to do so, her voice cracks and breaks. Her mouth is so very dry that she is sure she can feel her lips split and she can taste the metallic tang of her own blood. Her tongue is thick and heavy in her mouth, swollen.

It's certainly as tender as a fresh bruise and Bronagh can't help but wince when it rubs against her molars. Yes, she has definitely bitten it. That's probably the source of the blood rather than her lips, she realises, as her stomach threatens to turn.

It takes exceptional effort to tilt her head to the side to try and figure out where she is. Old-fashioned wood cladding covers the wall to her left – the kind she has seen in pictures from the seventies and eighties. It's oppressively dark, something that isn't helped by the busy floral-patterned curtains in hues of brown and orange which are blocking out all but the finest sliver of light. The malodorous aroma filling her nostrils could be damp, she thinks, or it could in fact be coming from her own body. She feels slick with sweat as she lies in sheets that feel stale and moist.

This is not her home. Her memories might be hazy at best, but she feels that deep in her soul. This is not a place she recognises. It's absolutely not a safe place either. That much is clear. Her body is screaming at her that she is in danger, but it's like her head is full of pieces of a jigsaw that she can't quite put together.

Like how she got here. She isn't sure if there has been an accident, or an illness or a... her head hurts too much to think. She wills herself to remember but all she gets are flashes of things that make no sense. Pink toenails, and switching the shower on. Her phone, charging. The sensation of cold rain beating against her skin – or was it the shower water beating against her skin?

Still, her voice remains stuck in her throat and her mouth, still dry, except for a trickle of blood mixed with saliva. Gagging, Bronagh wrenches herself onto her side, afraid that if she doesn't, she will choke either on sick or on her swollen tongue. The movement sends another bolt of pain directly to her head and she cries out – a garbled, rasping noise that is barely recognisable as her own voice.

Tears spring to her eyes. She wants this to be a bad dream. Any minute now she will hear Mal's soft Donegal accent call her name and she'll open her eyes in her own bed, this pain a distant, weird memory.

'You were shouting in your sleep again,' he'd tease.

'Hope I wasn't calling out another fellah's name,' she'd tease back. Mal would laugh and pull her to him, reminding her once again why she never so much as needs to look at another man. She has everything she wants with him.

He's her safe place. She's told him that – used those exact words, as it happens. Malachy Cooper is the prince she found after far too many years of kissing frogs. Almost three years in, she feels utterly safe and secure in their relationship – ready to take the next step. He's what is real. Not this. She's almost sure of it.

Wake up, she pleads internally. *Wake up now. This isn't real. Whatever the hell this is, it isn't real.*

The sound of a door opening, and the flooding of the dismal little room with artificial yellow light from the hallway, silence her inner screams.

'I see you're awake,' a deep male voice echoes through the room – much too loudly. She winces, not only at the loudness of his words, but at the realisation that it is not Mal who is talking to her. Just like the room she is in, she recognises nothing about this stranger at the door.

Slowly, aware that the pain will hit again at any moment, she rolls back and tries to pull herself to sitting.

'Settle yourself. Lie you where you are,' the man says, his accent one she can't immediately place. There are twangs of a Northern accent, for sure, but something else seems to run underneath it – something she can't place. 'You took quite a knock to the head there. You'll be feeling that for a couple of days,' the man says. 'You've been asleep a long time.'

Bronagh continues to pull herself to sitting. It will make her feel less vulnerable than just lying in this mouldy bed.

It hurts, and her stomach threatens once again to turn. She tries to speak, but her throat is still parched, and her tongue, still swollen.

'Yeah. You bit your tongue when you hurt yourself. It's

bound to be painful,' the man says. 'I've brought you some medicine and a little soup.'

She shakes her head. She doesn't intend on taking anything this man has to offer. God only knows what he could ply her with.

'You won't get better unless you have something to eat,' he says. 'And the medicine, it will make you feel better. Less pain.'

Raising her eyes to meet his, Bronagh takes him in for the first time – or at least as much as she can, given that he is still standing partially in shadow. Tall and broadly built, he has a thick head of dark hair, accompanied by an equally unkempt beard. It's hard to guess his age, but if pushed, she'd put him in his thirties or maybe early forties. Dressed in jeans and a checked shirt, he doesn't stand out as particularly different from many men of his age – except that the surly expression on his face seems to carry an extra layer of menace. He is carrying a wooden tray.

'No,' she stutters.

'But you want to feel better?' he asks as he takes a step forward. Every cell in her body feels repulsed by him. The very last thing she wants is for him to take even one more step towards her, but at the same time she knows that she is power-less to stop him. There's no strength in her body. She is as vulnerable as she has ever been – in a strange bed, in a strange house, her body broken and in pain.

'Surely you want to feel better?' he says, probing again and hoping for an answer. 'You'll want to be back on your feet? Yes? You'll have been missed.'

A glimmer of hope flickers inside her – she'll have been missed. Mal. Mal will have missed her and she has to go back to him. They had plans for something, didn't they? This man, this room – it doesn't mean something is wrong. It's not nice. It's not clean or well kept. But maybe this man is just helping her. Maybe he found her unconscious and brought her here until she came round. It might be okay.

'Hospital,' she rasps. 'I need to go.'

The man raises an eyebrow. 'You don't need to worry about that. We are taking care of you here.'

'Where am I?' she asks, hoping he will give her an explanation that both makes sense to her broken brain but also gives her hope that this is temporary and she'll be back with Mal soon.

'You are here,' he says. 'Where you need to be.'

'I want to go home,' she says, her voice muffled as he sits on the edge of the bed.

The man nods but doesn't speak. Instead he reaches his hand out towards her, palm upwards, and offers her two small white pills.

'No thank you,' she says, even though she'd sell a kidney for pain relief. 'Why am I here? What happened?'

Still not speaking, he thrusts his hand towards her, bringing the pills closer to her face. His expression leaves her in no doubt that he is not offering her a choice. There is nothing friendly in his demeanour.

With a shaking hand she lifts the pills and pops them in her mouth, wincing at the stiffness in her jaw. He nods and hands her a glass of water – which Bronagh soon discovers is tepid. While the taste is, at best, unpleasant, the water does manage to feel soothing as it washes over her sore tongue and down her throat.

'You'll need mouthwash,' he says. 'To stop infection setting in, but first you have to eat.'

'Not hungry,' she lies. Her stomach is grumbling but she doesn't want to eat anything. Certainly not here. She doesn't want to do anything here that she doesn't have to. 'I just want to go home.'

He shakes his head with a menacing slowness. His face is clearer now that he is no longer in shadow. Eyes like flint, he takes her in from head to foot. No physical touch could feel more intrusive. Instinctively she pulls the blankets up to her chest, even though she is still fully clothed. A person's body will give them all the signals they might need that they are not safe, and Bronagh does not feel safe. Why isn't he answering her when she tells him she wants to go home? He said himself that she will be missed.

Lifting a spoon from the tray, he stirs the soup before bringing it to her mouth. 'You were asleep for a very long time. Eat,' he says, and there's a hint of softness to him. It's unsettling. This harshness followed by softness. Threat, dressed as concern. It's making her dizzy. Or maybe that's just the concussion. Reluctantly she opens her mouth and allows him to feed her a spoonful of lukewarm cream of chicken soup. Its slimy texture makes her want to vomit.

'It's not too hot so it won't hurt your tongue,' he says, and she finds herself grateful for that small mercy, despite her ongoing fear. He said she'd been asleep for a long time. She wants to ask him how long, but she also doesn't want to talk to him any more than she needs to. Everything in her body is screaming at her to stay guarded.

They sit in silence for a bit – him spooning more soup into her mouth and her wondering if it will anger him if she asks once more about going home. She finds herself too nauseous to continue eating after a quarter of a bowl and she slumps back against the pillows, her eyes growing heavy.

'The painkillers are working,' the man says, but everything

is fuzzy around the edges. It doesn't feel real. None of this feels real.

'There is someone who is very eager to see you,' the man says. 'But he will wait until you have slept some more. You need to get better. He needs you.'

The room is dark again but Bronagh's not sure if it's because her eyes are closed, or if the door has been shut, cutting off the light from the hall. It doesn't matter, in the end. There is no choice but to give in to sleep.

6

MAL

Mal is growing agitated. He has barely slept and now, along with Shelley, he has been sitting in the waiting room at Strand Road Police station for over an hour, watching people come and go. It's busy – the dregs of the overnight public order offenders being claimed by solicitors or family members. Somewhere someone is singing a loud, tuneless drunken melody that makes it perfectly clear what he thinks of the PSNI. Much longer and Mal will join in, he thinks.

Shelley had arrived to his and Bronagh's home about an hour after Mal had phoned the police last night. She had helped him go through just about every contact on Bronagh's phone, checking if anyone had seen her or heard from her. She had called the police when, three hours after Mal's initial call, there was still no sign of a response car arriving, only to be fed the same lame excuses as he had been. A clash between football supporters had turned nasty – shades of sectarianism budding into violence. Mal had been impressed when he had heard her tell the dispatcher she didn't give two hoots about football – she wanted her friend prioritised.

It hadn't made any difference. After another hour, she had told Mal to try and get some sleep but he had been too on edge. He hadn't wanted to go into their bedroom and further disturb the items Bronagh had left on the bed, in case there was a clue he had missed that the police might see as evidence.

So, after ordering Shelley to get some shut-eye in the spare room, he had laid down on the sofa and failed to sleep – hoping the whole time his phone would ring or the police would arrive, or Bronagh would walk through the door.

By the time light was starting to creep across the sky, he'd had enough of waiting and had told Shelley he was going directly to the police station to make someone listen. She'd insisted on coming with him, and he had felt empowered by the notion he was actually doing something to help find Bronagh.

But he hadn't counted on being left to sit and wait for someone to be available to talk to. One man lumbers in, barely able to stand, and proceeds to shout abuse at the desk sergeant, threatening to 'smash his bloody face in'. It isn't until he spits at the sergeant that a uniformed officer intervenes and drags him through to the custody suite, reading him his rights as they go. The man, clearly not in the mood for calming down, shouts 'Up the IRA!' as he disappears through the double doors.

Mal doesn't know if the man is drunk or on drugs, or possibly a mixture of both. Whatever his story is, Mal can't help but feel sorry for a man who finds himself in that condition at eight in the morning – three sheets to the wind and in the bad books with the Police Service of Northern Ireland. Something must have gone badly wrong in his life to make him so angry – and so vulnerable.

No one is born a criminal. Sometimes things happen

though. Mistakes are made. That doesn't make them bad people.

The hard plastic seats are just a little too narrow to be comfortable, and the temperature inside the dark, artificially lit room is borderline tropical. The whole place looks and feels dystopian – a fallback to the Troubles, where police buildings were constructed with minimal windows and reinforced walls. Able to withstand the worst the IRA could throw at them.

The only reprieve from the humid heat is the occasional blast of wind and rain that floods through the door every time someone else walks in.

If Mal isn't mistaken, everyone else seems to be getting seen more quickly than him and Shelley. He's starting to wonder if they've been forgotten about. He's fighting the urge to shout at the desk sergeant too – demand to know why a missing woman doesn't seem to be a priority for the PSNI.

'Stuff this!' he says under his breath after a further ten minutes' waiting, as he stands up to march towards the desk. He's aware of Shelley reaching out to urge him to sit back down but he has no intention of doing so. He'll keep his calm. He'll be polite. He will say all the right things, but he is damned if he'll just continue to sit and wait like a good little boy when everyone else – even the drunks and the junkies – seem to be getting help before him.

'Excuse me,' he says, as he reaches the desk. The desk sergeant – a ruddy-faced man in his fifties, with a hairline as receding as his stomach is protruding – looks up from his seat behind the counter.

'Yes, sir. Can I help you?' he asks, almost as if this were the first time he's spoken with Mal.

'I very much hope you can,' Mal says. 'I spoke to you over

an hour ago. About my girlfriend Bronagh Murray. She's missing. You said you'd get someone to talk to me.'

The desk sergeant doesn't answer for a moment. He instead tilts his head as if trying to assess just how much of a threat Mal poses to him. Perhaps the spitting and the shouting of earlier has him on edge. Although Mal imagines he is well used to being abused. It no doubt comes with the job.

'Yes,' the sergeant says, 'that's right. You spoke to me and I said I'd get someone to come and see you. Nothing has changed about that.'

There's a beat as the sergeant looks Mal up and down. 'Unless, that is, you've come back here to tell me your girlfriend has turned up after all – after a bender perhaps with her pals, or maybe she's forgiven you for whatever fight you've had.'

Mal's fists clench, but he will not lose his cool. He will not do anything that will take away from the police doing the job he wants them to do, or bring attention to his behaviour. 'No. She *hasn't* come home. She's not been on a bender and we didn't have an argument. She's still missing and I was wondering when you might get round to actually having someone come down and talk to me.'

'Well, sir, we are getting through things as fast as we can. I'm sure someone will be with you soon.'

'All I'm hearing is "soon". But this is a missing woman. Our door was left open. Her belongings all still in the house. Shouldn't that be enough to speed the "soon" up a bit?' Mal is calm – but only just. How can the desk sergeant not see how worried he is, and how worried Shelley is? That they aren't the type of people who waste police time and that they wouldn't be here if they didn't feel it was really bloody important for them to be here.

'Sir, it's out of my hands. I'll ring upstairs again, but I'm afraid you'll have to wait just like everyone else here.'

'Look, pal,' Mal says, his teeth perhaps more gritted this time than before, 'I'm trying to keep this really polite but I'm worried about my girlfriend's safety. It would seem that I – and my cousin here – might be the only people who *are* worried about her but believe me, that should be enough for you to help us. No one has heard from her in coming up to forty-eight hours. How does that not set alarm bells ringing around here?'

Without realising it, his volume has increased and Shelley has got up from the godawful uncomfortable seats and come to stand beside him, her hand once again reaching out to act as a steadying force.

'Mal, come and sit down,' Shelley says, her voice soft but laden with all the same emotions he is feeling.

'Look, we would really appreciate it if someone took this seriously,' she says to the desk sergeant who, Mal notices, at least has the decency to look more than a little red-faced. Mal knows his type. All smart-arsed and holier-than-thou until confronted with their shitty attitude.

'I'll check with upstairs,' he says. 'Take a seat. I'll be with you in a couple of minutes.'

'I'd appreciate that,' Shelley says as she leads Mal back to the seating area. In the minutes he has been standing at the desk, his chair has been swooped on by a teenager who looks and smells like he hasn't seen a shampoo bottle in at least six weeks, and Shelley's seat is now occupied by a girl who looks much too young to be nursing a stomach as round and obviously pregnant as hers.

'I need some fresh air,' Mal snaps.

'It's freezing out there. And lashing from the heavens,' Shelley says.

'I still need some fresh air. This place is making me sick.'

He appreciates that Shelley follows him anyway and they stand huddled together outside, not quite able to escape the waft of smoke from the nearby smokers' hut.

'What I don't understand is why they don't seem to be taking this seriously.' His voice is an angry whisper.

'I know. I'm sure they will,' Shelley says. 'They have to.'

His stomach tightens. At the same time, tears prick at his eyes, which he quickly brushes away while telling himself to man up. Who the hell is *he* to fall apart? He's not the one in danger. He's supposed to be her protector. Isn't that a man's job?

'Mal, I know it's awful. It's just awful.' Shelley's voice is shaky. When he looks at her, pale-faced and exhausted, her eyes as red-rimmed as his, he thinks how she looks much younger than her years. So much more vulnerable.

He sniffs. 'I just need to feel as if someone is doing something. I don't care if it's the cops or a man in the street – it's this standing around, waiting, that's killing me. God knows where she is, or what the hell has happened. All I know is with every hour that passes, it's scarier.'

He watches as Shelley crumples, her composure lost as tears slide down her cheeks. He pulls her to him and hugs her – lets her cry into his shoulder. He can feel her shiver but he knows it's not from the cold or the rain. He knows how scared she is because he feels it too.

As they stand there, both trying to catch their breath amid a wave of fear, a well-dressed woman walks through the gates of the police compound and towards them. Her eyes are fixed on the door to reception, but Mal can't help but notice her assured manner. She's a solicitor, maybe. Possibly even a detective. Maybe, he thinks, it's worth a chance. He should talk to her. See if she can shake things up.

'Excuse me,' he says, as Shelley pulls back and dries her eyes on the sleeve of her coat. 'Excuse me, but do you work here?'

The woman looks at them both. Mal watches her take them in, as if she were making a mental note of every detail.

'Not as such,' she says.

He sags. Okay, so it was a long shot. What were the chances she would be a detective who would swoop in and take on this case? This is real life, not an episode of *Law & Order: SVU*. He nods, waits for her to walk on, but she stops and keeps looking at them.

'Are you okay?' she asks. 'Do you want me to get someone for you?'

Mal snorts. 'Chance would be a fine thing, but thank you. We're waiting to be seen. We've been trying to report a missing person.' God, even saying the words is painful. 'But it seems as if the PSNI aren't all that interested.' There's more than a hint of disgust in his voice.

'You've been *trying* to report a missing person?' the woman asks, one perfectly sculpted eyebrow raised. Mal can't help but feel it ironic that this complete stranger is more interested than the police force who are supposed to be protecting them.

'Yes. We called it in last night. We were told a response car would be sent out, but none came. We've been here for more than an hour. Meanwhile she... my girlfriend... has been missing for coming up on forty-eight hours. No one has heard from her. All her belongings are still at home. The front door was left open...'

The woman blinks. 'And no response team was sent out to you? They knew all the details, right?' The woman stares Mal directly in the eyes, as if trying to read him. She probably doesn't believe him either.

'That's what I've been trying to tell that desk sergeant in there. I called about eight or so last night. They said they were busy but someone would be sent out. I've seen enough cop shows to know these early days are important and we're losing hours here.'

'But you only called it in last night, and you say she has been missing for coming up on two days?'

It's a fair question. 'I didn't know she was missing until gone six yesterday. I've been away on business. I assumed she'd been caught up in work, or had lost her phone or something and that's why I hadn't heard from her...'

He doesn't add that a small part of him had been scared she might have run out on him. It's irrelevant now anyway.

'But when he got home it was clear something was wrong,' Shelley adds.

'And you are?' the woman asks.

'I'm Shelley. Mal's cousin.' Shelley nods her head towards him. 'And Bronagh... the missing woman... she's my best friend. But look, you don't work here and we don't want to waste any more of your time. Or our own for that matter.'

She takes him by the hand and turns to go back in through the door. Mal doesn't feel like getting on the wrong side of her so he follows her without complaint – only stopping when the woman calls their names.

'Shelley! Mal!'

They turn to see the woman rifling in her bag and pulling out a business card, which she hands over. Mal takes it from her and casts his eyes over the words written in 12pt Times New Roman.

Ingrid Devlin
Investigative Journalist

Non-fiction Author

'I don't work here, but that doesn't mean I can't help. You're telling me that you reported a missing woman to the PSNI almost thirteen hours ago and no one has helped you yet?'

Mal nods. 'That's exactly what I'm saying.'

'And your front door was left open? All her stuff still there?'

He nods in response to each question.

'And you're both as sure as you can be that she hasn't gone to see a friend, or family, or anything like that?'

'Absolutely sure. We've spent the night ringing everyone we could think of. No one has seen her or heard from her,' Shelley says.

Ingrid Devlin's eyes are wide with disbelief. 'I'd be happy to put pressure on the police on your behalf. Highlight how you feel the police have responded to this. Appeal for information about your girlfriend... Bronagh, isn't it? My details are all there on the card. You can look me up if you want. I have a meeting to get to, inside.' She nods towards the door. 'In fact I'm running late. But call me. Or better still, give me your number and I'll call you.' She reaches into her bag and pulls out her mobile phone, unlocking it and tapping on the screen before handing it over to Mal to input his number.

'Leave it with me,' she says before scurrying off.

As they walk back through the door, the blast of humid heat hitting them in the face, Mal immediately notices a tall woman in her mid to late thirties, dressed in a charcoal grey trouser suit standing by the double doors, looking directly at them.

The woman glances to the desk sergeant, who nods, before she starts walking across the room to Mal and Shelley.

'DS Eve King,' she says, extending her arm to shake Mal's hand. 'If you'd like to come through, I'll have a chat with you.'

7

INGRID

Okay. They have my attention. These two people standing outside the police station. A missing woman who has left all her things behind. It might be nothing, of course. A simple case of someone who has had enough and cleared out for a break, or an exercise in ghosting. It happens.

There have definitely been more than a few times in my life when I've felt like disappearing into the ether myself. But the open door – that feels like something more. It feels like something big. Which of course begs the question – why the hell have the police not acted on it?

I could see the worry on both Mal's and Shelley's faces. That expression of fear mixed with honest confusion that screams that they really can't understand why their loved one would be missing. I've come to learn that it's a look that can't be faked.

I've spoken in the past to many people who've tried. Who've adopted long faces and downturned mouths and sworn they couldn't think of a 'single reason' why someone would simply disappear. I've come to recognise the subtle shiftiness in their eyes. The performative worry and grief – and those are the ones I pay closest attention to.

And sure enough, sooner or later, evidence always seems to come to light that proves my gut was right. Sadly.

Maybe I've been in this job too long and am becoming much too jaded. The longer I spend at the coalface of journalism, or digging into the world of true crime, the more I see the same patterns of behaviour repeat again and again. I've been doing this for sixteen years. Seen too many people hurt. Too many women hurt, in particular. It's as depressing as it is predictable.

'Ms Devlin,' he says. DCI David Bradley. My nemesis in many ways, but someone I have come to perhaps reluctantly respect. Admire even. Our paths have crossed during many investigations in the past – and we most certainly have clashed on more than one or two occasions. But recent years have taught me that as far as coppers go, he's one of the decent ones. He doesn't just talk the talk, he walks the walk.

'DCI Bradley,' I say, standing up and shaking his hand. 'We meet again.'

'Still doing the Bond villain schtick?' he asks, his voice deadpan, but I know he has a begrudging respect for me these days too. I suspect he actually enjoys our banter.

'I've got to get my kicks somehow,' I say, following him into his office and taking a seat across the desk from him. He looks tired – the pressures of the job perhaps weighing down on him. If I'm jaded, he must be positively spent.

Even tired, however, he still manages to pull off that rugged George Clooney vibe. It's little wonder the PSNI wheel him out for almost every police press conference. He attracts attention – as shown in the comments section on social media every time I add his picture to a news article. Lots of 'He can arrest me any time' and 'Wonder whether he likes to play with his handcuffs?' type of jokes from middle-aged women. He's not my type – I'm not sure I even have a type any more. After my last and longest-running relationship, I'm quite content to be single – but I can understand how less disillusioned women might find him appealing.

'I'd have thought the love of your job would provide enough kicks,' he says with a wry smile playing on his lips.

'True. True. If you love your job, they say you never work a day in your life. Aren't we both lucky not to have to work for a living?' It's standard that we have to get these opening salvos over and done with before we get down to business.

'Indeed,' he replies. 'But on matters work-related. Maybe we could get going here?'

'Of course,' I tell him, reaching into my bag to grab my phone. It always helps to record these conversations.

'Ingrid, if you don't mind, I'd prefer you keep this off the record,' DCI Bradley says.

I pause and shake my head. 'No... I mean. You knew what I was coming here to discuss today. I assumed you'd be more than happy to go on the record with it? That's the whole point of my visit.' I can feel myself tense up. I swear, if I have come down here, having prepared all last night for an interview with Bradley about the growing incidents of violence against women and girls across the north, and he refuses to go on the record, I might just lose my shit. And not just because of my wasted time doing my research – but because this is a hugely important issue that needs to be highlighted again and again. Given my conversation with Mal and Shelley, it might actually need to be highlighted more than ever.

'I don't think it's very easy to get an interview if the interviewee insists on going off the record,' I say coolly. 'This has been arranged for a while. I even submitted some sample questions through the press office which, as you know, is not something I'm fond of doing.'

'Oh, I know. You prefer an ambush approach.' He smiles but it doesn't quite reach his lips.

'Not at all, I just don't like the whitewashed approach.'

'You know we have to be careful about what message we put out there,' Bradley says, leaning back in his chair. 'We have to make sure we get the wording exactly right. Treat things with the correct level of respect.'

'Well I assumed that's why you were selected for this interview,' I tell him. 'A man of your experience. You're well used to being in front of the press at this stage. And you're well versed on issues relating to domestic abuse and violence against women.'

He looks at me for a beat, not speaking. He knows I'm aware of his back story. Of his wife and her escape from an abusive relationship almost a decade ago. I'd covered that story back then. It all started with the death – well, the murder as it happened – of a young mother, Rose Graham. Bradley's now wife, Emily, happened to get herself mixed up with Rose's widower who, as we both learned to our horror, is not a very nice man.

'I am,' he says. 'Which is why I want to get it right. These are strange times, Ingrid. We have to be careful not to make the situation any worse than it already is.'

'Northern Ireland has one of the highest femicide rates in Europe. I'm not sure it could be any worse,' I tell him. 'What I think we have to be careful not to do is underplay it. This is a dangerous place to be a woman. Just as I arrived, for example, I met a man who was here to report his girlfriend missing. He seemed very worried indeed.'

This gets Bradley's attention. He sits straighter. 'Is that right?'

'Yes, and worse still, he said he reported it last night over the phone. No cops showed up so he came in this morning to speak to someone in person. It has the makings of a juicy story. Especially at a time when there is a degree of scrutiny around the thin blue line's attitude to women and crimes against them. It sounds to me like someone has dropped the ball. I do hope she turns out to be okay.'

'He reported it last night and no one came out?' His brow crinkles – that strong jawline of his tensing. He's not happy.

'That's what he said. He seemed beside himself, to be honest. His sister... no... his cousin, I think... she was there with him. Best friends with the missing woman, apparently. She seems just as rattled. I think he said he'd come back from a work trip and the front door was open. All her belongings still there – even her phone.'

If I'm expecting a comeback from him, I soon learn I'm not getting one. Instead he lifts his phone, jabs in a number and swears when no one answers. He quickly taps in another, and when that one is picked up, he asks if Eve King is about. I know Eve too – a detective sergeant who looks and behaves as if she has walked right out of a Lynda La Plante drama. She's his second in command.

There's some indistinct chattering from the other end of the phone before Bradley hangs up and tells me that, as it happens, DS King is currently speaking with the man and his cousin about the missing woman case.

'Bronagh Murray,' he says. 'That's her name, but given the gleeful look on your face as you told me about her boyfriend, I assume you already know that.'

I see no reason to correct him, so I just nod and smile.

'You can rest assured I will be investigating this thoroughly myself. If what you are telling me is true, this is an unacceptable lapse in procedure.'

'Are you saying that on the record, Detective Chief Inspector?' I ask, knowing full well that I am chancing my arm.

'Ingrid...' he says, 'such behaviour is beneath you.'

'As avoiding my questions is beneath *you*,' I say, starting to pack my things away. 'You've wasted my time bringing me here with no intention of answering my questions. Even about this live case and the possible mishandling of it. It's hugely disappointing and not a good look for the PSNI.'

'The PSNI has more important things to be worrying about than keeping the ladies and gentlemen of the press happy,' he says. 'We have actual work to do. Cases to follow up. Crimes to solve.'

'Missing women to find,' I say as I drop my phone into my bag. A mic drop moment. 'It's good to know you get round to looking for them eventually.' I make to stand up – anger starting to bubble in the pit of my stomach. I have promised this interview to one of the usual online outlets. They are counting on it to run as part of a special investigation into soaring crime rates against women in Northern Ireland.

'Hang on a minute,' he says, his own voice echoing the anger in mine. 'I can't speak to that individual case because as I have already stated to you—'

'Off the record,' I say with a roll of my eyes.

'On or off the record doesn't matter. I have told you I will be looking into the handling of this case personally. There may well be a legitimate reason that officers were not tasked to this case. Without knowing all the details, it would be foolish of me to say anything on or off the record. And I'd urge caution in reporting the same just now. I'm not the only person who could end up with egg on their face. I know you love a good story, Ingrid, but perhaps it would be wise not to jump to conclusions.'

I shake my head. 'Perhaps not. But if it turns out that she has been hurt, or worse, do you think people will be shocked or surprised? Sadly, we both know it's much more likely something bad has happened, and that once again we will all enter another circular discussion about the rising number of incidents of violence against women and girls, both in the home and outside of it.'

I know he can't challenge my position. We've been down this road several times before, Bradley and me. Investigating some of the more heinous crimes against women. We could be Derry's very own Benson and Stabler if only I were a cop too. I've made that joke to him before. I don't think he likes it.

'You want an on-the-record sound bite? How's this – I'm not at liberty to comment on this individual case at the moment,' he says, his patience clearly wearing thin. Good. I hope I do get under his skin. I should. This is too serious an issue to brush away for another time.

'Noted. And can I say, on the record, that I'm not at liberty to spike my story about violence against women and girls at the moment. I may give my sources a call and see if they have anything they can tell me,' I say, and stand up to leave again.

He leans forward, runs his hand through his hair and lets out a deep sigh. 'Look, I will give you your interview, on the record, no prepared questions. But not today. Today we have other things to deal with. Give us a chance, Ingrid.' There's a pause. 'I'll leave it with you to think about,' he says, before turning his attention back to his computer – international sign language for: 'This conversation is over and you can go now'.

Frustrated, I leave. It's all well and good him offering me

another interview at another time. But what am I going to do now? Work instead on hanging the PSNI out to dry over dropping the ball on Mal's report? Instinct tells me this is a big story but damn it, I can hear Bradley in my head. *'Give us a chance, Ingrid.'* And: *'There may be a legitimate reason why officers were not tasked to that case.'* I'm going to have to be careful about this.

As I leave the station, I take my phone from my bag and tap in a quick message to send to my sources inside the PSNI. They've proven to be very useful in giving me the inside track on investigations. I hope they can give me a steer on this.

I do experience a moment of self-disgust though. The kind of disgust only a journalist knows – when we get that little fizz of excitement at the thought of a great story only to remember our great story is often someone else's great misfortune.

I don't make the news though, I remind myself as the message pings off into the mobile network. I only report on it. And people have a right to know what kind of a world we are really living in.

8

MAL

'If you'd like to follow me through, we can chat somewhere quieter,' DS Eve King says, leading them through a door away from the increasingly manic reception area.

'I'm sorry to have kept you waiting. I wanted to check a few things before I came to speak to you,' she adds, as she walks with remarkable pace and purpose down a long, narrow corridor leading farther and farther into the heart of the building.

'I called last night and reported it, and I don't think it was taken seriously,' Mal says, keeping up with her. 'They said she was an adult and that most missing people turn up, but obviously I don't think this is a case of her having got lost at the shops, or gone to see her mum. I know her. She wouldn't just up and go.'

'Besides, we spoke to her mum,' Shelley interjects. 'She lives in Spain, you see. And no, she hasn't heard from her either.'

King comes to stop in front a nondescript door, brown and shiny from one too many coats of varnish. When she opens it, it reveals a liminal space, painted in shades of bland, and what could only be described as mushroom. The only furniture is a well-worn wooden table, with four metal chairs – two on either side. A plastic coffee cup lolls on its side, its decanted contents dried to a stain. It's a portrait of bleakness.

'Take a seat,' she says. 'Can I get you a tea or coffee? Full disclosure: both are pretty rank but of the two, the coffee is the least offensive option.'

Mal shakes his head. Now that he is in the bowels of the police station, his stomach is tense and he's not sure he'd be able to keep anything – especially not coffee sold as 'the least offensive' choice – down. Shelley asks for a glass of water and DS King nods and says she'll be back in a minute.

As soon as she leaves the room, Mal takes a breath. 'I wasn't expecting this,' he says. 'A detective sergeant.'

'But it's a good thing, isn't it?' Shelley asks. 'Maybe it means they've decided to take it seriously? That's what we want.'

'I hope so,' he says, reaching for the coffee cup and setting it right, grimacing at the blooms of mould festering inside the plastic. God knows when this room was last used. If the dead air – scented with a heady combination of body odour and damp carpet – is anything to go by, it has been a while.

Straightening himself, he wonders how long King will be. It can't take that long, surely, to pour a glass of water. Nervous energy fizzes through his veins and he stands up, knowing he needs to move to keep himself from losing it.

'Mal. She'll be okay,' Shelley says, in a less than convincing voice. He doesn't want to be the one to say out loud that she might not be, so he just nods, makes a vaguely affirmative 'uh-huh' noise and keeps walking, feeling as if the walls of the room are closing in on him.

The arrival of King, carrying two cups of water, is a welcome distraction from his growing panic.

'Sorry again for keeping you,' King says, handing one of the cups to Shelley before offering the other to Mal. 'I thought you might want some too. I'm sure this is very stressful for you.'

He nods, thanks her and takes the cup before sitting down.

'I wanted to get a colleague to come and help me with some notes,' King says as the door opens again and a uniformed officer – definitely more in the line of the just-out-of-Garnerville-and-still-on-probation – walks in with a notepad. At best, Mal would put him at twenty-five, although since hitting his thirties, Mal is definitely finding it harder to gauge the age of younger people.

'This is Constable Dean Morrison,' DS King says.

Constable Morrison nods and takes a seat beside his superior officer.

There's a hushed air of expectation as Mal waits to hear what DS King will say next. He can feel the tension coming off Shelley in waves. She shifts in her seat and coughs – the sound of it echoing around the room.

'Mr Cooper,' she begins.

'Mal. Call me Mal.'

There's a beat before she replies. 'Okay, Mal. You reported your girlfriend, Bronagh Murray, missing last night.'

'Yes, and I had to come down here to follow up on it because I waited all night for the police to show up as I was told they would, but none did.' He can't keep the bitterness from his voice.

DS King, he notices, at least has the good grace to look ashamed. 'I'm very sorry for that,' she says. 'The division is facing huge operational pressures at the moment but regardless, having read over the report taken by our dispatcher, I agree that someone should have been with you last night. I can assure you that this matter has my full attention and the full attention of the PSNI. Of course, should you wish to make a complaint to the Police Ombudsman, you would be well within your rights to do so and we can provide you with the relevant contact information.'

By the well-rehearsed way in which she speaks, Mal is sure this is not her first rodeo. He doesn't care that the police are under pressure though – they should be taking steps to ensure each division is properly staffed. What if there had been a murder?

What if there *has* been a murder?

He swallows that thought down. He will make a complaint to the Police Ombudsman, but hopefully only once they are out the other side of this and Bronagh is safe home with them. Which is the only outcome he wants to give any serious contemplation to.

An elbow from Shelley pulls him back into the moment. He glances at her.

'DS King asked you a question. You looked like you were in your own wee world there,' Shelley says.

'Sorry,' he apologises. 'I'm tired. My mind wandered. What was it you were asking?'

DS King glances towards Constable Morrison. They exchange a look which Mal reads as 'not impressed' before she turns her head back towards him.

'We will be sending a few officers to your house imminently, if that is okay with you?'

'Yes. Of course. Anything you need. I'd have been happier if you'd sent them last night when I called.' He knows he probably shouldn't make that quip but they need to know he's not going to let this go.

'You told the dispatcher all her personal belongings were still in the house?' King asks, not taking the bait.

'Yes. Yes, well I think so. No. I did. I definitely did. And they are still there. I didn't want to pick through everything in case I was disturbing evidence or something. All I lifted was her phone, because it was lighting up with notifications. But her keys are still there. Her bag. Her car. Her jacket is still hanging at the bottom of the stairs,' he says.

'And you told the dispatcher that a neighbour had found your front door open and had closed it herself. When was this?'

'The day before yesterday. She said it was around lunchtime. Her name is Mrs Cosgrove. She lives next door. I'm sure she would confirm this for you.'

DS King nods.

'And she said there were no lights on in the house that night. She didn't see Bronagh come home,' Shelley interjects.

'And she would normally see Bronagh come home?'

'She'd normally see everything. She likes to keep an eye on the street,' Mal replies, wondering how on earth she managed to miss the most important thing of all – actually seeing what happened. It seems DS King has the same thoughts.

'But she didn't see any suspicious activity, apart from your front door being left open?'

There's something he can't quite pinpoint in her tone that makes Mal think this DS King doesn't believe him. Confirmation bias on her part perhaps. A belief that it's always the boyfriend, or the husband, or the father.

'Not that she mentioned. I think she said she had been out. As I said, I'm sure she will talk to you herself.'

DS King nods. 'And to be clear, you can't think of any reason why Miss Murray would be absent? Perhaps you'd had a disagreement? Or she is visiting friends and family? I see from the dispatcher report you hadn't contacted—'

'We spent last night doing your job and calling around

everyone we could think of,' Shelley interjects, and Mal is grateful for it. 'Mal's right when he says no one has heard from her and I've been her best friend for the last sixteen years, so take it from me when I say that this is not usual behaviour from Bronagh. I have no doubt something is very wrong.'

DS King nods, her face softening as Shelley's voice cracks. She believes *her*, Mal thinks. That will have to be enough.

'And this is another sensitive question,' she continues. 'Do either of you have any concerns, or can you think of any reason or likelihood, that Miss Murray may be in a fragile emotional state, and may have been, or could be, a danger to herself or others?'

Mal feels the blood drain from his face. What is being suggested here? That Bronagh might have had some kind of breakdown? That she might have hurt herself? Taken herself away somewhere and... it doesn't bear thinking about.

'No,' he says confidently, yet not quite believing he has to say this out loud. 'She was... is... happy. She wouldn't hurt herself or anyone else.'

'If she were in trouble she'd have asked for help,' Shelley says, and Mal doesn't have to look at her to know she is crying. 'She'd have come to me. No. She hasn't done *anything* to herself.'

'I know these are unpleasant questions,' DS King says, 'but we need to get a full picture so it is important you tell us anything at all that you think might be relevant. It's just— well, we had a quick search of our system and it appears Miss Murray was involved in a very traumatic incident in the first half of last year.'

Mal's stomach seizes. He should've known it was only a matter of time before this was brought up. No doubt it will help convince the police that he is a bad egg. A man of poor character. A man who, they might think, could hurt a woman.

'That's right,' Shelley says. 'But she has worked through that. We've all worked through that.'

DS King looks at Mal, as if watching for a reaction. He's determined he will not give her one. He keeps his face as non-expressive as possible. She nods, looks down at the file in front of her and continues.

'So, have you noticed any changes in her behaviour? Any run-ins with someone who might hold a grudge? Any enemies we should be aware of?'

'No one holds a grudge against Bronagh,' Mal says. 'Everyone loves her. Ask anybody. She isn't the kind of person who makes enemies. If anything, she can be too soft with people. Afraid to offend them. I don't know what has happened here but I do know whatever it is, it isn't her fault.'

'I'm sure that's true,' DS King says. 'So let's focus on what we do know.'

The reality, Mal thinks, is that they know very little. Bronagh is missing. None of their friends, nor her parents in Spain, have heard from her. She left her phone at home, so no one trying to get in touch with her has reached her. There is no sign of a struggle, or a break-in. Everything in their home in Springbrooke Avenue looked remarkably normal – just as he would expect it to look, except of course for the absence of Bronagh herself.

Still, he straightens himself and vows to do the very best he can to answer as many questions as DS King can throw at him. He'll do whatever it takes, he thinks, as long as they find her.

9

BRONAGH

There's a new voice. Female. It slices through her sleep until she has no choice but to open her eyes. As the room is no longer dark, she regrets this move immediately. The heavy curtains have been opened. Turning her head towards the window, she sees that light is doing its very best to stream in through the glass, which could benefit from a good clean.

But even though the light is muted, it is still strong enough to hurt her eyes. Now is not the time for giving in to the urge to close them again though. It's a time instead for having her wits about her, no matter how much pain she is in.

The bed dips beside her and turning her head to see a woman, she immediately startles. This is someone she has seen before. It's a face she could never forget, no matter how much she might want to. Only the last time she saw this woman, she had been slumped in a passenger seat, pale with her eyes closed, and looking to all intents and purposes as if she could be dead.

'It's you,' Bronagh says, as she watches the woman silently

pour two more white pills from the bottle on the tray in front of
her into her own hand.

The woman says nothing but unlike the man who has been
here before, she doesn't so much as raise her eyes to meet
Bronagh's.

'You were in the car,' Bronagh says, trying to gauge her pain
levels as she speaks. 'I came to help you. You were hurt. The
boy, he was—'

'Take these,' the woman interrupts, her accent hard to pin
down. Welsh maybe? Bronagh can't quite tell. 'They'll help.'

'No,' Bronagh says, feeling braver than before. She absolutely does not want to take these tablets and slip back into a
nothing existence. She needs to be in control and she is hungry
for as much information as she can get her hands on. 'Tell me
who you are. What's happening? Why am I here? Are you
hurt?'

'You must take the tablets,' the woman says, ignoring the
questions. Her eyes are still lowered as she gestures the pills
towards Bronagh.

'No. I don't want them.' Her voice is firm and her tone tense.
She wills herself to think fast, and think clearly, feeling in her
very bones that she needs to get out of here. To her surprise,
the woman cowers away as if scared by her refusal to do as she's
told. This, Bronagh realises, is something she might be able to
use to her advantage.

'I... need to go to the bathroom,' she says. It's not a lie, she
realises, suddenly aware of a growing pressure in her bladder.
How long has it been since she last urinated? How long as she
been here? She has no clue. 'Please,' she says, sensing a weak-
ness in the woman. 'I really need to pee.'

The woman raises her gaze and Bronagh can see her face
properly for the first time since the car. She is still almost as

pale as she was when Bronagh tried to rouse her and find her pulse. There are still dark circles under her eyes but also something more – the shadow of a fading bruise is still visible along her left cheekbone.

'Come with me,' the woman says in a quiet voice, putting the pills back on the tray and walking to the other side of the bed. 'I'll help.'

'I'll be fine,' Bronagh says as she pushes off the covers, not knowing at all if she *will* be fine. With the sheets pulled back she catches a glimpse of the raspberry pink of her toenails and remembers her pedicure, her holiday, and Mal. Her heart lurches.

'Please,' the woman says, reaching out a hand to steady Bronagh as she tries to stand.

The effort of getting to her feet causes Bronagh to groan loudly, but even though she has the urge to slump back against the pillows, she knows she has to make it to the bathroom or she will have even more to worry about.

'This way,' the woman says, leading her slowly around the bed. The carpet feels thick with grime and dust beneath her bare feet. She wonders momentarily where her sandals are, the memory of them slapping against her feet in wet grass beside the car returning.

'You were in the car,' Bronagh says again still hoping for an explanation, but the woman simply shakes her head.

'You were. I came to help you. With the little boy.' The woman looks at her, her eyes wide with fear, and she shakes her head again. 'No. Please, the bathroom is here.'

If the bedroom was dank and grotty, the bathroom is borderline putrid. God only knows the last time it was given a proper clean, or aired out for that matter. The smell of damp and stagnant piss is heavy in the air – the old wooden window frames painted shut. There is an extractor fan, which is yellowed, and the vents are coated in some unholy mix of grime, cobwebs and insect corpses. Even if the fan worked, Bronagh is quite sure it would be even more of a health hazard than this airless room.

Only the desperation to pee forces her to actually sit on the toilet and do what she needs to do. There is no toilet paper. There isn't even any soap to wash her hands after, or a towel to dry them with. She twists the tap on and waits for a second before water spatters the sink, in gulping bursts from pipes that clearly are airlocked. Do these people actually live here? The man and woman? And what of the child?

Drying her hands on her T-shirt, she opens the door to where the woman waits to help her back to bed.

'I want to go home,' Bronagh says. 'Can you help me downstairs? Maybe call me a taxi?' Truth be told, she will walk barefoot, however far it takes to get away from here, but she is trying her best to cling on to some hope that she has interpreted all of this wrong and these are simply people helping her before bringing her back to Mal.

'You have to rest,' the woman tells her, leading her back towards the bedroom.

'I have rested. I need to go now. Thank you for your help.'

'No, no. You must have something to eat and some medication. Before he comes home.'

'He? Who is he? The man who came before?'

The woman shakes her head and tugs at Bronagh's arm. She is remarkably strong for someone who looks so frail, or maybe it's just that the blow to her head has left Bronagh weaker than normal.

'Can you at least tell me where I am? Who are you? What is your name? My name is Bronagh.'

The woman shakes her head again and continues to lead the way towards the bedroom.

'I tried to help you. I remember that. You were in the car and the little boy... he came and got me. Please, can you help me?' She knows there is more than a hint of desperation in her voice.

The woman pauses, stops tugging, and turns to look at her. Bronagh thinks she can see a glimmer of compassion in her expression, but just as she goes to speak, there is the sound of a door opening and any compassion that may or may not have been there is replaced by a look of fear.

'Please!' the woman whispers. 'Go to bed.' There is pleading behind her eyes. She doesn't need to say any more for Bronagh to sense that both of them may be at risk if she doesn't comply. This is clearly the only way in which the woman feels she can help her at the moment. She doesn't need to say any more for Bronagh to get the message loud and clear, so she nods and with her heart thudding in her chest, she makes her way back to the bed and tries not to cry with fear and frustration.

The woman takes her place seated behind the tray on the opposite side of the bed to Bronagh. Again, she tries to get her to take the white pills but Bronagh still wants to have her wits about her, even if it comes with a strong dose of pain.

It's impossible, however, to be immune to the fear on the face of the woman opposite her, so she takes the pills with a nod, before sliding them into the pocket of her joggers. If the woman objects to this, she stays silent, but then again that could be because the sound of the man's heavy footsteps on the stairs makes it clear he will be with them any second.

If she's not mistaken, Bronagh is sure she can hear more than just the thudding of the man's approach. There is a second sound. A lighter set of footsteps. It's hard to pick out exactly above the persistent ringing in her ears.

Bronagh is pretty sure there's no point in hoping for some sort of clue or camaraderie from the woman opposite her. She has dropped her gaze once again and has fallen mute. She is lifting a spoon and stirring the gloopy mixture in a bowl on the tray. Rice pudding perhaps. Or porridge. Whatever it is, it looks distinctly unappealing.

The opening of the bedroom door makes her jump, despite her expecting it, and draws her attention immediately away from the tray. Looking up, she sees not only the same man who was there the last time she was conscious but also the small, familiar frame of the little boy who had pounded on her door.

Still dressed in the same clothes he had been wearing when he had taken her by the hand and led her to the car at the top of the street, his appearance is just as unkempt as it was. His face is still pale and his hair, still messy.

However, when he sees her, his face breaks into a wide smile – one that instantly makes him look healthier and more alive – as carefree as a child should look. He glances to the man as if seeking approval and when the man nods back to him, he launches himself towards the bed and towards Bronagh, paying no heed whatsoever to the other woman.

Clambering onto Bronagh's lap, he wraps his arms tightly around her, burying his face in her neck as if she were a long-lost best friend, and grips on so tightly that she can feel the fluttering of his heart in his chest and the warmth of his breath on her skin.

Confusion washes over her. It makes no sense that this little boy is clinging on to her for dear life when his mother is inches away. No one speaks and Bronagh starts to feel uncomfortable.

He's only a child, she tells herself. She doesn't want to push him away, but there is something about how he is holding on to her – as if he needs this hug to exist – that makes her feel deeply uneasy. Soon she feels warm, wet tears starting to slide down her neck as the boy starts to weep. She pats him gently on the back, comforting him as she would her best friend Shelley's children but at the same time not understanding – at all – what is going on.

Eventually the boy pushes back and looks at her directly. His tears have made his blue eyes even brighter – forming a stark contrast to the dull and dirty pallor of his skin. Blinking at her, he raises his hand and places it very gently on her cheek, and the warmth of it makes her feel sad for a reason she doesn't quite understand. Maybe it's because she can be angry with the man and the woman, but this is a young child. One who is clearly neglected and caught up in some strange way in something she, as an adult, cannot even comprehend herself.

Bronagh places her own hand on top of the boy's. None of this is his fault. She feels a need to let him know that she is a safe person. That if her instincts are right, he is as much of a victim in all this as she is.

He blinks, sending two more fat tears rolling down his cheeks. His nose has started to run and he pulls his hand from her face so that he can draw the cuff of his anorak under his nose before reaching back out towards her. There is silence from the other two people in the room. It's almost as if they have ceased to exist and in this moment, it is just Bronagh and this pale little boy.

He opens his mouth to speak and she waits, eager to know what he has to say. The same instinct that is telling her he is a victim in all this too is telling her that he is also the key to it all.

'Mumma!' he says, his voice cracking as he throws himself towards her again and pulls her into a hug.

She blinks.

This doesn't make sense. She's not his mother. She has no idea why he is calling her by that name – and yet he is clinging on to her with such ferocity and saying that word again and again, just as he had done when he knocked on her door and led her out of her house and away from the safety of her life.

As he cries 'Mumma' again and again, she glances to the woman – the woman she had taken to be the boy's mother, but her head is still bowed and she is not meeting her gaze.

'Your mummy is here,' Bronagh says to the boy. 'Look, there she is!'

She can feel him shake his head and grip on even tighter. 'Mumma!' he says.

No, Bronagh thinks, this absolutely does not make any sense of at all. 'I'm not your mummy, darling. This is your mummy.'

She looks to the woman, who is once again gazing downwards, her hair, unwashed and uncombed, falling forward and shielding her expression. That's when Bronagh notices for the first time that she too is in dirty clothes – clothes that look as if they have been worn for too long but also look as if, at one time, they might have been nice, expensive even. A pair of linen trousers, a fitted T-shirt. Completely unsuitable for the cold weather, of course, as are the sandals on her feet.

The only person in the room dressed in clean clothes is him. This man – tall and well built. Dark hair and dark jeans. A dark shirt with a crisp white T-shirt underneath. There is little about him that reminds her of the boy except, she realises, he has the same piercing light blue eyes.

'Where is this boy's mum?' Bronagh asks as the boy clings tighter still. 'What is going on here?' She might have taken a knock to the head but she is pretty sure she knows fundamentally that she is not a mother, she does not know these people, and she does not belong here. This is not her life.

She should be at home, among her own things. Her books, her knick-knacks and her half-packed suitcase. She should be waiting on Mal to come through the door and whisk her upstairs for some reunion sex. She should be trying to find her damn passport.

The man, his face in shadow as rain starts to beat down on the filthy windowpane, shrugs as the boy tightens his grip, nestling his bird-like frame back into hers. He's so thin – just a fine wee thing. It's impossible not to feel protective of him.

'Where is this child's mother?' she asks again, her voice louder this time.

'You,' the man says in that strange accent of his. 'You are his mother. You see how he clings to you. You hear him? You're his mother, just like he says. All we did was bring you back to him.'

10

MAL

It feels even stranger than before for Mal to return home knowing that Bronagh is not there, and that at any moment the police will arrive to kick off what DS King has promised will be a very thorough investigation. They will search this house. Speak to their neighbours. Examine every detail of his and Bronagh's lives, no doubt.

'No stone will be left unturned until we know where she is,' King had said.

'And presumably no stones will be left unturned until you know why I had to come here myself to get any of you to take this seriously?' he had replied, before watching DS King swallow and nod.

'I can assure you of that,' she'd told him. 'We are taking this matter incredibly seriously and it is already in the hands of our most senior officers.'

He has to take her at her word, just as he has to believe they really will do everything they can to bring Bronagh home.

The house is much too quiet without her chatter, or her

music, or her singing to herself as she goes about her chores. He can't help but think that they should be in the air, almost in Alicante and tantalisingly close to a fortnight of sunshine and no worries.

Instead he is here looking at his own home in a whole new, uncomfortable light. DS King had asked him all manner of questions about their relationship, about Bronagh's work life and her past. He understands why the questions needed to be asked but it all felt like such a colossal waste of time when they are already so far behind. If only he had come home earlier – skipped the last day of the conference, which wasn't even all that productive anyway. He would have known earlier. Been able to sound the alarm earlier.

Or even if he had skipped the conference altogether. If he had only worked from home instead, then maybe Bronagh would be okay and none of this would've happened.

'It's not your fault, Mal,' Shelley had told him as they'd left the police station. 'And no one who knows you and Bronagh would ever think you could be in any way responsible for her disappearance.'

He'd shrugged. He wanted to believe her but he knows as well as anyone else that he will be Suspect Number One. Just as he knows that not everyone will believe him to be incapable of harming a hair on his girlfriend's head.

That for some of them it will feel like the obvious answer. After all, he has hurt her in the past. Shame makes him nauseous. That had been different, he tells himself. Things were messier then.

But he can't even begin to think of a scenario that makes sense to his tired brain. He can't think why his girlfriend would be targeted by anyone. Or why, he thinks as his stomach clenches, she would just walk away and leave everything behind. Is there some secret part of her life he knows nothing about? Has he missed some pretty big warning signs along the way? Maybe because he'd yearned to believe in the happy ending he wanted so much for them.

Making a coffee, hopeful that another dose of caffeine will keep him awake and alert, he pops two paracetamols in his mouth and washes them down with a glass of tap water. His head hurts – no doubt due to lack of sleep. He feels so utterly useless.

The police had told him officers would be on the scene within the hour. Not just a response car, but a team. All available resources. Every officer who isn't currently sleeping off last night's policing operation. He is grateful for that. But it doesn't make him feel any less impotent. There has to be something more he can do himself to help. He can't be expected to sit and wait, drinking coffee and popping pills and watching his phone light up with notifications every few seconds. Friends of his and Bronagh's checking to see if he has heard anything yet. People asking if there is anything they can do. The odd ill-timed, poor-taste joke about her finally having realised what a loser he is and having dumped him. He'd switch the damn phone off if he weren't still living in hope that the next message or the next call could be from Bronagh.

This, he thinks, is insufferable. It is driving him mad. He has to do *something*. Digging in his pocket, he pulls out the card that Ingrid Devlin woman gave him outside the police station. It couldn't hurt to have a journalist on board. Shelley had said she'd heard of Ingrid – had even read a couple of her books about crimes that had happened in Derry. The murder of a wife and mother, the murder of a child back in the nineties... She sounds like the kind of woman who has her ear to the ground, so surely she will be able to help? She'd seemed keen to talk to him.

Without procrastinating any further, he opens his phone screen and taps in the number on the card. Ingrid doesn't sound at all surprised to hear from him. If anything she sounds a little confused as to why it took him so long.

'I was wondering when you'd get around to calling,' she says on the phone. 'In fact I was giving you another fifteen minutes and then I was going to call you myself.' There is a teasing lilt to her voice, an attempt to be overly friendly. Mal's not entirely sure how he feels about that.

'I'm just back from the police station,' he says. 'I've been trying to think straight.'

'I can imagine this is very difficult. Your head must be all over the place,' Ingrid says confidently, but not without a hint of compassion this time. This is a woman, Mal thinks, who has made a career of inserting herself into the very centre of a lot of crime-related drama over the years. She has just cause for her confidence – none of this is new to her.

'Don't worry too much about trying to think straight. That's the job of the police. I assume they've launched an investigation?'

He opens his mouth to speak.

'Actually, don't worry about answering that. I know they've launched an investigation. I have little mice with big ears in that building.'

Mal isn't sure whether to be impressed or aggravated by this woman, deciding for his own sanity to choose to believe that her confidence is bordering on the right side of cocky. 'So you probably know more than I do, then,' he says. 'Maybe I should be the one asking you questions?'

'Not at all,' she snaps back. 'Yes, I have some sources in the

PSNI, but that just means that what I know is targeted, strategic information and clear of emotion – specific to police procedure. You know, about Bronagh. Who she is. Her strengths and her personality. You know, all these little details that you don't even realise will be helpful. Right now all the different versions of the woman you love will be dancing through your head trying to get your attention. They'll all be dropping their own clues but there's just too much noise to pick out the right ones. If you'd let me, I'd be happy to help you wade through them all.'

He sighs. 'I'm not sure I've the energy to talk in riddles or to try and work out what exactly it is you're saying,' he says wearily.

'Of course you don't,' Ingrid tells him, and there's a hint of an apology in her tone. 'And of course you'll be exhausted. Let me try and keep it simple. There are two angles to this. The first, and most important, is finding Bronagh. The second is finding out what caused the monumental cock-up in police procedure. Are they sniffing around your house yet?'

'No. Not yet. But I'm expecting them any minute.'

She sighs. 'They really should be there by now. It's not good enough, is it?'

She doesn't give him the chance to answer, probably realising as much as Mal does that there is no need to state the obvious.

'Why don't you let me know your address and I'll come round. Believe me, there is nothing the PSNI love more than when I turn up during an investigation. They know they're in for some extra scrutiny. It always puts a light under their arses, you know?'

'Anything that gets her back here safer and quicker is fine by me,' he tells her and immediately rhymes off his address.

'Give me an hour. I've a couple of things I want to double-check – a few mice I want to chat to – and I'll be with you as soon as I can and we can really get things moving.'

'Okay,' he says, flopping down on the sofa, feeling his exhaustion in every single one of his bones 'I'll see you in an hour. Do you really think you can help?'

'I've learned not to make promises,' she says. 'But I wouldn't be coming to see you if I didn't think I could.'

He can't help but feel a flicker of hope as he ends the call. At least, he thinks, he's being proactive. It has to count for something.

But just as quickly as the hope comes, it is crushed by a thought, unbidden, entering his mind and making his blood run cold. He has no idea whether or not she is even still alive.

For the love of God, Cooper, he tells himself. *There's no need to be jumping to conclusions like that. Don't allow that stuff in your head.* But how can he not? How can his mind not race to images of her picture all over the news? Of reading reports about a missing woman – only this time it will be describing her.

Immediately his mind starts to paint a picture of Bronagh in the language the police are likely to use. Thirty-two years old, slim build, five foot six... or is it seven... or five. He doesn't know. He only knows where the top of her head reaches when he holds her close for a hug. Just like he knows she has blue eyes – a grey blue, like the water at Buncrana beach on a sunny day. Freckles, which she hates, but he loves. Brown hair, silky soft and smelling of apples, and she pays a clean fortune to add those whatever-they're-called highlighty things to it. What was she wearing the day she went missing? He doesn't know. He wasn't here. He didn't see her. But her favourite jacket – the khaki denim one with the camouflage patch pockets that she wears everywhere, is still hanging at the bottom of the stairs and her trainers are by the door.

He wants to run upstairs and pull through her clothes, see if he can work out what is missing from her drawers, but that's a fool's errand. Bronagh Murray has so many clothes it would be a near impossible task for him to figure out what wasn't there. He's always teasingly asking her just how many pairs of joggers a woman needs, or why she has to have so many oversized hoodies when she will just steal his anyway.

Maybe he should've paid more attention to which ones are her favourites. Maybe that's the kind of thing a boyfriend should know, especially one who has been trying to prove himself worthy of her.

The police will be here soon to look around, he tells himself. There's a chance they would view it as highly suspicious if they landed to find he has pulled everything from her chest of drawers and wardrobe. They'll think he's trying to hide something. Fuck, he thinks, it will probably look suspicious to them that he bundled his dirty clothes from his work trip into the washing machine last night and washed them. There will be questions to answer about that. Will they think he was washing away evidence? Will they arrive with that spray that makes blood glow in the dark?

How is anyone supposed to keep their sanity through this? Without thinking, he lifts his phone and calls her number, momentarily forgetting that, of course, her phone is sitting on the coffee table in front of him and nowhere near her. That particular realisation, as her phone lights ups, comes like a punch right to the gut.

A knock on the door pulls him from his thoughts, and he's immediately on his feet. A tiny voice is whispering in his head:

it might be her; she might be back. She doesn't have her keys with her.

His hope is short-lived, however, when he opens the door to find Constable Morrison and a female colleague on his doorstep. In the street he sees another unmarked police car pull up, and a number of uniformed officers step out. It will only be a matter of seconds before the curtains start twitching and neighbours start popping their heads out of their front doors to see if they can be of any help. This is it, he thinks. This is where it all starts. Mal is vaguely aware of Morrison talking to him as he watches the other police officers walk up and down the street, looking at each of the houses. They'll be knocking on doors soon.

Mrs Cosgrove has, of course, come outside and hobbled her way over to Mal's house with remarkable speed for one who claims to be infirm.

She's doing a good job of looking deeply concerned, but Mal knows her well enough to also recognise that wee glint in her eyes that belies her excitement at some real drama happening right on her street.

'Oh Mal, love, is something wrong? Is it Bronagh? Is she hurt? Maybe I should've had a good look around the other day when the door was open, but I didn't think!' Her voice is trembling, her hand shaking. She does a great impression of a feeble old lady but Mal knows different.

'So it was yourself who found the front door open then?' Morrison asks. 'Mr Cooper here was telling us that a neighbour closed it.'

'Yes, son. It was me. I always like to keep a wee eye out for my neighbours, you know. We're like that here. Always watching out for one another. Isn't that what community should be about?'

'Indeed. Mrs Cosgrove, is it?' Morrison says.

'Yes, that's me. Eilish Cosgrove. That's E.I.L.I.S.H. – just to make sure you spell it right. I live next door.' She jerks her head towards her house. 'I've been there fifty-something years. A lifetime.'

'Well, we'll absolutely have to have one of our officers come and have a chat with you, if that's okay,' Morrison says, his notebook in hand as he writes her name down.

'Ask me anything you want. I'll answer you.' She's beaming with pride, delighted at being useful. Mal has never wanted more to tell her to get lost.

'We'll keep that in mind. But first, we have to have a chat with your neighbour here and see if we can help him. So if you don't mind heading back over home, someone will be with you shortly. We can't have you standing out here in the cold on our conscience.'

She makes to protest. Mal knows her well enough to know she will tell the officer she doesn't mind the cold. That she just wants to help. But Morrison must have at least enough experience to know full well how to deal with interfering neighbours. 'Why don't you go and pop the kettle on?' he says before turning his back to her and letting his female colleague lead Mrs C back across the double driveways to her own front door.

'How about we go inside?' Morrison says. 'Save ourselves from any more interruptions by well-meaning folk. A couple of my colleagues will come in and have a little look around, if that's okay? Nothing too invasive. It's surprising what you can miss when you're used to seeing everything every day.'

Mal nods, even though it doesn't make sense to him. Surely being familiar with the house means he's exactly the right person to see if something is amiss. It should stick out like a sore thumb. Except that Bronagh is always telling him he can't see what's in front of his own face half the time.

Morrison turns down Mal's offer of a tea or coffee, which is probably a good thing. There isn't much milk left in the fridge. They were running all their fresh supplies down before their holiday. Mal hasn't had the chance, or the wherewithal, to go to the shops and restock.

He walks through to the living room and sits down, as Morrison follows suit on the armchair by the window. *Bronagh hates that seat,* he thinks. *She says it's the least comfortable in the house. No one ever sits there.*

Morrison seems to find it perfectly comfortable and he looks at ease as he glances around the room. Mal wonders if there are certain things he is looking for. Anything here that declares itself a big, fat clue. To Mal's eyes, it looks like it normally does – save for the mug on the floor.

'That's... that is Bronagh's mug,' he says. 'She must've left it on the coffee table there before she... before she went. There was still tea in it. I'm afraid I had a moment of frustration at everything last night and lost my cool. I meant to pick it up...' The excuse sounds feeble and he's annoyed with himself for not cleaning it up before.

'It's fine, Mal. We all get frustrated sometimes. Don't worry about it. Our officers will know what to look for.'

Mal nods, wondering if he should feel nervous despite the reassurance. No, he tells himself. He can see that Morrison, for all his youth and puppy-like enthusiasm, actually does seem to care about his work, and the people he is talking to. Mal wonders if he can use that to his advantage. Perhaps get him to give him some sort of insider scoop on the investigation. Maybe there is something the police know that they're keeping from him. Ingrid Devlin certainly seems to think there might be. She needs to talk to her 'mice'.

He's about to ask Morrison when there are three knocks on the door, followed by the sound of a female voice calling, 'Hello?'

This time he knows immediately it's not Bronagh – and not just because she sounds different, but because the part of him that has hoped she will just walk through the door is increasingly sure of the fact she won't.

11

BRONAGH

The little boy still clings to Bronagh, burying his head in her neck, curling his legs up and leaning the whole weight of his body against hers. She feels his hand grip her top tightly, pulling it away from her chest slightly.

Her head spins as she tries to process what this man has just told her. That they are her family. They are most certainly not. She has a family. At least she has Mal. And Shelley. Her parents too, not that they are particularly close. They left as soon as they deemed her independent, and started their new life in Spain. It's a life that largely does not involve or include Bronagh and she has made her peace with that. Still, they – and not this man, woman and child – are her family.

'I don't know what you're talking about,' Bronagh says in a hushed tone, wary of upsetting the boy. He may well be a part of whatever the hell this is, but he is a child – and clearly one who is very confused. The last thing she wants to do is cause him any upset. He's little more than a baby and she can feel his frailness as he nestles against her.

God only knows what this little boy has been told – what he

has been through. She has no idea what kind of sick scheme is at play here, but her life no longer feels real. It's madness. Maybe, when she took the knock to the head, she was injured much worse than she thought and she is in some dreamlike state – a coma or something – and this is just a crazy, drug-fuelled dream.

If she's struggling to make sense of it, she can't imagine the mental gymnastics the little boy on her lap is going through. And yet, he seems utterly convinced that she is his mother.

The man glowers at her, his brow furrowed. 'How can you say we aren't your family? Are we not taking care of you? Feeding you? Giving you medicine for your injury? Have we not given you a bed to sleep in? Is that not what a family does?'

A growing panic constricts her breathing and her head, still fuzzy, tries to process his words and the situation as best she can. The little boy clings to her tightly once again, and she can feel the warmth of him and the fierceness of his hold as if he needs her in this very moment to protect him.

Glancing to the woman, in the hope of some sort of help or even an acknowledgement of the man's completely insane behaviour, Bronagh is soon disappointed.

The woman's gaze is still downwards and her concentration is on stirring whatever porridge or gruel appears to be in the bowl in front of her. There is no allyship to be found here. Just as there's not a chance Bronagh is going to eat whatever that concoction is – even if she didn't feel as if she might be sick at any second.

It looks so unpalatable – like everything else in her surroundings. It's like something from a dystopian nightmare. Only the soft, warm breath of the boy on her skin is grounding her in the here and now and convincing her this isn't all some epic illusion. And still, the man stares at her, waiting for a response to his question as if it is she who has wronged him.

'I appreciate that you have helped me,' she says, though it pains her to do so. There's a cruelty in having to thank someone for tending to an injury you're pretty sure they intentionally caused in the first place. 'That was very considerate of you. But that doesn't make me a part of your family. I have my own family and they'll be worried about me.'

'We are your family,' the man repeats. 'Zachary,' he says, and the boy turns towards him. 'Who is this woman?'

'Mumma,' the little boy says without hesitation. It's the only word she has heard him utter.

'Are you calling Zachary a liar?' the man asks, and the boy blinks and stares at her as if awaiting her response as eagerly as the man in the doorway.

'I... I don't know. He is confused, perhaps.' She reaches out to the woman, who pulls her arm away before Bronagh can make any contact. 'He called *you* Mumma when he brought me to you. After he knocked at my door. It was all he said.'

The woman looks up just long enough for Bronagh to see the pleading in her eyes. Or maybe it's a warning. It's difficult to tell, but what isn't difficult – what is as plain as the nose on her face – is that she wants her to stop talking. Nothing good will come from her questioning the man – no matter how desperate she feels. She doesn't want to stay quiet. She wants to get up and get the hell out of this house as quickly as she can, but she knows she is weak, and her trip to the bathroom proved that she was still very unsteady on her feet. She's not sure she could walk downstairs without falling. She's pretty certain that if the man tried to stop her, he would be able to in a matter of seconds. Probably not even as long as that, if she is being honest with herself. She'd not even get past the door. He might not even let her get off the bed. And what of the boy?

How would Zachary react if she pushed him aside and tried to bundle out of the house? What if she took a dizzy spell and tumbled down the stairs? And, of course, she has no clue where she is. This house could be three doors down from her, or three towns away for all she knows.

'It's very strange,' the man says, 'for a mother not to acknowledge her own child. And yet here he is, clinging to you. Ask yourself why would we care for you, or feed you, or tend to your injuries if you were not truly one of our family?' The tone of his voice is confusing. There is a sincerity in his words as if he truly believes what he is saying. He believes she is part of whatever the fuck this twisted 'family' of his is. She's not sure if that scares her more than anything else. If there is one thing she has learned in all her thirty-two years, it is that it's a waste of breath and energy to argue with a man who believes he is right. Especially when she is at a physical disadvantage.

'I don't know,' she says, biting back the urge to tell him that it would only be right for him to look after her since, she suspects, he caused her injuries in the first place.

The woman *was* unconscious. Bronagh doesn't think that was an act. She had seen the pallor on her face, and how unreactive she was. Her mind goes to the pills secreted in the pocket of her joggers and to how the same pills had affected her when she had taken them earlier, at the man's request. It's possible, she supposes, that the woman could have been under the influence of the same medication, or something similar, when she was slumped in the car looking as if she might be dead.

If only she had turned back as soon as she had seen the woman was unconscious. If only she had run back home and called for help, or lifted her phone, or shouted as loud as she could. She had been so stupid to get so close. As soon as she had seen that both the passenger and driver doors were open – that the driver had clearly absconded – she should've been on high alert. She has never considered herself to be a stupid woman, but she had been high on adrenaline and in a state of panic while the boy had cried beside her. She had just wanted to help. She didn't have time to think about it. Or the headspace to think about it. All she could see was this distressed child and a woman in a state somewhere between life and death. She did what anyone would do when confronted with a crying child in this situation. She'd tried to help. She'd just wanted to make things better and instead, she's here in God-knows-what-hell-hole trying to make sense of something so bizarre and twisted that it doesn't seem real.

If this is some sort of kidnapping, there is a big disappoint-ment coming for her captors when they realise she is no one of importance, and does not come from money. There is no one – not even her lovely Mal – who would be able to access more than a couple of thousand pounds at the very most. Even that would require a level of begging, borrowing and stealing. Her captors are going to a lot of effort for very little reward.

Unless the endgame is something else. Something worse.

'Tell me why you want me here,' she says, unable to force herself to play along with his twisted happy-families game. 'What do you want from me?'

He moves so fast that she barely registers his crossing the room until he is right beside the bed, close enough to grab her by the chin with one of his meaty, pungent hands.

In the next second he has dragged her across the bed towards him, knocking both Zachary and the woman out of his path. Bronagh is vaguely aware of someone crying out but, even if she had to swear on her own life, she would be unable to tell who the noise came from. It's entirely possible it escaped her own throat. There is no chance of her being able to turn her face away from his. The hold he has on her is simply too tight.

Her heart is thumping so hard that she dreads it may burst from her chest, but she vows she will not betray her fear entirely. Fighting with her instincts, she keeps her eyes open as he grips her jawline tighter, forcing her mouth open.

'You are *my* family,' he sneers. 'You do what I say. I say jump, you jump. I say bark like a dog, you will bark like a dog. I say smile and you *will* smile. Do you understand?'

She tries to answer him but with his clinch so tight on her jaw, she cannot speak, nor can she nod. But she realises that he isn't really waiting for an answer. He knows she understands. She has no choice but to understand. This – it dawns on Bronagh with a sickening realisation – is likely not the first time he has threatened someone. Even without the bruises on the face of the other woman, she'd know this was a violent man in front of her. As he tightens his grip, pain searing through her, she knows this is not a discussion or even an argument. He is putting her very squarely in her place. He is exerting his power and his control.

All she can do is keep breathing and watch, in horror, as he brings his face even closer to hers – so close she can almost taste him. Her stomach lurches. Just as she has convinced herself that he is going to assault her with a kiss, he turns his head ever so slightly that he swerves her mouth and instead is just millimetres from her ear.

'You do not question me ever again. I won't be so understanding next time.' She feels the slick sensation of his tongue circling the folds of her ear before feeling his teeth nip slightly at her lobe. 'Next time, I bite,' he says with a laugh before releasing his grasp and pushing her backwards onto the bed.

Her head misses connecting with the wall behind her by centimetres.

She closes her eyes and curls up in a ball, her instincts screaming at her to protect herself at all costs. Hands over her ears, she wants to simply disappear. *Dear Jesus,* she thinks, *what is this?*

Shaking, shock and fear taking over her body, she feels a hopelessness wash over her – one that was not there before. Before, she could tell herself it was a little strange, and definitely a lot creepy, but there could still be an innocent – if bizarre – explanation for it all. Now, though, she knows that this is real. She is living a nightmare and there is no easy way to wake up from it. Try as she might, she cannot stop herself from crying. As she rocks herself in the foetal position, she feels a small body lying beside her, and a small arm wraps itself around her middle.

'Don't cry, Mumma,' Zachary says, his own voice breaking. *May God forgive me,* she thinks, but she has to fight the urge to push him away. It's his fault she is here in the first instance. It is he who tricked her into following him. It is he who continues to call her 'Mumma' in that creepy, babyish voice of his. She wants to scream at him that she is not his 'mama' and that she wants nothing to do with him, or this house, this woman and this brute of a man.

He is only a baby himself, Bronagh reminds herself. Still, that does not stop the touch of his hand, as he wipes a tear from her cheek, from making her skin crawl.

12

INGRID

The police have beaten me here to Mal and Bronagh's house, although of course they should have been here hours ago. Still, it appears to be all systems go. Bradley must be panicking about how bad this is going to look for the PSNI. And he should be. It's about as big of a gaffe as you could imagine.

They are already causing quite a stir, I see, as I wait for a response to my knock at the door. Despite the inclement weather, a few neighbours have come out of their houses and wandered to the bottom of their garden paths and are standing in little huddles, eyeing up the cop cars parked outside number twenty-four.

It's exactly what you expect it to look like. Just like any number of crime scenes I've had cause to visit it over the years, because I have no doubt there is some kind of crime going on here.

It makes for quite a depressing tableau. Women standing with their arms crossed. Hiding under the hoods of their coats or huddled beneath shared umbrellas. Heads bowed together. There is chat – wicked whispers no doubt. Everyone loves a bit of scandal. Given the average age of the neighbours I see gathered, I'd hazard this is the most exciting thing to happen in months for many of them. I make a mental note of which houses the nosy neighbours appear to belong to before calling 'Hello!' again in through the door. A uniformed officer appears behind me and I flash my press pass.

'Mal's expecting me,' I tell her.

She nods and to my surprise, doesn't double-check, instead directing me to go on in. Perhaps she has been prepared for my arrival. I follow the voices to the living room where Mal, looking understandably even more wrecked than when I first met him two hours ago, is sitting on the sofa, his head in his hands.

He looks up and disappointment is written large across his face. Of course, I think, he's at the stage in these investigations where he still thinks his loved one is going to come through the door at any second. Something tells me – and it's not just the heavy police presence – that no one actually thinks that's likely to happen in this case.

'The officer outside told me to come on in,' I say, nodding back towards the hall in the direction of the officer who let me in.

There's another young officer in the room – uniformed. Looks about twelve, but then again I'm finding that increasingly, as forty looms larger, anyone under the age of thirty 'looks about twelve' to me. The joys of ageing. This one does look particularly fresh-faced though. Probably new to the job.

'Do you know this woman?' he asks, getting to his feet and walking towards me.

'Well... not really, but I did invite her round,' Mal says. 'She says she can help. This is—'

'Ingrid Devlin,' I interrupt. 'You must be new? I don't think we've met before?'

'Three months on the beat. Constable Morrison,' he says. 'And who exactly are you, Ms Devlin?'

'It's actually quite reassuring that my reputation has not preceded me,' I say with a soft smile, reaching out to shake his hand. This is definitely the time to play it cool – keep the newbie sweet and onside. This job is all about building relationships – especially with people who could perhaps become one of my sneaky sources.

'I'm an investigative journalist. I used to work for *The Chronicle*, but I'm freelance now. I focus on true crime. You might have seen my books in Waterstones or Little Acorns?'

'I'm not really a book person,' Morrison says. 'I don't have much call to go into bookshops.'

'You don't know what you're missing,' I tell him. 'You find out all manner of things in bookshops.'

'I'll keep that in mind,' Morrison says with the air of someone who has already forgotten which shops I named. It's clear he's not quite sure what to make of me and that's okay. I'm used to that, and when push comes to shove, he is not who I'm here to speak with. And he absolutely won't be in a position of authority to reveal anything too sensitive about the investigation to me.

I turn my attention to Mal. 'So, I see the police are doing some door-to-door interviews.'

'Yes, and DS King will be here shortly,' Morrison interjects.

'I don't imagine she'll be too happy to find me here,' I say. DCI Bradley tolerates me. Eve King on the other hand? Definitely in the 'not a fan' category.

'Mal, are you okay to talk to me? Maybe this isn't the best time for me to call.' I say this knowing that he of course will talk to me. However, in situations like this, when someone is experiencing the worst day of their lives, it's good to make them feel as if they have some sort of control over proceedings.

'Of course I can talk. Did you find anything out?' he asks.

That gets the attention of Morrison, who immediately straightens up. 'Ms Devlin, if you have any information on the whereabouts of Ms Murray, it would be helpful if you shared it with the police.' From the look on his face I'd say he's delighted at speaking up, but also not yet confident enough to be sure I won't just tell him to get lost, or worse, laugh at him.

I take a breath and stay perfectly poised. 'If I feel I have information that is relevant to your inquiry, and which you are not already in possession of, then I will be sure to share it.'

Mal looks between the two of us, unsure what to think of our exchange, no doubt. I feel for him. This is a game of sorts – and I can't give anything away. Not – I think with a sour, sinking feeling – that I have anything of any significance to give away. The truth is, my sources have been remarkably quiet – safe to say it's all hands on deck with this investigation. Whether it's because they have reason to take it particularly seriously, or because Bradley is panicking I'm about to sink the PSNI for their lack of action, I don't know. But it certainly won't do Bronagh any harm.

'Look, I don't care much who knows what,' Mal says. 'What I do care about is getting Bronagh back. Quickly. Constable Morrison, you said you are here to do your job so please do it. Look wherever you need to look, and ask whatever you need to ask. You and your team can pull this house apart if it helps. Ingrid? Is it okay if I call you Ingrid and not Ms Devlin?'

'Ingrid is perfectly fine,' I say.

'Maybe we can have a chat in the kitchen.'

I nod and follow him out of the living room, down the hall

and through to the small, modern kitchen. There are little touches of their life together everywhere. Photos stuck to the fridge with magnets from sunny holiday destinations. Mugs with their names on upturned on the drainer. A calendar with what I assume to be Bronagh's writing outlining their holiday dates and decorated with love heart doodles. It's little things like this that bring a person and a story to life for me, so I try to store them in my memory.

'DS King will be here shortly,' Morrison calls down the hall, as Mal encourages me to take a seat. I can't help but hear the young officer's words as some kind of warning. The kind, perhaps, a mother would give to her children when the end of the working day approaches and their authoritarian father is on his way home. Perhaps my reputation does precede me after all.

'Tea? Coffee? No... hang on. We're out of milk. Glass of water?' Mal asks.

'I'm good, thanks,' I say as he switches on the kettle. 'The police certainly didn't waste their time getting here.'

'Well, it depends how you look at it. I called them first last night. About, God—sixteen hours ago actually.'

It's unthinkable. No matter what DCI Bradley might do to try and make up for this, or how many heads may roll, it won't give those hours back to the investigation. I only hope – for everyone's sake – it's not too late for Bronagh.

Mal opens the cupboard and takes out a mug.

'So, these sources of yours? Have they heard anything about Bronagh?'

I feel bad that I don't have much at all of substance to tell him. My sources within the PSNI are as clueless about the whole situation as Bradley was this morning before I spoke to him. Although... I did hear something that may or may not be related.

'To be honest? Very little. It's too early in the investigation. But one of them did say there seems to have been something in the wind these past few days at the station, among the higher-ups. As if they were expecting something big to happen. It might be this... it might be something else. I know that's not very helpful but I'll keep you posted as I get information, as long as you're open and honest with me, Mal.'

'I've nothing to hide,' he says. 'I'll do whatever it takes to get her back here safe and sound.'

He sounds genuine. Not that you can always tell, but most of the time there are some tells. A shiftiness about the eyes. Something in their body language that screams 'liar' or 'cover-up'. I'm not getting those vibes from Mal, but that doesn't mean I trust him. First rule of journalism – question everything.

'Did they give you any clue about what this something big is?' he asks.

I wish I could give him a helpful answer but I can't. My source did tell me they would see what they could find out and get back to me ASAP though. He didn't want to say too much, other than something has them rattled. That certainly seemed to be the case with Bradley this morning, but I'd put it down to the disturbance in town last night, and the delay in their response to this call. I imagine either of those would be enough to rattle even the most experienced officer.

'Nothing I can tell you with 100 per cent certainty,' I tell him. 'But let's focus on what we do know. Tell me about Bronagh and tell me about the last time you saw her or heard from her.'

He pours the boiling water from the kettle over a teabag in his mug before walking to the fridge, opening it, swearing and closing it again, perhaps a little too forcefully. 'No milk,' he says as if it is a surprise to him and he hadn't already told me that just minutes before.

I can see it now, a little hint of anger in his face. Justified, maybe. He's under incredible stress, but still I make a mental note of it as he sits down in front of me and, looking at me straight in the face says, 'Tell me what you need to know.'

13

BRONAGH

'Get up,' the man says. 'Your son needs you.'

Bronagh looks from the man to the woman, and then to the boy. He stares up at her with those blue eyes, his face pleading. The child is clearly desperate for attention and affection, but she isn't the person to give it to him. He's a stranger. She knows nothing more about him than that his name is Zachary and he has clearly been neglected.

Of course she feels sorry for him. He's just a baby. But he is not *her* baby, and is instead just part of whatever sick fantasy is being played out in this house.

'He's not my s—' she begins, only to be silenced by a glare from the man and the slightest raising of his hand. A warning that he is not afraid to use brute force. To punish her if necessary. She has no doubt at all that he means it.

'Sorry,' she mutters as desperation claws at her. She can't understand what game is being played here.

'Good. You should be,' he says. 'Now. You eat something and you get up.'

'I'm not hungry,' she says.

'You eat something,' he says, his eyes like flint. All she can do is nod, while he turns on his heel and leaves the room.

'What is this?' she asks as soon as she hears his footsteps fade on the stairs. 'What is going on?'

The woman shakes her head. 'You heard him. You are the boy's mother. Take my advice. Do not argue with him. Do what he says. You don't know what he's capable of.' She leans in, places her hands over Zachary's ears. There is something touching about the protectiveness of the gesture. 'He is not normal. He is a monster.'

Bronagh feels sick but this time she doesn't know if it is her injuries or fear causing her stomach to turn. But she sees that this woman is terrified too. Whatever game is being played here, she is sure the woman is as much of a pawn as she is. It's possible that's what they all are – even this child.

'Can we play, Mumma?' the boy asks. 'I have a car. And a lorry. And a boat.' His eyes are wide with excitement. In any other situation she would push aside her lack of maternal instinct and tell him of course they can play. But this isn't any other situation.

'I'm not feeling very well,' she says and it's not a lie. She just wants to lie down and have a nice long sleep. In her own bed, preferably. The realisation that that is beyond her reach makes her want to sob.

'Be careful,' the other woman says. It's not a warning as much as well-meant advice. 'If you want my opinion? Keep the child happy. He...' she nods in the direction of the door and the stairs '...does not like it when the boy isn't happy. And if he tells you to eat something, then eat something. You can't guarantee when you'll eat again.'

She pushes the bowl towards Bronagh, a mulchy beige sludge. Porridge. Bronagh hates porridge but she can't deny she is hungry, and the woman's warning that she may not have access to food again any time soon weighs heavy on her.

'What is going on here?' Bronagh asks, an air of pleading in her voice. 'Are you the child's mother?'

'Mumma!' Zachary calls again, sliding back onto her knee and curling once more into her. Bronagh feels herself recoil from him but forces herself to allow him space on her knee. She must not upset the child.

The woman shakes her head. 'It doesn't matter. It just matters that you keep yourself safe. It's the only way to get out of this.' There is a pleading in her voice that both scares Bronagh but also gives her a sliver of hope. She may get out of this. All she has to do is follow the rules.

'Do you really believe that?' she asks, as she tentatively brings a mouthful of the lukewarm porridge to her lips. The texture of it makes her gag. She knows immediately that it doesn't matter how hungry she is, she won't be able to eat it. At the same time she notices Zachary eyeing it hungrily. He's so thin, just skin and bones; she can't help but wonder when he last ate.

'Would you like this food?' she asks him, and he nods enthusiastically.

'You'll be hungry,' the woman warns as Bronagh hands her spoon to the little boy and he immediately starts devouring it.

'I can't eat it,' she says. 'I just want to go home.' To her shame her voice cracks and she worries for a moment that she might break down.

'Then follow his rules,' the woman says. 'Don't question him. It's the only way if we want to get home.'

That's the moment it dawns on Bronagh for sure that she is not the only person there against their will. The woman may not be as big a part of this operation as she first thought. In fact there's a chance she could turn out to be a valuable ally. She absolutely needs to get her onside and that means taking her advice in the here and now.

'Okay,' she says, trying to get a grip on her emotions. 'Okay.' She will have to push down her fear, push aside her instincts to get as far away from Zachary as possible and play this game. She has to get out of here and this might be the only way to do so.

14

MAL

Mal has spent the last half hour outlining the full details surrounding Bronagh's disappearance. Ingrid recorded everything he said on her phone, but also took notes. She has promised to get a news article circulated to her usual contacts as soon as possible.

'Police procedure regarding getting these appeals out can be a little slow and a little bland,' she'd told him, before scrolling through her phone and waving her screen under his nose. Slow, she'd said. As if he didn't already know that all too well.

Looking down, he reads: 'Police in Derry are becoming increasingly concerned for the safety of missing thirty-two-year-old Bronagh Murray, who has not been seen since leaving a beauty appointment in the city centre early on Monday afternoon. It is believed Miss Murray left the salon on Sackville Street at around noon and made her way back to her home in Springbrooke Avenue. She has not been seen since. If you have any information about her whereabouts, please call Strand Road PSNI Station,' et cetera, et cetera.

There is no picture and no description. There are just these words buried at the bottom of a news site.

'Is that it?' he asks. 'Is that the sum total of their appeal for information?' Frustration nips at him, putting him on edge and making him want to slam his fists onto the table.

'It's a start,' Ingrid says, 'But it's not enough. Don't worry, I'll put some pressure on them. If you send me an up-to-date photo, I can get this distributed within the hour.' She promises him she will send it to the BBC, to UTV and Sky News. As well as the newspapers.

'Once we get her picture out there, humanise it all a bit, we should see a bigger response.'

It all still feels as if it's moving too slowly, but what can he do? These things take time, but time may well be something they don't have.

A flurry of voices from the hall lets Mal know that once again they are being joined by new people.

More police. More questions. A senior officer who seems more than a little flustered to see Ingrid Devlin standing in the kitchen with Mal.

'I should've known you'd beat me here,' he says.

'You should have.' Ingrid smiles back at him. *There's clearly history between these two*, Mal thinks. There is something about the reporter that gets under this older man's skin.

'Mal, this is Detective Chief Inspector David Bradley,' Ingrid says. 'You should consider yourself very lucky to have the big guns on this case.'

'Mal, I'm very sorry for what you're going through. DS King is leading this investigation but I'll be keeping a close eye on things. Have you been offered access to a family liaison officer?'

Mal shrugs, shakes his head. He doesn't think so. But he is so tired that he knows he hasn't picked up on everything that has been said to him. Questions have been coming from all directions. His phone has been lighting up with notifications. People have been walking in and out of the house as if they own it, and he feels like he is in a TV show or a play, or something that is very much not his real life.

'I don't think so.'

'He hasn't yet, sir,' King chimes in. 'But it's on my list.'

Bradley nods before turning his attention back to Mal. 'As our friend Ms Devlin has said, I'm DCI David Bradley. Our officers are just starting a door-to-door investigation – hopefully they'll find someone who saw Bronagh leaving here, or noticed some other unusual activity. It's possible that there may be a camera doorbell or two, which might have picked up some CCTV images as well. You don't have one yourself?'

Mal feels a wave of guilt. 'No. Well, yes, we have one but I hadn't got round to putting it up yet.' He could kick himself. It must've been sitting on their hall table for the past month.

'We're all guilty of putting things off from time to time,' Bradley says, but even though his tone is loaded with compassion, Mal knows he won't forgive himself. If he had just bothered to get it done, chances are it would've picked something up. Maybe he'd have received a notification of something that would have sounded immediate alarm bells. He wouldn't be sitting here trying to stop the most horrific of mental images from creeping into his thoughts.

Panic stirs in his gut. He doesn't want to give in to it. He doesn't want to break down and make a show of himself in front of this Bradley character, or Ingrid... or anyone for that matter... but once it starts to fizz and ferment, it's hard for him to control it.

It's been months since he had a full-on panic attack but it's shocking just how quickly that gut-wrenching sensation can kick in, and how quickly adrenaline and cortisol can flood his system – stronger than any drug.

'Mal,' he hears a voice say. 'You've gone a little pale. Do you want to sit down?'

He's lost in a moment where he can't tell if this is real or not. The fizzing in his stomach is spitting, gurgling, volcanic. Feeling like he is being burnt alive from the inside, he gasps for air – sucking it in, in small gulps that are never quite enough, so he tries to gulp faster as his chest tightens. *This must be how it feels to die,* his mind screams. Sweat beads and falls from the edges of his hairline, and down his back.

There is a hand on his arm, gently trying to guide him to sit, but his muscles have tensed, are aching, and the pain of even this soft touch is excruciating to him.

Images – horrific images – flash through his mind. Bronagh hurt. Bronagh dead. Bronagh lost in the dark. Bronagh being violated. Closing his eyes as tight as he can doesn't stop the images coming, and even though he knows they aren't real, they are as vivid as they would be if the horrors in them were being played out here in front of his eyes.

He feels himself sit down, his legs buckling beneath him, and becomes aware of a voice counting with him as he tries to gain control of his breathing. The storm is doing its best to pass but as it does, he feels embarrassment rush in. All eyes are on him. What if they're thinking this is all an act?

'Mal. It's okay. Listen to my voice. And keep breathing. Try to slow it down.' He remembers what he was told the last time the panic attacks came for him – to breathe in slowly through the mouth for seven, hold for four, and exhale slowly for seven. Each breath makes his chest tremble as if his lungs no longer remember how to do the job they've been doing for the rest of his life, but he persists. The voice, which sounds less robotic and which he can identify as Ingrid's, continues to instruct him, gently, to breathe. The rest of the room seems to have fallen silent, but he knows it isn't empty. Bradley, King and at least one other officer are in the kitchen and Mal's face blazes with the shame of losing his cool. A sudden, almost overwhelming urge to pour himself a stiff drink washes over him and he is glad there is no alcohol in the house. The worst thing he could do right now is start drinking.

'I'm sorry,' he stutters as soon as his body allows him to speak. 'I just need you to get her back. I need her to be safe.'

'Please don't apologise,' Bradley says, taking a seat on the coffee table in front of Mal and looking directly into his eyes. 'I want you to believe me that we will do everything within our power to find Bronagh. As for getting upset or overwhelmed – it's perfectly natural under the circumstances. None of us are immune to our emotions. Especially when a team of police officers arrive at your door. Even more so when we should have been here long before now. I want you to know I am personally looking into this and trying to work out where things went wrong.'

Mal sniffs and nods. Okay, so maybe this Bradley fellah isn't as obnoxious as he first thought. Or maybe he is just playing good cop and the bad cop schtick will come later.

'Okay, so keeping this all rolling. Bronagh's parents are in Spain?'

'Yes,' Mal tells him.

'And you've spoken to them?'

'Yes.'

'And she's made no contact with them or arrived on their doorstep... anything like that?'

Mal shakes his head. 'No. Besides, her passport is here. It's up with all our travel documents ready for our holiday.'

Bradley nods. 'You've given her parents' details to DS King?'
'Yes.'

From across the room King nods in agreement. 'We've spoken with them this morning and they have asked us to keep them abreast of the investigation. They don't want to fly over if there is nothing to worry about.'

That this does not impress Eve King is obvious. Her body language, from the subtle roll of her eyes to her pursed lips, screams it. But then, Mal thinks, she doesn't know the kind of people Bronagh's parents are. The kind who always put themselves first. He could've known they wouldn't come running. A sadness washes over him, weighed heavier by his lack of sleep and his post-panic-attack exhaustion.

'Sir!' There's a voice from the hall as another uniformed officer walks in – his police-issue shoes leaving sopping wet footprints on the wooden floors. He spots Mal and freezes, his eyes wide. Clearly he'd been about to say something but has decided it's probably not best to say it in front of the missing woman's boyfriend.

'There's something that we think you should see.'

'I'm on my way,' Bradley says standing up, and Mal makes to leave with him.

'I think it's probably best if you stay here,' DS King says, raising a hand to stop Mal in his tracks. 'Let DCI Bradley have a look at things.'

'But if it's about Bronagh? I need to see...' His pleading falls on deaf ears as King looks at him with a pitying expression on her face.

'You need to let us do our jobs,' King says. 'We will keep you informed as appropriate. This is where you need to put your trust in us.'

Mal can feel his chest tighten. He doesn't have much faith

left to put in the police – and it's surprising that they expect him to be trusting after last night's debacle.

'Constable Morrison, perhaps you could sit with Mr Cooper here, while we go and check this out?' King's voice is authoritative. She isn't really asking – she's very much telling the newbie officer what to do.

The younger man looks at Mal, eyes pleading for him not to kick up any more fuss and to come and sit down and wait with him. Reluctantly, adrenaline still powering through his body, Mal sits down and tries to ignore the anxiety that is gnawing at every part of him.

'I don't know how I'm supposed to just sit here and not actually *do* anything,' he mutters.

'It must be very difficult,' Morrison says. 'But it's important to try and keep your cool. There will be a hundred leads and you'll wear yourself out chasing them all. Let the police do that for you. That's our job.'

It strikes Mal that Morrison is still so wet behind the ears that he believes in his profession with such absolute devotion that he'll parrot sound bites and sing its praises. Give it time, Mal thinks. The rose-coloured glasses will come off.

Standing up, he walks to the window to try and see what is going on outside. Where has Bradley gone? What is it that he has gone to see? It's excruciating to wait and not have a single clue as to what is going on.

A small crowd of nosy neighbours – Mrs C chief among them – has gathered outside near one of the police cars, despite the fact it is raining. Mrs C has put on her best coat and boots, and her plastic rain hood. She must be loving every single minute of this drama.

After a few minutes he sees Bradley and King emerge from number thirty-seven, where the Vij family live, their facial expressions giving nothing away. The rabble of neighbours and ear-wiggers stop their chatter for a moment to see if they can catch a juicy morsel of gossip on the wind – but Bradley and King are giving them nothing. As much as Mal wants to know what they have seen, he is glad they aren't playing to the crowd – who will no doubt have their own take on what is unfolding on their street.

As he hears them walk back in through his front door, he tries to brace himself for what will come next. Hopefully it will be something that answers more questions than it asks.

'Well?' he says before they've even fully entered the living room. 'Was it something useful?'

Bradley and King exchange glances, before King takes the lead. 'Mal, can I ask you, do you and Bronagh... together or separately... have a child?'

'What?' Mal can't understand where this complete curve ball is coming from. 'No. No. Neither of us are parents. The only kids Bronagh really spends much time with are Shelley's twins. Why are you asking that?'

'Okay, so your neighbours have a Ring Doorbell and captured some footage on the day we suspect Bronagh disappeared. Only, well... she appears to be with a child. Looks like a young boy from the angle the shot was captured. I'm afraid it's a bit blurry and the sound is hammered on the camera, so it didn't pick up any conversation.'

'And Bronagh was definitely with the child? Not just walking on the path at the same time?' He's confused. This is, frankly, bizarre.

'She was holding his hand. They were walking up the street – towards the fields there – the child looks quite distressed and, well... Bronagh appears to be hurrying. She's not wearing a coat, just what looks like joggers and a light top. We've scanned through it for a few hours, but no further footage of her was captured, which would lead us to believe that wherever she went with this child, she didn't come back. So you definitely can't think of any child this might be?'

Mal shakes his head.

15

BRONAGH

She had followed the woman downstairs after Zachary had finished eating the porridge. She had felt unsteady still, and her feet had stuck to the grimy linoleum floor in the hall as she was led through to a kitchen that clearly had not been updated since the seventies or eighties. Chipped melamine, rusted chrome and grease-splattered worktops make up the grim space. An old refrigerator – one that really should have been long retired by the look and sound of it – rattles and hums in the corner.

The room smells of damp, mixed with decaying food from the overflowing bin, and with undertones of cigarette smoke. Zachary takes her hand and leads her towards a varnished pine wooden table, which he immediately climbs under, beckoning for her to follow him.

She glances at the woman, looking for some sort of reassurance or guidance, but all she does is nod back in Bronagh's direction.

She doesn't particularly want to get down on the floor. She feels grotty enough – still dressed in the clothes she wore when she followed Zachary to the top of the street. They'd been soaked through as she followed him, and lying in that stuffy, damp bedroom on sheets that appeared less than fresh had not helped matters. She'd give anything for a long, hot shower and those fluffy joggers she had planned on putting on before her whole life was turned upside down. But she is heeding the warning to do what Zachary asks of her, and she gets on her hands and knees and crawls on the sticky floor and under the table to where Zachary appears to have made himself a little den.

He is sitting on a blanket, a series of small toys – the car, lorry and boat he told her about upstairs – lined up in front of him. In his hand he holds a toy, plastic in bold colours of red and yellow and blue, probably more suitable for a toddler, but Zachary eyes it with wonder as he makes it swoop and rise again and again. All of the toys are well loved – a polite way of saying past their best – but that doesn't seem to matter to the child. For a moment she thinks of how childhood can find a place to grow in even the most barren soil. Zachary grins, as he pushes the plane in her direction, urging her to take a turn playing with it. Someone has clearly taught this little boy how to play – how to uncover his imagination, she thinks. She doubts very much it's the brute of a man who made her skin crawl upstairs. Maybe, she thinks, it was the woman with the haunted expression on her face.

'Thank you, Zachary,' she says, as she takes the plane from him and makes it loop the loop, much to his delight. It's easier, she thinks, to be here, under this table, and pretend that she is not in the middle of a nightmare. One she has no idea how to escape from.

She's not sure how long they play for, long enough for her stomach to cramp with hunger pains and her head to throb.

She looks to the woman, who is sitting stock-still on a kitchen chair. She's not looking around her. She doesn't get up and stretch her legs or wander around the kitchen. She doesn't even join in their games. She just sits like a statue in the fading light of the day, the shadows mirroring the bruises on her cheeks.

'Will you come and play with us?' Bronagh asks, when her legs start to cramp and she knows she must get out from under the table to stretch.

The woman shakes her head but does not speak.

'Do you have a name? I'm Bronagh.'

'No,' Zachary says shaking his head. 'Mumma.'

She is afraid to correct him, she realises, so she just nods and turns her attention back to the woman on the chair. 'Please, tell me your name. It's strange not knowing.'

The woman shakes her head again. A small shake, almost imperceptible, as if she is trying to hide it. Bronagh stares at her until she feels Zachary's hand on her cheek trying to turn her head back towards him. The touch of his hand makes her jump, which sends shockwaves through her battered head. Instinctively, she pulls away and watches in horror as his mouth widens and tears fill his eyes.

Before he can so much as exhale, the woman moves at last and is on the floor, consoling him. 'Don't cry, Zachary. Mumma didn't mean to frighten you. She just has a sore head.'

The woman's voice is shaking. She is scared, Bronagh realises. No... not scared. She is terrified. She looks to Zachary who is staring at her as if she has just physically assaulted him, and not that he was merely startled. 'Please don't cry,' the woman pleads, her own voice thick with tears. 'Please,' she begs Bronagh. 'Please, he needs his mumma!'

Bronagh isn't sure exactly what is going on here, but it's clear that she has to do something. 'Zachary,' she says, reaching out to him. 'I'm sorry. I was frightened. I didn't mean to scare you. Please, come and sit here on my lap and we'll play again.'

He eyes her suspiciously and she realises this child is perhaps just as nervous as she is. Imagine being told this complete stranger is your mother and immediately being expected to have a bond with her. None of this is his fault.

She sags with relief when he clambers onto her knee and allows her to soothe him. It might feel alien to her, but clearly this is what she has to do if she is to get home. Like the woman said – they have to follow the rules.

'Thank you,' the woman mouths, as she returns to the chair and her same static pose. Bronagh gets it now. They must keep Zachary happy at all costs.

Later, as the woman helps Bronagh back up the stairs to that damp, miserable bedroom, she whispers under her breath, 'My name is Maria.' Bronagh knows not to say anything in return. She just gives Maria's arm a little squeeze of gratitude in response.

16

MAL

'No. I don't know that child. Never seen him before.' Mal is staring at the screenshot of the doorbell footage that DS Eve King is showing him. Raindrops have obviously hit the camera lens, distorting the image a little, but nonetheless it's clear to Mal that he is looking at Bronagh – who is being led by the hand by a child dressed in joggers and an anorak.

The camera only captures a couple of seconds at most before they move out of its range of vision again, but DS King was right before. They definitely do seem to be in a rush.

'So, it's not one of the neighbours' kids maybe?' King asks.

'No... well, I don't know. I don't think so. There aren't many kids on this street – a lot of our neighbours are older and past that stage.'

'A grandchild perhaps?' Constable Morrison asks. 'Someone visiting?'

'I don't know,' Mal says again, becoming frustrated. Okay so this is a possible lead, but what use is a blurry image of a child to anyone? It's not like a child is likely to have kidnapped his girlfriend, for goodness' sake.

'And the direction they're walking in,' King asks. 'That leads to where, exactly? Is it the greenway?'

Mal nods. 'Yes, the greenway and then into the woods.' He and Bronagh often go walking there themselves, taking advantage of the council's adoption of land near parks and woodland to create a route suitable for walkers, runners, cyclists and whoever else might make use of it.

'So it would be busy enough then?'

Mal shrugs. 'I suppose so, but to be honest there's a bit of a drainage problem so when the rain's heavy it turns into a total mud bath and people tend to give it a wide berth.'

King turns to Morrison and instructs him to get a few of his fellow officers to go and check it out.

'What do you think, sir?' she says to her senior officer. Bradley looks at Mal briefly before ushering King out of the room to talk to her. Mal's determined to hear what he has to say, however, and moves to the other side of the door. He notices Morrison gesturing to him to come away but he ignores him. This is his house and his girlfriend, and if he wants to stand where he can hear what is being said then he bloody well will!

'I think we need to get a proper search of the area, just in case Miss Murray has had a fall or become injured in some way. The River Faughan flows through the woods alongside the path, doesn't it?' Bradley asks.

'I think so,' he hears King reply. Mal knows it does and wonders if he should butt in with an answer. Before he has the chance, Bradley speaks again.

'The Faughan can get right and high, and fast-flowing too, when we've heavy rain. It would be easy to get swept away.'

'Jesus Christ!' Mal exclaims, unable to keep quiet. Pulling the door fully open, he walks into the hall. 'You don't think that she's been swept away? No. She wouldn't. She wouldn't have any need to be near the river and she's sensible. She wouldn't take any risks.' He feels sick at the thought of what they're suggesting.

'If a child were in peril, maybe,' King says before stopping talking and shaking her head.

'Mal,' Bradley says, 'we're just discussing all possibilities, and chances are they will sound distressing to you. It's really better that you let us get on with things and if we need to talk to you or ask you questions, then we will. Is there anyone who can come and sit with you? Or I can get a family liaison officer to support you.'

Mal shakes his head. How can the police expect him to wander away from this discussion? This is about his girlfriend. The woman he was going to ask to marry him.

'I don't know,' Mal mutters, feeling defeated, and his head too full of horrifying images – all the what-ifs fighting for attention.

'Sir, I will take a couple of colleagues and look up along the greenway towards the river,' Morrison says while Mal feels his chest tighten again. He wants to tell all these people to go away. The police. Ingrid. His neighbours. He wants them all to fuck off and for none of this to be true. He wants to wake up and find it's all been a dream. He wants the cliché. He wants the impossible. He just wants Bronagh.

Feeling like his legs might give out from underneath him, he sits down before he falls down. He doesn't want a liaison officer. He doesn't want a stranger – a cop at that – hovering around him, watching his every move or making endless cups of tea and indulging in small talk.

'Shelley will be back in a bit,' he says. 'She was just going home to have a nap and a shower. That will be enough. I don't need a liaison officer. I think, maybe, I just need some space to think. When your officers are done looking around, of course.'

He doesn't want them to think he's hiding anything or shooing them out the door. That's simply not true, but it's impossible to think with people coming in and out. It's impossible to relax knowing they're going through his and Bronagh's belongings, looking for evidence of God knows what.

He barely registers when Ingrid tells him she's leaving to get the news article circulated as quickly as possible. She might as well be speaking another language. His mind is too caught up in trying not to think the very worst. It feels as if every other ounce of energy is draining from his body but he knows he has to keep going. Now is not the time to flag.

His thoughts are interrupted by the return of Constable Morrison whom Bradley and King immediately usher out of the house, all three talking as they walk back down the garden path.

He wants to run out and see what Morrison has to say, but he knows he will be ushered back inside. They'll give him the same 'we'll tell you when there is something to tell' response they did before. He wonders if they have any idea how this feels. How hellish this entire experience is.

He can't help watching their expressions for subtle and not-so-subtle clues. If Morrison has nothing to report, this should all be over and done with quickly. They will go back to door-to-door interviews, or go back to the station to co-ordinate their approach.

But there is no shaking of heads, or rubbing of chins. There are nods and animated expressions. They all look in the direction of the greenway before looking back to the house, through the window, and catching him gawping at them. Maybe he should move, try to hide his nosiness, but he doesn't want to. Of course he wants to know what exactly is going on and the expression on their faces tells him, in no uncertain terms, they have found something.

Frozen for a moment, Mal watches Bradley speak into a two-way radio, while King makes a quick phone call. His heart starts to thud as he sees some of the other officers turn their attention to the top of the street. The domino effect of whatever news Morrison has come back with continues as one by one, they begin to walk up towards the greenway. There's no way they can expect him to just wait here. He has every right to leave his house and go where he wants to, and before he even really thinks about it, he is already walking out of his front door with the full intention of finding out exactly what is going on.

17

INGRID

I decided on my way back to my apartment to not only send a pre-alert to news editors I normally work with about the incoming appeal for information, but also to pop a quick email to the editor who commissioned my piece on the PSNI's attitudes to violence against women and pitch them a whole new idea.

I'm in on the ground level, and for whatever reason, Mal seems to trust me. DCI Bradley didn't turf me out of the house when he landed, so I'll accept that as a begrudging acceptance of my value in this case. I'm absolutely going to use that to my advantage. I'm going to follow this investigation from the start to the conclusion – whatever that may be – and report on what happens when the alert is raised about a missing woman. I intend to eat, breathe and sleep this investigation for as long as it takes.

I'll have to play this all very carefully of course. I have to keep Mal onside. I have to do my best not to annoy Bradley and King. Access on the level I currently have is invaluable. I don't want to risk that.

After I left Mal, I had a quick chat with some of the neighbours and got a little insight into what had been found on the Ring Doorbell footage. The homeowner – a perfectly groomed Indian woman in her sixties called Rupi Vij – had been only too happy to show me the footage she had on her phone, and had even been kind enough to send it on to me so that I can screenshot it and get it out there as quickly as possible.

None of the neighbours I spoke with have any idea who the child in the video is, which gives this particular story an edge that will hopefully get it front and centre of the news agenda just in time for those evening bulletins. Woman goes missing with unknown child? It screams of being a lead story.

I have no time to waste on getting this story out there and replacing that awful dry rubbish the police press office has come out with. No doubt they'll update their statement soon, given the newer information, so I absolutely want to beat them to it. I want the scoop, but I also want to show Bradley how it should be done.

Switching on my laptop, I grab myself a coffee and a sneaky chocolate biscuit before sitting down at my desk and starting to write. I can't forget that while this is a story that gives me a little bit of a buzz, it is also about a woman. A woman whom I suspect may be in serious danger right now. A woman that the press have a chance to help. Wasn't it Voltaire who said great power brings great responsibility with it? As journalists, and not just social media gossips, we have to remember that.

Maybe it's that the industry has changed so dramatically in the last couple of decades, but I feel that responsibility more than ever before. It's too important.

I've not always got it right. To my shame – in the pursuit of a good story – I have rushed ahead. Published without due diligence or pushed people who didn't really want to talk to speak up, without thinking of the possible consequences. I've put people at risk. I've put myself at risk, I think with a shudder, remembering how gung-ho I had been in the past.

I'm not proud of it, and I've tried my very best to change in the years that followed. I've learned I can still be ambitious and determined to break a story, but I've learned to manage it all better. To look at the big picture instead of focusing on the byline I hope to get. That's what I will do now.

Sticking my earbuds in and hitting my latest Spotify playlist, I get to work. The sooner I can get this out there, the sooner I can be back at Springbrooke Avenue and talk to more neighbours. I absolutely want to get a proper chat with Shelley, too. I need to be all over this because once it's out there properly, I have no doubt the other media outlets in town – and no doubt further afield – will come in their droves.

18

MAL

Mal is halfway down his garden path when he sees Shelley heading in his direction, although she keeps shooting glances towards the top of the street where the police are gathering, as are many of their neighbours.

'Mal? What's going on?' she asks as she walks towards him. Her voice is shaking, and the colour is drained from her face.

'I don't know but I'm about to go and find out,' Mal says. 'They've all headed up there. There was some discussion, out of earshot, before they did. I don't know how they expect me to just sit inside and wait for news like a big bloody eejit.'

'I'm coming with you.' Shelley grabs his hand and he realises how much he needed to feel that human contact. Something that grounds him right in the here and now. 'We'll do this together, Mal. It will be okay. She will be okay. This will be something and nothing.'

He wishes he had her confidence. Not that he actually believes she means what she says. He can feel her hand trembling in his.

They walk, heads down, in the fine, misting rain towards

two unmarked police cars close to the edge of the greenway. Several officers are walking along the path and into the grass, shining their torches now that daylight is fading quickly. He wonders how long they will keep looking once it is dark?

As Mal and Shelley approach, he becomes aware that all eyes are on him. The groups of neighbours now staring him down but talking among themselves.

'They'll still think I've hurt her,' he says, his voice low. 'Look how they're all staring at me.'

'Keep your cool,' Shelley says, squeezing his hand. 'It doesn't matter a damn what they think. People are going to gossip no matter what. But don't lose your head and give them a reason to spread shit about you. They'll all find out about the video and that child soon enough. You can do this.'

She's right. Mal knows that. It really doesn't matter what people think, but it does matter how he conducts himself. He doesn't want the cops to think he's some sort of hot-headed oaf. He doesn't want to come across as an angry Neanderthal. He needs to make sure the police are focused on finding out what has really happened. Spotting Constable Morrison, Mal makes a beeline for him – hoping to be able to capitalise on the younger man's lack of experience and knowing neither Bradley nor King are likely to be loose-lipped.

Morrison looks up as Mal and Shelley approach and immediately starts walking towards the cousins.

'Mal, why don't you go back to the house? We'll come and talk to you soon.'

Mal's chest tightens. 'I'm here now. Just tell me, have you found something?'

'Look, there's some ground kicked up, ploughed through by a car maybe. It doesn't necessarily mean anything. Could be young ones joyriding. We're having a look. Honestly, you'd be better going back to the house. Get a cup of tea. We'll let you know if there's anything we think you should know.'

'How about we help search?' Shelley says. 'Get some folks together – neighbours and the like. Have a good look around the woods and fields. Down by the river. We'd cover more ground.'

'That would be something to discuss with DS King,' Morrison says. 'But I don't think it would be something she'd be keen on, not as it starts to get dark anyway. It wouldn't be safe, and we don't know for sure she came this way.'

'This is the only place the street leads to,' Mal says, looking over Morrison's shoulder as the tyre tracks he spoke about catch his eye. But there is something else there too that catches his eye.

He's trying to focus on his conversation with Morrison but he can't quite figure out what it is he sees. 'We know she walked in this direction,' he says. 'We've seen the footage. So surely we should be searching in the...' His voice tapers off as he realises what it is beside the tyre tracks that has caught his attention.

One of the officers guarding the scene bends down and picks it up, confirming that he is right. It's one of Bronagh's beloved Birkenstocks. He'd recognise it anywhere. He used to tell her they were the ugliest shoes she owned, but she'd shrug and tell him he had no taste.

'Besides, they are the comfiest things I've ever put on my feet,' she'd say, and they became her staple from May to September each year, and in the winter on occasions when she'd gone and had a spray tan, or – like this week – a pedicure.

Without even realising it, he has started walking towards the tracks and towards the officer, desperate to see up close for himself. As if him looking will somehow magic her in front of them, looking mightily cross that she's lost one of her favourite shoes.

It's as if he is being pulled towards the officer – desperate to be close to Bronagh in whatever little way he can.

'Mal!' he hears Shelley shout. 'Hang on!'

He's vaguely aware of other voices calling to him to stop but he doesn't think he could even if he wanted to. And he doesn't want to.

He's not even aware that someone is coming up behind him until he feels hands grabbing at his arms, and trying to pull him to a stop.

'Let go!' he rages. 'That's Bronagh's. That sandal is hers. She's been here. You have proof now!' His voice is breaking, his anger peaking as he realises the likelihood that the car that made the tracks also carried his girlfriend away to God knows where.

'Mal, if it's Bronagh's, we need to do as much as we can to gather any forensic evidence that might help.' Morrison's voice is more authoritative than it had been previously and even though Mal desperately wants to keep moving, he stops as his legs buckle beneath him. Falling to his knees on the sodden grass he realises that he didn't fully believe that something bad had happened to his girlfriend until right now.

19

BRONAGH

Bronagh lies back on the pillow, her eyes drooping and her head aching. She knows it would be so easy to take the little white pills she hid away earlier. She could take one and be rewarded with a few hours of oblivion, when she doesn't feel as if she might combust under the pressure of the anxiety she's feeling. She could build up the strength that Maria tells her she will need.

But she doesn't want to give up control entirely and she fears that taking these pills – whatever they are – will render her unable to function. Instead, she closes her eyes and hopes that sleep will soon come. Her body is healing after all.

To her relief she drifts off and when she wakes the house is quiet, bar the occasional creak and rattle so typical in an older home. It's dark outside and Bronagh's pretty sure no one is awake. There is no dull hum of conversation sneaking in through the cracks in the floorboards. No opening and closing of doors, or heavy thud of footsteps on the stairs.

She wonders how much time has passed since Zachary first knocked on her door. She has no idea how long she was unconscious for after she was taken, or how long the pills knocked her out for. She might have been gone for just a day, or it could be longer. She has no way of knowing for certain.

But what she does believe – and hope – is that someone must be looking for her by now.

Surely enough time has passed that Mal, or her mum, or her friends will have realised something is very wrong. She won't have been replying to messages, or active across her social media. She won't have returned work emails. Surely enough time has passed now that Mal has arrived home to find it deserted. He'll have twigged something is wrong when he spots that she doesn't have her phone with her, or her bag, or any of her things. Those will be unmissable clues, surely? Even for Mal who isn't the most observant soul on the planet.

He has to be looking for her. He'll find some way to locate her, or at the very least let the police do their job. Someone will have seen her with Zachary, surely? Her street is filled with nosy neighbours and curtain-twitchers. Mal always jokes that they moved into 'Retirement Row' and many of the residents have little better to do with their time than nosy at everyone else's business.

Maybe one of them will have one of those video doorbell yokes – just like the one she has, still in its box on the sideboard, waiting for her and Mal to get round to fitting the damn thing. There'd be footage at least, and sound too, of the boy coming to her door and asking for her help. The police would be able to see what direction she had run off in and maybe picked up CCTV from elsewhere, or that... what do you call it... the thing police use to trace and follow cars? She's seen that on TV. ANPR, she thinks. Automatic Number Plate Recognition. Yes. That's it.

Bronagh's feelings of elation at remembering its name are

fleeting as she realises that even with all the possible aids available to keep tabs on people these days, clearly no one has traced her to this address. Wherever the hell it is.

Having watched enough true crime shows in her lifetime, she knows to listen for clues and hints of her possible location. The sounds of traffic or sirens. The sounds of trains passing by or planes overhead. Cows mooing in the nearby fields. Or factory horns. Or even bloody birdsong. But she has little to go on. Apart from the rain beating on the window occasionally and the creaking of the house, she hasn't heard much due to the persistent ringing in her ears from the blow to her head.

After pulling herself back up to sitting, Bronagh shuffles to the edge of the bed and very slowly eases herself to standing. Her eyes closed, she tries to gauge how steady she is on her feet before she dares open them. Okay, she thinks, as she finds her balance. She's doing okay.

Eyes now open, she shuffles towards the window, holding her breath lest she makes the slightest noise that will send her captor racing upstairs to put her back in her place. With a shaking hand, she reaches for the threadbare curtain and gently eases it a couple of inches aside so that she can see the window itself.

For all the light that shines back in, it might as well be painted black. There are no street lights, no passing headlights from cars. She can't even see any hint of a skyglow, no light pollution from a nearby town or village. Where on earth have they taken her?

Slowly her eyes adjust and she starts to be able to make out the form of some trees, maybe, their branches nudged by the breeze. In the black sky she sees, at first, the smallest of lights. The dot of a star, light years away. As she continues to search the skies, she spots another star just fighting to be seen.

And another. And another.

She reaches for the handle and tries to lift it, hoping she can push the old window open even just a crack and breathe in some fresh air. But the old metal framework is rusted. Flakes of rust and white paint fall away as she uses all her strength to try and open it. It's no use. It's tightly sealed. She is a prisoner here.

Exhausted and defeated, she shuffles back to the bed and lies down. She will not allow herself to panic. Not yet anyway. She has Maria as an ally now. That counts for something. If she does what she's told and plays the man's game of acting like Zachary's mother, she has a chance of getting out of here. Doesn't she? And if those stars can be found in the night sky, whatever distance she is from home, then surely someone can find her.

As she loses the battle against the need to sleep, she just hopes that happens before it's too late.

20

MAL

Re-examined Ring Doorbell footage from Mrs Vij shows a battered Ford Focus, at least fifteen years old, being driven up the street towards the greenway approximately half an hour before the footage of Bronagh running with the little boy.

The same car is seen driving back down the street about fifteen minutes after Bronagh was captured on film. The registration plates on the car – both front and rear – were hidden under a covering of mud and dirt. Forensics will look at the footage, Mal has been assured, but it's not likely they'll be able to get any kind of a read from it.

'This isn't *CSI* unfortunately,' DS King says. 'People think we can do a lot more with CCTV footage than we actually can because of that show. The reality is if a number plate is caked in dirt, it's not likely we'll be able to pick anything up. Still, you never know.'

Mal can't help but feel defeated. Surely the PSNI have more resources at hand than this. There can't just be a shrug of the shoulders and a 'sorry, it's muddy' response.

'It's not all negative. This footage does give us some things to go on. We will maybe be able to identify the exact model and year of the car. We know its colour now...'

Silver, Mal thinks. Like ninety per cent of the other cars being driven in this town. It's not likely to be useful to know that.

'We know the windows are tinted – by the looks of it, to a level that is definitely not legal. We can get our traffic division to keep a look out for it, add it to the media appeal. I get it's not much to go on but it's something.'

Mal nods, but inside he can't help but feel it might as well be nothing. It's not like it's an unusual make of car, or that there aren't any number of boy racers flying about the place in souped-up modified cars with windows so tinted it's a wonder they can see out of them. It's not quite a needle in a haystack – but it's not far off.

The police have taken the sandal away in an evidence bag. As if it might reveal some big secret. As if a shoe can somehow be tethered to the owner and will be able to locate her. It all seemed a bit pointless, but he didn't argue. He just handed it over and let Shelley walk him back to the house, ignoring the stares of the neighbours and the car that pulled up and offloaded a journalist who ran towards him with questions.

The shoe has made everything worse. It has reinforced the horror of what he is thinking – of what he fears might have happened.

There's no reasonable explanation for Bronagh to leave one shoe in the field. She isn't Cinderella and she wasn't running away from Prince Charming. It can't be a coincidence that it was found right beside tyre tracks. The car that drove down their street, away from the greenway, shortly after the time Bronagh sent her last message, screams of abduction, doesn't it?

They're all beyond simply catastrophising at this stage. This isn't his imagination running wild.

And he can't stand how this is making him feel. Impotent. Useless in every way.

How on earth can somebody pull up in a car, grab someone and disappear again during the daytime and no one notices, or has any helpful information?

'Look, not all your neighbours are in; there are two near the top of the street who appear to have doorbell camera devices but with whom we haven't been able to speak yet. There may well be something more helpful in their footage. A close-up of the boy, perhaps? Or a different angle of the car driving away. Don't give up hope. Definitely not at this stage of the game,' DS King reassures him.

'Plus, Ingrid's story is getting a lot of coverage,' Shelley adds, turning her phone towards his face so he can see the legions of comments readers have left.

'Lots of people having a good nosy, you mean,' he says bitterly, guessing that most of those who have commented will already have forgotten about Bronagh, distracted by a new TikTok or Instagram Reel. That's the way the world works now. Nobody really pays attention. Not even when the most important person in someone's life is missing.

Shelley bristles at his response, pulls her phone away from him and holds it close to her chest. 'I'm just trying to stay positive,' she says, a break in her voice. Mal immediately feels guilty. The last thing he wants to do is upset Shelley. The woman doesn't have a bad bone in her body and has been an incredible friend to Bronagh, especially over the last year when she needed a friend more than ever before.

More guilt nips at him, but he pushes it away. He can't keep punishing himself for something that he can't undo. Hadn't they worked hard to get over it? Things were finally back on an even keel, or so he'd thought. He had actually been looking forward to the future again for the first time in months. And then this happens...

Maybe this is his karma, he thinks, as his stomach sinks farther than he thought possible. If so, karma really is a bitch because it's making Bronagh suffer for his mistake, as if she weren't the person made to suffer by his behaviour in the first place. It's no wonder the police are eyeing him suspiciously. He would be doing the exact same thing if he were in their position.

God, but he really hates himself right now because nothing he can say can bring her back to him. There's nothing he can do but apologise to Shelley for being such a dick, and fight off the urge to go and buy some whiskey.

21

INGRID

I stretch, trying to correct my posture. If I keep this up – sitting over a computer for hours on end – I will end up with a hunch-back and that is definitely not the look I'm hoping to rock in my forties. No longer able to hold it in, I yawn, desperately trying to wake myself up. There is much more work to do before I can even consider going back to sleep.

I didn't know, this morning, when I headed out for my appointment with DCI Bradley, that by bedtime I would be balls-deep in a breaking news story that is garnering attention from across the country and beyond.

A missing woman always attracts attention. A missing attractive woman attracts even more. It's sad, but true: even the news subscribes to patriarchal standards of beauty. At least, on this occasion, that will work in Bronagh's favour.

She fits all the criteria of the 'perfect victim'. Young (well, relatively; thirty-two isn't old these days, is it?), beautiful and popular. The kind of woman her friends describe as the life and soul of the party. Whom Mal describes as the 'best and most loving woman he could ever have hoped for'. Who works for an exclusive beauty clinic specialising in high-end treatments and designer fillers. No lumpy lips here. The aestheticians Bronagh works for are artists who have the city's elite among their clientele. Bronagh has been described as the 'backbone' of the clinic by her tearful boss, an impossibly perfect-looking woman called Sandra who might be twenty-five or forty-five – I found it impossible to tell.

That there is intrigue surrounding the little boy in the CCTV clip simply added more fuel to an already smouldering social media fire and now it has ignited and is burning bright.

No one seems to know who the child is. There have been attempts by AI experts to zoom in and clean up the image to get a better look at him, but I don't hold much court with those. AI is only ever an approximation of what someone might look like. There's a good chance the boy looks absolutely nothing like the almost cartoonish figures the armchair sleuths have come up with.

But surely someone must know who he is? Mal swears he has never seen him on Springbrooke Avenue before and does not recognise him at all. None of the neighbours seem to know him, which seems strange. He doesn't look terribly old. Five or six maybe. Certainly not of an age where he should be wandering the streets during the day on his own. Surely he should be at school. But it's quite useful to me to have the angle of both the perfect victim in the form of Bronagh, and a mysterious child to hook this story on.

Feeling the need to stretch further still, I get up from my desk and walk to the window, staring out over the River Foyle for a moment or two before closing the curtains and becoming enveloped in my own little cosy corner of the world. Putting the kettle on, I run everything I know so far through my head over and over – pushing down the feelings of guilt that arise from the flutters of excitement in the pit of my stomach.

There is a woman somewhere who might be in huge danger. She might be cold, and hungry, or scared. She's slipping into the third night away from her home and I wonder whether she knows that people are looking for her? Does she know she's firmly in the news agenda? I try not to think about her too much – not get inside her head. Not at this stage. As I've grown older it seems harder and harder to hold on to my journalistic objectivity. Maybe I've just seen too much and heard too much.

I have to keep my focus on my work. I know the police, and even with my little mice scurrying away inside the walls of the Strand Road PSNI station, I know I will only ever hear so much. Some mice are chattier than others and my current collection aren't the best. It's not easy to get sources inside the police – especially not in Northern Ireland – but I've made it my place to build a rapport with a number of officers over the years.

Then I'll start asking for a little guidance. A little advice, maybe. The men in particular like this. I'd say the majority of them love a good mansplain and if I can use that to my advantage, I will. Over a matter of months, and sometimes years, I build on those conversations. Sometimes I take them up on the offer for a coffee, or a drink. I'm friendly, but careful to always stay just the right side of professional and, sooner or later, I push for a little more information and extend our boundaries a bit. If it works well, we reach the point where they contact me when they hear of any juicy cases in the station. I am always overly grateful and it works incredibly well for all of us.

Or it can. My current cohort are requiring a little more wooing than their predecessors, which isn't ideal when such a time-sensitive case is unfolding. So far they've not provided anything much that I don't already know. It's really very disappointing.

I bring my coffee cup over to my sofa, curl my legs under me and pop my laptop on a cushion on my knee. I know it's not the best move for a laptop – that it might overheat – but my back aches from sitting at my desk all evening.

I've spoken to some of Bronagh's friends and colleagues, all of whom seemed delighted to talk to me and enjoyed their fifteen minutes in the spotlight. I've yet to speak to her parents, who are in Spain, but I will do that in the morning.

For now, I'll do another scan of her social media and any other internet hits that might pop up. It's amazing how much you can find out about someone with the assistance of Google.

So I tap in her name and Mal's too and wait to see what juicy little titbits pop up on my screen. In my experience there is always something.

Very quickly I learn that Bronagh is a fan of Instagram. It seems to be her social media network of choice. There's no evidence she has a TikTok account and her Facebook page is locked down pretty tight, but carries a profile picture from two years ago, which would indicate to me that she doesn't update it all that often.

Instagram, however, offers a heavily populated grid of pictures, quotes and reels. Her with Shelley. Her with her work colleagues. Pictures of various lunches and breakfasts and brunches in nice cafés. Inspirational quotes about life and love and seeing the world. I don't find any sneaky little quotes that feel like subtle nods towards people who have wronged her. Although I am intrigued to find, going back about fourteen months, a picture of her bandaged and bruised, giving a thumbs-up while lying on a hospital bed.

The caption reads:

> Thanks for all your thoughts, prayers and supportive
> messages. Mal and I are fine. A little bruised and battered
> but there's no lasting damage. It has been a nightmare week
> for everyone concerned. It just goes to prove that your life
> can change in a heartbeat. Don't take any day, or any
> person for granted.

I jot down the date of the post and type the month into Google along with Bronagh's name to see if there are any hits. The screen comes back with no suitable matches.

I go back to her Instagram account and examine the picture again. She's a popular girl. There are close to three hundred likes and more than one hundred comments. I scroll them, my brain rotting at all the textspeak. Give me strength but there are only so many 'OMG, babez. R U okay? You still slay, even in a cast! LOL' and 'Praying 4 u, doll' comments I can read without fearing for the future of the English language. About halfway down the comments, something catches my eye. Among the sea of heart emojis there is one statement, in stark black and white: 'Get rid of him! What if it's worse next time? You deserve better!'

I immediately wonder what this could be referencing. Is she blaming Mal? Sweet, lovely Mal who tells me they are deliriously in love?

The person commenting is registered as Debbie Young, but when I click on her profile I see that it is private and there are no further details as to her identity. Damn.

I tap on her name to send a private message and hope she is the kind of nosy person who looks in her spam folders. Too many messages can get lost in those.

Debbie,

My name is Ingrid Devlin and I'm a journalist investigating Bronagh Murray's disappearance. I saw your comment on an old post of Bronagh's – 'Get rid of him! What if it's worse next time? You deserve better!' and I wondered whether this was about Mal? I've spoken with him and he seems besotted, but I'm just wondering if there is something else going on behind the scenes? Perhaps something the police should know about? Obviously we all just want to get Bronagh home safe and sound. I'd appreciate it if you could message me back or call me on this number…

I tap in my mobile number and sit back. I'd believed in Mal – what little I know of him. I'd thought him genuine. His fear seemed to be real. His love for Bronagh, very much so. But Debbie Young's words? They have planted a seed of fear deep in my gut.

22

BRONAGH

Morning arrives and Bronagh is awake and listening intently for sounds in the house. She so very desperately wants to hear sounds that are comfortingly familiar to her. The sound of Mal listening to Biffy Clyro and singing along badly as he showers. The clatter of pots and pans as he puts away the dishes from last night and, as usual, can't seem to manage to do so quietly.

But she hears none of these and the longer she lies in hope, the more she comes to accept that they are not coming. In their place, silence is punctuated by the sound of shoes on tiled floors every few minutes. It's comforting at least that the footsteps do not sound closer. There has been no creaking of the stairs, or the wooden floorboards in the landing. It sounds as if the footsteps are downstairs and she'd be delighted if they stayed that way. Or if someone has to come to her room – which she supposes will happen sooner or later – she hopes with her whole heart that it isn't that man. The heat and smell of him, coupled with the wildness in his eyes, have been haunting her all night – slipping into her pain-scored dreams. Turning them into the worst of nightmares.

If only all of this were one big nightmare that she will eventually wake from.

Forcing herself to open her eyes, clinging on to that smallest shred of hope, she wants to weep when she sees the same ramshackle bedroom she fell asleep in last night. Momentarily she once more considers trying to shift the chest of drawers in front of the door, but then the memory of him – the man – towering over her, making sure she knew without doubt that he would hurt her if she so much as tried to stop him – rushes in and she knows it would be self-defeating.

As she sits up, the pain intensifies in her head and a wave of nausea rises in her gut. Unable to stop herself, she retches, but while her stomach twists and contracts, it's empty and nothing comes up, except for some foul-tasting acid – enough in itself to make her gag again.

A loud thump at the bedroom door makes her jump. She hadn't heard anyone on the stairs. The handle turns as Bronagh shuffles backwards to the top of the bed – as if that will provide her with any protection.

As the door opens, she hopes with every part of her that it is Maria. Maybe, she thinks, there's half a chance she can get her to share more information.

After yesterday, when they had been in the kitchen together, she thinks it might just be possible to get her onside. There has to be hope in this somewhere. Bronagh can't bring herself to think any other outcome is possible.

As she watches Maria back into the room carrying a tray, she takes a deep breath. If she can just play this very carefully, it could be her chance to get out of here – or at least to start sowing the seeds of her escape.

Slowly Maria turns around and as she goes to put her foot to the door, Zachary runs in, almost knocking her over. Maria's eyes widen, and her mouth opens as if she were going to exclaim in shock and surprise. She stops though, as if she is afraid of making a sound.

'Mumma!' Zachary shouts and jumps on the bed, the movement sending Bronagh's head swimming once again.

'Breakfast,' Maria says and sits the tray down on the bed before taking a seat herself. It's grimly unappetising. Two slices of barely browned toast with the lightest scrape of butter. There is no tea or coffee, only a glass of water. Bronagh can't tell if it looks murky because the water is dirty, or because the glass is old and worn. Whatever the reason, she doesn't really want to drink it and yet her mouth is so dry she absolutely needs to drink something.

As with her other visits, Maria also has some pills on the tray. 'You must take those for your injury,' she says.

Shaking her head, Bronagh keeps her voice low as she speaks. 'My head isn't as sore today,' she lies. 'I don't think I need them.'

Maria doesn't try to persuade her like she did last night. Instead she shrugs her shoulders, reaches for the pills, and slips them under her top and presumably in her bra. All Bronagh can do is look on, wishing she'd done the same thing. She'd had the wherewithal to hide them last night and they had come in handy when she was desperate for sleep.

Clearly her regret is written all over her face, as the woman shrugs in a gesture which Bronagh reads as 'You snooze, you lose'.

She takes a drink of the tepid water, and is relieved to find it doesn't taste as foul as she feared, but Bronagh can't bring herself to eat. Even though her stomach is empty, she feels too nauseous to even consider trying.

'You need to eat,' Maria says. 'Even if you aren't hungry.'

'I feel sick,' Bronagh replies.

'Then you eat and hope you keep it down. We don't waste food here. He doesn't like it.' She says the last four words in a whisper, her eyes darting to the door.

'Who *is* he?' Bronagh whispers back, tentatively lifting a piece of toast and breaking off a corner. She watches as Zachary's hand reaches for the other slice, those blue eyes of his darting upwards for approval. 'Go ahead,' she tells him, and watches as he takes a large bite before she turns her attention back to Maria.

'His name doesn't matter,' the woman says, her eyes downwards again.

'But—'

'But nothing. Don't ask questions. Believe me, it will be better for you.'

'I can't just give in. I need to know what he wants. When I can go home.' Bronagh knows she sounds like a whiny child. But she has every right to be whining right now as far as she can see.

'He has told you. This is your home now. Zachary is your child. It will be better for everyone if you just accept that.'

The bite of toast Bronagh has been eating sticks in her throat, making her gag then choke.

'Drink the water,' Maria says, in a hushed but urgent tone, her eyes panicked, darting between Bronagh and the door. Bronagh takes a sip, which thankfully is enough to dislodge the toast and allow her to breathe freely. She won't be eating any more though. She has had enough. Her throat hurts – the force of gagging and choking also causes the pain in the back of her head to flare again.

'You're scared of him too,' Bronagh whispers urgently, her voice now hoarse. 'I saw it last night. I see the way you keep looking to the door now. We could work together? Help each other out. Zachary, he is your little boy?'

Maria shakes her head. 'Please, you have to stop asking questions. Your boy can hear you.' She nods towards Zachary who is already finishing his slice of toast and eyeing the discarded remains of Bronagh's slice.

'I need to know what this is about,' Bronagh says as desperation starts to set in. How can Maria hold the line that Zachary is Bronagh's child when they both know that to be a lie? Is it fear or loyalty to that brute of a man that motivates her – or some twisted combination of the two? Bronagh knows what she saw last night – how Maria cowered under his gaze. The traces of bruises on her face can still be seen. The way she keeps looking towards the door as if terrified he will storm in at any moment and... and do what?

Who knows how far he will go, or what he is capable of. Maria has no doubt that his threats last night were genuine. There is something dark in his eyes that screams of a lack of conscience. As if he doesn't see them as human.

'Please, you must stop,' Maria says again, her voice breaking. This causes Zachary to look up at her, his little face contorting with concern. He reaches his hand with his toast out towards Maria who gives him a small smile and a shake of her head. 'No, you eat up, darling boy. You need to grow big and strong.'

Like his father, Bronagh thinks with a shiver.

Maria is rewarded with a bright smile from Zachary and Bronagh swears she can see her sag with relief. She really is terrified. No doubt she feels powerless on her own to take him on. It's not surprising she has grown to be scared. Everything about her screams broken – from the bruises on her body to her gaunt appearance, and the lack of light in her eyes – but she can't always have been like that. She must want to get away from here as much as Bronagh does.

She reaches out to touch Maria's hand – to try and offer her some comfort and reassurance that they are in this together, but the other woman simply snatches her hand away as if Bronagh's touch has burned her. She doesn't speak but simply shakes her head.

'There are two of us; if we work together, we have a better chance of getting away from whatever the hell is going on in this house,' Bronagh whispers. 'We can take Zachary too. We can get him away from here. Go to the police.'

Maria shakes her head again. 'No. We're safe here. You don't understand.' Her eyes are pleading, her pale face pathetic-looking in the half-light of this bedroom – which might as well be a cell.

'Then help me to understand!' Bronagh begs, desperation clawing at whatever tiny part of her is just about managing to hold it together. 'I don't know what you've been through but—'

'This!' Maria says before putting her hands over Zachary's ears so he can't hear. 'What you just said. You don't know what I have been through. You don't know anything about this, but you think you can just fix it all in a heartbeat? You think it's that easy? Do you think I haven't tried?'

This is the most animated the woman has been, her eyes wide and flushed with rage. She might be keeping her voice low, but there is no mistaking the anger in her tone. 'Perhaps you think I'm that stupid. Just a weak little victim. You don't know anything about me or this place. You have no idea what you're caught up in.'

Bronagh can't help but feel wounded by Maria's words. She has only been trying to help get them both out of this house. She hasn't meant to cause offence to anyone.

'Arrogance,' the woman adds. 'That's the word, isn't it? Arrogance. To think that you know more about what risks I'm taking than I do. You don't know me, or what I've been through, but you think I'm stupid.'

'I don't!' Bronagh protests, her own gaze darting to the door almost as often as Maria's, increasingly aware that this is not a safe space. This is not a safe conversation. Any minute now things could get worse for them both.

'I don't think you're stupid at all. I just want to go home.' Her voice cracks. 'I have a home. A job. Friends. A man who loves me.' The thought of Mal coming back from his work trip to find the house empty makes her heart ache. He will be so worried. Or maybe he'll think she's left him. The thought of that is almost too much. Especially after everything they've been through these last few months...

No. She can't allow herself to think about that. Certainly not now. She will crumple altogether if she gives those thoughts any room to grow.

Maria stares at her with a gaze so penetrating, Bronagh can't help but wonder if she's reading her mind.

'We all have things we would like but can't have,' Maria says, with less fight in her voice now. 'If you want my advice, you forget about it. Keep your head down. Be compliant. Focus on Zachary. He's a good boy.'

'But he's not *my* boy,' she replies.

The woman just stares at her, those dark, dull eyes taking in every detail and again making Bronagh feel as if she were utterly transparent.

'Please believe me,' the woman says softly, taking her hands away from Zachary's ears, 'he is your boy. And he needs you to be there for him.'

With that she lifts the tray and makes to leave the room.

'What will I do with him?' Bronagh asks, nodding to Zachary who is now looking at her expectantly, no doubt hoping for some interaction or entertainment.

The woman shrugs her shoulders before leaving and closing the door behind her. Sagging with disappointment and the realisation she isn't going to find a comrade in arms under this roof, Bronagh slumps backwards, barely able to wrap her mind around what the fuck is going on, while Zachary shuffles up the bed towards her once again, looking for a cuddle.

23

BRONAGH

Not long has passed before Bronagh decides she can no longer wait before using the toilet.

Surely the others in the house must know it's impossible for any human not to have to carry out their basic bodily functions. She's fairly sure none of them would want her peeing on the floor in this room – not that it would do much to make the place smell worse. The stench of mould and dry rot hangs heavy in the air – urine would only add a little extra seasoning.

The smell doesn't seem to bother Zachary who has sat humming on the bed, playing with his little green toy car – occasionally running to the window to try and peek out. She wonders how often he has been outside and been allowed to run freely, to play with other children. Has he ever gone to school? Surely he must have family other than these captors? Surely there must be someone out there who misses him?

She's still not sure if she is permitted to leave the room on her own. She's still feeling her way around. Maria told her she had to get up but then she had left, closing the door behind her.

The only times Bronagh has left this room before now have been when escorted to and from the bathroom or the kitchen.

She doesn't revel in the thought of going back to that disgusting bathroom again. She already feels filthy enough.

But she cannot allow herself to fall into melancholy. Not now. She has to keep her fighting spirit, even if the only prize she is likely to win in the here and now is the chance to pee before she wets herself.

Pushing down her nerves, she stands up and ignores the thumping in the back of her head. Dizziness follows, of course – and she catches herself swaying before reaching for the wall for support. *You can do this,* she tells herself, putting one foot in front of the other and moving across the room, hyperaware of each creak of the floorboards. Her eyes are on the door, her ears straining for any sound of someone on the stairs.

'Where are you going, Mumma?' Zachary asks, jumping off the bed and running to grab her by the hand.

'I need to go to the loo,' she says. 'Be a good boy and I'll be back in a minute.'

He eyes her suspiciously, his expression mirroring the same paranoia she has seen on the man's face. Two peas in a pod, only she hopes that the boy will not share his father's temperament.

There's no doubt in her mind the child is sorely neglected. Of course, children come in all shapes and sizes, but his weight, along with his pallor and the unwashed smell that comes from him, make Bronagh's heart ache for him. This is not what childhood should be – not that she knows much about raising children.

The only children she has any regular contact with are Shelley's twins; that hardly makes her an expert. Without warning, a wave of fear – so strong she feels it like a physical punch –

threatens to floor her. Will she see those babies again? Will she see Shelley again? Not wanting to frighten Zachary, she stifles the urge to sob, using every ounce of willpower she has to stop herself from screaming, and takes another step.

She needs to do this one step at a time. One foot in front of the other. She can worry about the bigger picture in a couple of minutes. For now, her most pressing need is just moments away from being tended to.

'Be careful, Mumma.' Zachary's voice is thin and reedy. With a stuttered breath, her very soul shaking, she tells him she will and opens the bedroom door only to be greeted by an empty hall. All seems quiet downstairs. She can absolutely do this. She does not need a permission slip.

The elation that comes from being able to relieve her bladder is incredible, if short-lived. What is she supposed to do now? Just go back to that cell of a room and play with the child? Wait for Maria to come back with some unappetising food and a look of terror on her face? Wait for the man to come back and shout his orders?

Stuff this, she thinks. If the man has said this is her home now, then surely she doesn't have to be confined to one small part of it. Surely she can have a look around and investigate. Maybe she can talk to Maria again – persuade her that they really should be allies in all this.

Standing at the top of the bare wooden stairs, she calls out a very tentative 'Hello?', fully expecting to hear Maria call back, but there is nothing.

No answer. Surely Maria hasn't gone out. Where would she go?

'Hello!' she calls again, a little louder this time, as she takes a first step downwards. 'Is anyone here?' She takes another step, trying to assess her surroundings. A creak from the bedroom draws her attention behind her, and she sees Zachary's face peeking out the side of the door.

She's going to have to take him with her to talk to Maria, and hope that his presence doesn't silence the other woman. 'Come on, let's go downstairs!' she says, forcing false jollity into her voice. He smiles and comes towards her, once more taking her hand.

'Shall we go and see Maria?' she asks, and he nods.

Together they take another step, and another. Still there is no sound from below. No loud voice of the man barking orders, or tinny rattle of the radio. No opening and closing of doors, or heavy thudding footsteps.

At the bottom of the stairs now, she surveys the hallway properly, unlike yesterday when she was still woozy and not quite with it. It's as dank and depressing as the upstairs. The walls are painted in shades of green so dark and dismal it's astounding anyone could ever have found them soothing and pleasing to the eye. The peeling wallpaper and the dappled black mould on the ceiling complete the look and feel of decrepitude. A lack of adequate natural light doesn't help. With the three doors off the hall closed, the only light in this liminal space is from a small glass panel on the top left of the front door – the top right panel having been boarded over, and by the looks of it, some time ago.

'Hello?' she calls again, wanting to make sure that whatever she does, she does not startle anyone. There's no telling what these people could do, or how they could react if they are frightened by her.

'It's me,' she says, her voice hoarse, chills prickling her skin. It's impossible to tell if it's from the cold or something much deeper – much darker. Zachary squeezes her hand. 'It's Bronagh!'

As she says her name, she wonders if the man even knows, or cares, what it is. He hasn't asked her – at least, not in her memory. There's every chance she might have said something to him while three sheets to the wind on whatever horse tablet they fed her, but she's not sure she was even in a fit state to remember her own name back then, never mind tell him. She'd told Maria though. Last night. Maybe she'll have told him. Maybe her fear is an act.

'Mumma,' Zachary says. 'Your name is Mumma. Not Bronagh.'

He came to your house, a voice whispers in the back of her mind. *The little boy. He knocked on your door.*

Not on the door of Mrs Cosgrove, or any of the other curtain-twitchers in Springbrooke Avenue. Other women more likely to be at home during the day. She's never usually home.

Her blood runs cold. Was she targeted? Watched? Waited for? It's hardly likely that this little boy just picked her door out of the blue. It's not the nearest to the top of the street or the greenway. There are maybe twelve other houses before Zachary would have reached hers. Had he knocked at other doors first? Or had they planned to take her all along? Maybe they saw her come back from her appointment. Could it have been that random? It doesn't feel like it. Would they have taken the risk of letting the child wander alone on the street? Knocking on random doors, not knowing what reception he would receive. Anything could've happened to him. Anyone could've opened the door. Anyone could've snatched the child. Or not been fit to follow him. Or not been in. It was too risky to take the chance if they were targeting her over everyone else. This had to have been planned.

Perhaps simply because whatever was going on in this house required them to have a woman who could easily pass for Zachary's mother. Although for the life of her, Bronagh can't understand why that woman isn't Maria.

It's enough to make her head spin, but at the same time the only conclusion she can come to is that, for some reason, she has been chosen.

Gripped with fear at the realisation all this might have been more calculated than she could ever have imagined, adrenaline spikes through her veins like a tidal wave. She turns and walks back towards the front door.

'Where are we going?' Zachary asks, his hand still in hers.

This isn't the time for half-baked plans to try and get Maria on her side. For all she knows she is complicit in the abduction. It's time to see if she can get the hell out of there and fast. 'Sshh!' she says, raising her finger to her lips.

With a trembling hand she reaches for the door, in her heart knowing it's not likely to open – it can't be that easy – but she is trying to hold on to hope.

The door is an old wooden one with both a Yale and mortice lock. Please God, they will both turn and she will be able to leave. There could be someone, silently, in any other room who could be on top of her in seconds, but here she is with a door to the outside world. If she can just get out, they can start running and let her feet carry her as far away from here as possible, as quickly as possible.

Offering up a silent prayer – not that she believes in God all that much – she takes the snib of the Yale lock and starts to turn it. To her relief, it moves without hesitation, so now she just has to pray that the mortice lock isn't bolted. There's no key in sight so she knows this could be the end of her grand plans – before they've had a chance to get going. Taking a deep breath, Bronagh pulls gently at the door, hoping both that it opens and that it doesn't creak loudly enough to alert anyone.

It gives, immediately, letting an extra crack of light into the mouldy hall, and the hope is almost enough to take the legs from under her. Except of course she knows she cannot stop. She cannot give in to the waves of emotion crashing into her. She has to go. Fast.

Taking another deep breath, she turns to Zachary. 'You must do exactly as I say. When I say run, we run.'

'Like a game?' he asks.

'Exactly,' she says, pulling the door open entirely and allowing the bright light of the sun and its glare on the rain-soaked ground to blind her momentarily. Her eyes watering, she takes a step into the fresh, cool air, hope driving her forward. She's ready to lift Zachary if need be and to run with him in her arms. He weighs next to nothing anyway.

Still trying to adapt to the light and the glare, she looks at the ground, keen to follow the path out of the garden and away from here.

It's the sight of his dark, heavy boots that stops her in her tracks. Instantly, although she is still blinded by the glare, she knows it is him. She can feel his energy, smell his musky, dirty scent. She knows she has been too hopeful. It was never going to be this easy. She was stupid to think, even for a second, that it could be.

As he steps closer, his bulky frame blocking out the brightness of the sun, she looks up and sees him – and his mood – come into focus.

Though her ears are ringing and her heart is thudding loudly, she hears a small voice at her side call 'Daddy!' and feels the boy let go of her hand.

The man's eyes are dark, and his brow furrowed – each line and wrinkle looking as though they have been carved in his face by anger and hate. His stubbled jawline is rigid with tension. Though the sight of him is terrifying and she immediately knows she is in trouble, she cannot look away. Nor can she run. Fear has her frozen to the spot, her mind whirring, trying to think of something to say that could possibly make this better and improve her chances of surviving what is to come.

She is so lost in her own internal panic that she doesn't even register his arm, with open hand, as it swoops in the air and grabs her by the throat.

24

MAL

He hasn't slept again. Not properly. He probably drifted off a couple of times only to jump awake as the horror of what's happening hauls him from his half-sleep. Waking to see the other side of the bed empty has been like a punch in the gut.

He has been trying his very best not to spiral and give in to the wave of self-loathing that is washing over him, but all he can think is that the universe has ways of making itself known. Some kind of cosmic karma.

Eventually, unable to continue lying in their bed and feeling her absence for a moment longer, he gets up and pads downstairs where Shelley is sitting at the kitchen table looking as wrecked as he is.

'You didn't sleep either?' she asks.

'How could I? Knowing she's out there. Knowing that someone has likely taken her. I can't believe no one has come forward recognising the wee boy. At least that would've given us something.'

He walks towards the counter and reaches to switch the kettle on.

'It's just boiled,' Shelley says, raising her coffee cup to show him. 'Should be enough there for you.'

'Cheers,' he says and savours the robotic motions of making tea.

'What time do you think the police will be back?' she asks.

'Constable Morrison called me just before I came down. Said they'd be up at the abduction site soon.'

'The abduction site,' she says, putting her cup back on the table and hugging her arms around herself. 'Jesus Christ, Mal. Can this really be happening?'

He sighs. He's asked himself that question a million times overnight, and come to the conclusion that it doesn't really matter what he thinks or doesn't think. This is what is happening. Constable Morrison might still be on his way to the site, but all Mal needs to do is pop his head out the front door to see the police cars at the top of the street, see the uniformed officers standing guard. They have been there all night. Floodlights shining on the dug-up grass. Press arriving and leaving, posting their stories, walking past his house and looking up at the bedroom window. A uniformed officer at the bottom of the garden has, at least, stopped the press from hounding them.

He lifts the sodden teabag from the cup and flings it into the sink. 'Yeah, I think it can really be happening. I think it *is* really happening. At least people are looking. Ingrid did a good job getting it out onto the news like that. It seems to be everywhere.'

Shelley lifts her phone. 'Yeah, I've been doomscrolling. Amazing, all these people claiming to be her best pal now,' she says with a grimace.

'The cheek of them,' Mal says, sitting down. 'We all know that's you.'

'I think, cousin of mine, you'll find it's you. Is she not always banging on about how she is so blessed to be with her best friend?' Shelley mimes sticking her fingers down her throat and being sick, but Mal knows she's joking. Usually she's delighted to tell people how she brought these two lovebirds together.

He feels something crack inside him. Bronagh is his best friend and what is he going to do if she doesn't come back? He feels his chest tighten again – the threat of another panic attack in the wings waiting to swoop in.

'Take a breath, cous. This will come good. She'll be okay. I insist on it, so drink your tea and we'll face whatever we have to together.'

'What if she's not okay?' Mal says, his voice almost a whisper.

'It's Bronagh. She'll be grand. She's tougher than the rest of us put together,' Shelley says, as if she were trying to convince herself.

'I'm scared,' Mal says, feeling pathetic. He's a man. He should be taking charge of this situation and yet here he is whimpering like a six-year-old.

'I know,' she tells him. 'I think we're all a bit scared.'

Those words are enough to bring tears to his eyes and even though he feels he is now fully in the realm of humiliating himself, he can't stop the tears from falling.

'I thought all our troubles were behind us,' he says.

'Ah now. They will be again, Mal. You'll look back on this just like you look back on last year and wonder how the hell you got through it, but you'll get through it.'

Instantly he's back to a year ago when it looked like they were falling apart. When he had ended up begging her, on his knees, to give him another chance and had agreed to do whatever it took to win back her respect and her love.

When she'd shocked him by agreeing to give him the

chance to prove himself, he had done what she'd asked. He didn't even have to think about it. He wanted her and he was prepared to do whatever it took to keep her.

Bronagh had been nothing but supportive, and he'd thought they'd come out of this stronger than ever, but now – was there a possibility they had come through everything just to have it all ripped away? The universe has a sick sense of humour.

25

BRONAGH

The man shakes his head as his grasp tightens around Bronagh's throat. Right there on the path outside the house. Just when she had hoped she would be able to run.

Finger by finger he applies extra pressure, crushing her windpipe and leaving only the smallest space for air to try and fight its way to and from her lungs. It's a losing battle.

'I thought I warned you already,' he says staccato, although it's hard for her to make him out over the roar of her own blood in her ears as it fights to move around her body. 'Stupid. Stupid bitch!' he sneers.

Lifting her hands from her sides, she pulls at his fingers, hoping to force him to release his hold – even just a little. Even just enough to allow her a single deep breath to stop the world fading to black around her.

She can hear Zachary asking what is happening. To her horror, he doesn't sound surprised nor particularly scared. It's bizarre how normal he sounds.

Meanwhile she is desperately clawing at the man, tearing at his skin with her sharp, manicured nails, his only reaction being to squeeze harder still while using his free hand to fight off her attack. 'Stupid bitch,' he repeats, his face still uncomfortably close to hers, his warm breath damp on her skin. She isn't strong enough to turn her head away. He is holding her too tight.

Her arms feel looser. Slack. No longer belonging to her. She can't lift them, let alone fight him off. Her legs too... they lose all sensation as the black dots in the periphery of her vision start to multiply.

Zachary's voice is fading away.

Her bladder releases. Whatever little urine was left, after her recent toilet trip, trickles down her thighs, but she is past caring at this stage. There's nothing she can do about it anyway. There's nothing she can do about anything. She has failed. Let herself down. Let everyone down. And she'll never know why, or what happens next. Her body can't fight any more. Can't fight him any more. Can't hold on. There is no air. It has been cut off, just like the hope she carried. She swears she can feel the capillaries in her eyes bursting, the burning in her lungs, her muscles contracting in their desperate need for oxygen. Her body is trying to fight, but it's no match for this man. This man who warned her what would happen if she disobeyed him again. He was only doing what he had said he would, she thinks, and her vision fades through red to black as she closes her eyes and lets go.

26

INGRID

I love rabbit holes. I love how one story can lead to another, which can lead to another, which can track its way right to something really juicy.

I know a lot of people hate research, but I thrive on it. I can lose hours to it, and that's exactly what I did last night. Cocooned in my apartment on the banks of the River Foyle, I started to dig deeper and deeper into the lives and dramas of Mal Cooper and Bronagh Murray.

Debbie Young has not read my message yet, but that hasn't stopped me from finding out what had happened to give her cause for concern.

They had been involved in a crash. One the media had rightly described at the time as a 'horror crash'.

I read about it when it happened. I was on holiday so wasn't around to get my own boots on the ground at the accident site. Part of me – the part that is always on alert for the next breaking headline – was raging to have missed such a juicy story. The more human and empathic side of me was glad not to be anywhere near this awful mess of pain and misery.

It had been a rainy evening on the Glenshane Pass – a section of the main route between Derry and Belfast which cuts through a scene of impressive natural beauty. Between the rain and the spray misting from the road, visibility was shocking. Traffic was moving slowly, except for one car. A boy racer who it seems didn't believe the rules of the road applied to him, with devastating consequences for everyone whose life he altered that day.

The nineteen-year-old driver, not long having passed his driving test, had been overtaking where the road narrows to descend from the top of the hill travelling towards Belfast when, instead of merging with the outside lane, he aquaplaned, resulting in a five-car pile-up. There was one fatality. A man in his sixties, travelling alone – on his way to an appointment at the Royal Victoria Hospital.

A woman in a different car sustained what the papers described as 'life-changing injuries', which in my experience tends to mean an amputation, or paralysis, or possibly a traumatic brain injury. The other drivers and passengers sustained a series of injuries – some minor, some not so minor.

In among the melee of crushed metal and the bloodied and shell-shocked were Bronagh Murray and her boyfriend Mal Cooper who, according to the reports I have read, was arrested at the scene and was charged with driving under the influence of alcohol.

For reasons I can't quite understand, I've not been able to find any reporting on his eventual court appearance. And that's why I want to do some digging now. Just in case there is something murkier lurking under his perfect boyfriend persona. Drink driving is pretty serious – what caused him to get behind the wheel that day after drinking? Does he have a drink problem? Did Bronagh know about it? Did it cause tension between them? Was their relationship troubled? Yes, her work colleagues and other associates have described them both in glowing terms but behind closed doors, who really knows what happens. If Debbie Young's comment can be taken at face value, then it's clear there has been something not quite perfect about their pairing. I should probably try and talk to Shelley on her own at some stage. Since she's Bronagh's best friend. Then again, she's Mal's cousin so her loyalty may ultimately be to him.

I spent the wee small hours scouring through coverage of the aftermath of the crash. Groups of survivors and relatives standing at the crash site calling for traffic-calming measures to be implemented in rogue weather conditions. Others calling for tougher sentences for reckless drivers, speeders, like the boy racer, and for those who drive under the influence of drugs or alcohol – like Mal.

In a statement issued by the group of survivors and relatives, Lisa McGinley – daughter of Henry, the man who died – said 'This was the worst day of my life. Of my whole family's life. Every person here is carrying the scars of that day – be they physical or emotional. Lives have been changed irreparably. For my father, there will never be a chance to enjoy the retirement he so looked forward to. And to what end? So someone could get to their destination quicker? Someone took a risk because they thought somehow their needs mattered more than those of our loved ones. We will never forgive them.'

It is with 'We will never forgive them' that I grab my keys and my coat, as well as my laptop bag, and head straight for my car to make the first of a number of stops I have earmarked for today.

27

BRONAGH

The man releases his grasp from around Bronagh's neck, dropping her to the ground.

She hadn't even realised before that point that she had been lifted off her feet – she had stopped being able to feel anything at all except the burning in her lungs. They were all that was left of her – these oxygen-starved organs begging for life while giving up on it at the same time.

She doesn't feel the ground as her body lands, limp, on it. Not at first anyway. She doesn't feel the shocking impact of her already bruised and bloodied head hitting the concrete of the pavement. She is in a state of near-death bliss, her body protecting her from the fear and pain that comes with losing the toughest battle of all. All she feels is relief that he is no longer squeezing the life from her.

The fuzzy outline of Zachary's legs, and his worn-out trainers. She can't move yet. She had already surrendered to her fate, accepted that there was nothing she could do to change the outcome. She had made peace with her death in the seconds it had taken for him to change her from a woman determined to fight for her freedom to one who had no more fight left to give.

A crushed windpipe will do that to a girl.

And yet Bronagh hadn't counted on the body's unconscious determination to fight for survival. With one deep, burning inhalation, the life she was letting go of rushes back into being. Her lungs fill. The darkness lifts and in its place, everything becomes pain.

She coughs, the inside of her throat feeling as if it has been attacked with a cheese grater, and she spits a mixture of blood and saliva. Her head throbs. Every nerve ending fizzes and burns as it comes back to life. It's almost – almost – too much to take. She doesn't want to feel this. She might never know why she is here, or what this man wants from her, or why she was targeted. She might never know why Zachary calls her his mother. But she doesn't care any more. She just wants the pain – and the fear – to stop.

Tears pool and slide down her face, stinging her cheeks. She's vaguely aware of this man towering over her, of his strange voice ranting. She hears Zachary too. The lighter cadence of his voice. Their mixture of accents. It's possible they're speaking a mixture of languages or maybe she just can't comprehend him any longer.

If he'd just held on to her a little more, this could have been all over. Defeated, her heart hurts at the knowledge that it isn't and that there will be more pain to face.

It's just too much, she thinks as the pain overcomes her and she slips back under, grateful for the temporary reprieve.

* * *

When Bronagh wakes, the floor is cold below her. Cold and hard. The room is dark but it's not the kind of dark that comes from the turning of the clock and the slipping from day into night. It is black. So black, in fact, that she cannot see what is in front of her – or under her, or behind her. For a moment she wonders if she can see at all. All she can do is feel the rough ground – concrete, she'd guess. She tells herself to keep breathing. In and out. Do not panic. Do not give in to the urge to scream. It will just hurt more. But God, it already hurts. Her throat, her neck, her back...

She knows for certain she is not in the bedroom upstairs. How bizarre that she wishes right now that she were. She would love the comfort of a soft pillow under her head. The taste of tepid water to wet her lips, to soothe her throat. God, what she would give for one of those white pills to take her out of all this and make the pain stop.

Tentatively, unsure of where the room begins and ends, she sits up, reaching her arms in front of her. No walls. Not this close anyway. Bronagh wills her eyes to adjust to the dark, to start being able to decipher shapes and objects. She's not sure she has ever experienced darkness like this before. A basement maybe. Maybe the same house. If it's a basement, then there must be stairs – a way in and a way out. There has to be a door, or a window – something capable of letting in light. Maybe even a light switch.

If she can feel around, move around, she might find something. She might find a way.

But what if he is waiting? Just like before. What if he is waiting and he grabs her throat again – bringing her just to the point of death again before bringing all that pain rushing back in? Is she a mere plaything to him? Maybe he's getting some sort of perverse pleasure from all of this. He might have some sort of BDSM kink – getting off on causing women pain. But where does Zachary come into it? Why is he using the boy as bait? Does Zachary even know he is little more than a pawn? Bronagh wants to cry – for herself and for the boy who is forced to act like a lapdog to a cruel man.

But she finds she is too tired and too sore to cry. Her body is burning and the urge to sleep is so strong. Maybe when she has rested a little more she will be able to focus her eyes on this room and see a way out. Maybe she'll be able to find a crack in the dark that lets in light. There has to be a way.

28

INGRID

The courthouse is a bust. Their systems are down and the staff are not able to search their online database for Mal's name.

The dark-haired clerk looks as if she has already had more than enough of this day, even though it is only nine thirty.

'Look, we really are up to our eyes in it at the moment. Petty sessions are due to begin in half an hour and we're having issues accessing the list and arranging the video remands. I'm really sorry I can't help you at the moment but maybe come back this afternoon? Hopefully it will all be fixed by then and we can get you sorted. The Magistrate's Court usually finishes up around two, so maybe call around three to give us the best chance of being available to you?'

She looks on the verge of tears and I can only imagine the pressure of trying to make sure the right paperwork is in front of the judge in time. I don't want to make her job worse but still, there could be something really key in this information if only I can get access to it.

'Would there be a central office I could call? Someone higher up maybe who can help? It's rather urgent.'

The woman looks at me again, an expression of disbelief settling on her face. 'No,' she says, still polite but her tone is sharp. 'The system is down across the country – not just here in these court buildings. It's a software issue. As I said, my advice is to call back this afternoon and I'm sure we'll help you in whatever capacity we can then.'

Disappointed but not defeated, I leave her to her technology nightmare and head for my car.

A voice whispers in my ear that I should check to see if the police are following this line of inquiry, maybe see if DCI Bradley will fill me in on any relevant convictions.

Surely the police will have at the very least run Mal's name through their system to assess if there is any relevant history they need to know. Any domestic violence. Any paramilitary-related activity. Drug dealing. Burglary. Public disorder. Anything that might indicate he is not of good character. As the boyfriend or husband is usually Suspect Number One, I am sure it would have been one of the first things they would've done to uncover this offence. But whether or not Bradley would divulge any of that information to me, without going through the proper channels first, is of concern. He might be more friendly to me than he has been in the past but that doesn't make him any less of a stickler for the rules.

I pop off a message to one of my PSNI sources asking them if they can do a search for me on Mal. It's a big ask. It's not as easy as the TV shows might have you believe. Computers in the police station are fitted with keyboard trackers – there are systems in place to flag when databases are searched. It can only be done if there is just cause to do so, and not just because you want to be nosy. I don't want my source to put their livelihood at risk.

As I put my seatbelt on, I wonder if I am softening in my

advancing years. I still love the chase. I love the feeling of digging deep into the very soul of a story, but I'm not entirely sure I have the same killer instinct as before – the same all-consuming need to be the person who controls and breaks the story. I was that person for more than a decade until I decided to pull back from breaking news stories and focus on more in-depth feature writing, and on my own non-fiction career. It has served me well. I live a nice life. I have a nice home – one I hope to clear the mortgage on early. Away from the pressure of constant rolling deadlines in the newsroom, I've even managed to start building a bit of a social life for myself. I've reconnected with old friends. Made new ones. It's been good, but nothing beats the buzz of solving puzzles. There's an addictive quality to it.

It certainly won't hurt to try and find out a little more about the crash and the survivors.

First on my list is Lisa – daughter of the man who was killed in the smash. Her house is a well-kept chalet bungalow in a lovely little cul-de-sac just off the Buncrana Road. Her garden is well tended, a gorgeous autumn wreath hanging on her door. I remember seeing Lisa on the news at the time of the accident – looking hollowed out with grief, her face grey against her dark brown hair as she cried about the loss of her daddy. I've seen, and conducted, countless interviews with the families of those killed or injured in any number of tragedies, and you might think they all meld into one, but they don't. Some stick out. Lisa being one of them. I remember thinking that her father, a smiling man in his sixties, looked not too dissimilar to my own father. Things always stick in your mind when they feel a little close to home.

There's a car in the driveway, which gives me a flicker of hope that she might actually be home. The contemporaneous news reports of the time listed her as a childminder, so chances are she might well be surrounded by a gaggle of preschoolers. I hope she can take time away from them to talk.

It doesn't take her long to come to the door after I ring the bell. She looks much better than she did that day on the news. There is colour in her cheeks and her hair is not as dark and flat. Instead it is peppered with highlights. She smiles broadly when she sees me, as if she's expecting someone, and then her brow furrows. 'Sorry... are you Liam's auntie? I don't think I've met you before?' A loud squeal of excitement echoes from a room to her right. 'The wains are painting today. Making a total mess but having fun.'

I smile back, noticing the splodges of bold red and yellow on her hands. She looks down at them. 'Autumn leaves,' she says. 'Finger painting. All good fun. Anyway, I'll get Liam.'

'No!' I say, stopping her before she goes into the room. The last thing I want is to be accused of kidnapping a child. 'You've got me mixed up with someone else. I'm not Liam's auntie. Or anyone's auntie for that matter. Not one of your charges anyway! I'm Ingrid Devlin, and I'm a journalist work—'

'A journalist?' She cuts me off. 'Why would there be a journalist at my door?' Immediately she is on edge. 'No offence, love, but I've had my fill of your lot. The way yous barged in at my poor daddy's funeral like you had more of a right to get close to his coffin that his own family did.' Lisa shakes her head. 'And not so many of you were interested in helping with the campaign after either, so I don't think there's anything here for you, love.' She moves to close the door.

Immediately I spring into damage-control mode – sometimes necessary after the less scrupulous in the profession have done their damage. To my shame, I used to number amongst them.

'Lisa, look, I'm so sorry that you had such an awful experience at what was clearly a terrible time in your life. I can't imagine the pain you endured.'

She blinks and I see tears forming in her eyes. 'I really am very busy. With the children,' she says, clearly still eager to get away.

'I appreciate that, and I won't keep you long. I'm researching a story and I'm a bit stuck and, well, there's a woman missing. One of the women who was in the crash, it seems.'

'Aye. I saw that on the news. The poor Murray girl. But it has nothing to do with me. I don't want to get involved in any of this. I just want to get on with my life, and with my job. So thank you, but no.'

I open my mouth to speak but she is already pushing the door closed and this time, no amount of pleading or pitiful looks seem to be able to make a difference. It clicks shut and I'm left standing on the doorstep looking at my own reflection in the glass.

I think about knocking again, but sense it wouldn't end well. She clearly has a house full of children to get back to and that doesn't afford me the opportunity to try my usual soft-soap approach. She doesn't have half an hour to chat over a mug of tea before feeling able to open up.

This is not going how I hoped. And to top it all off, it has started to rain. Heavy, fat blobs of icy cold rain that are wasting no time coming down. After scurrying back to my car, I climb into the driver's seat and try to regroup. It's a bit like resetting your internal satnav – a little posh voice in my head might as well be saying 'Recalculating' just now.

I really had thought Lisa would talk. She talked a lot last year – was happy to share her story, and her father's story, even with the media being overly intrusive at the funeral. But clearly the passing of time has had an impact.

As my windows start to steam up, I turn on the engine and the blowers to clear the glass before lifting my phone to check if anyone has been trying to call me. Of course there are a number of missed calls – some I'm familiar with and some I'm not. I do, however, see a notification informing me that I have a new message on Instagram. My heart leaps when I click in and see Debbie Young's name on my phone screen. It leaps even higher when I click into it and see her reply.

> Yes! Call me now! I'm only too happy to talk about this. No one is going to tell me that Mal isn't involved in this. He's a dangerous man.

29

BRONAGH

There's a persistent drip, which seems to hit its target with a small splash every second. Sometimes it gets louder. Sometimes, it's as if it skips a beat, and she dares to hope that it will stop – only for it to start again. Like the ticking of a clock, but louder. In the darkness, Bronagh's senses are heightened. There is no other noise to catch her ear, so the drip drip drip seems to become louder and louder – the constant beat of a drum that she can't escape from.

She's no longer able to tell which part of her body hurts the most – her head, her throat, her bruised and battered legs, her arms which are scored with scratches she doesn't even know how she got.

Still, it is silent and dark. She has tried to feel her away around the room and get some idea of the dimensions of the place. Having located wooden stairs, she is now pretty sure she is in a basement. A metal gate two stairs up, which is locked and too tall to climb over – especially in the dark – makes it impossible for her to get through. It is bolted tight, barely making a sound even when she tries to rattle it.

There has been no noise overhead. No muffled murmur of voices. No footsteps or creaks. No feeling of dust or debris raining down on her – it's just her, the damn forsaken drip, and the darkness.

She doesn't know if it is night or day. She hopes that Mal is looking for her. That the police are looking for her. That someone knows something and that any minute now there will be an almighty banging on the doors of whatever building this is, and the police will rush in and rescue her. Just like it happens in the movies.

Her stomach tightens and groans with hunger – her lips are dry and she's not sure how long it's been since she last had something to eat or drink. Maybe that's all part of his plan. Killing her quickly was never it – what if he leaves her here in some anonymous, unknown building to rot? She wants to cry. She feels herself crumple but no tears fall. Instead, she shouts, again, for help. Pain tears through her, and for nothing. The voice that emerges from her is almost inaudible, her throat still too swollen and sore from when he almost choked the life from her.

He's the kind of man, Bronagh thinks, who could very easily leave a woman in a cellar and forget she ever existed. Why had she not listened to Maria's warnings to behave? She told her that her arrogance would get her into trouble but no, she had to push it. Had to make it all worse.

She cradles her knees to her chest, tears falling silently, and she shivers on the floor. She wishes she'd just been a few minutes faster when she'd gotten home from her pedicure. If Zachary had knocked on her door three or four minutes later, she'd have been in the shower and would probably not even have heard him. She'd have been having a shower disco to herself, singing her heart out and getting in the mood for her fortnight in the sun.

Or what if she'd not gone with him, but had instead lifted her phone and called emergency services? But she didn't know what had been happening. She saw a little boy in distress and she ran to help him. She did what any decent human being would do, and this is how she was being rewarded for it. As if she hadn't been through enough.

But no, she thinks, as the dripping gets louder still. She can't think about that now. Or about Maria and her warnings. She can't allow herself to fall into melancholy – that won't help. She has to focus her energies on staying alive and getting out of whatever rat hole she's in.

If she can't shout, she can make other noise. She's sure of it. She makes her way across the floor until she reaches the stairs again and feels the cold metal of the gate bars on her hands. She starts to shake it with all her might. It doesn't rattle loud enough to attract attention and she wants to fall back to the floor and cry more, but she knows there has to be something she can use. Running her hands down the length of the individual metal bars, she happens upon the bolt and a padlock hanging from it on the other side of the gate to where she stands.

This, she thinks, this she can use. She can make some noise. Bending her wrist at an uncomfortable angle, she's able to reach the lock and lift it, using all her strength to bring it down onto the metal gate.

The clang of metal on metal is satisfying, and more so because she can't scream. It feels like a win and she's so exhilarated that she crashes the lock onto the gate again. And again. Her anger and fear fuelling her more than any food or drink of water could. She will not be kept here – caged like an animal –

in this hole until someone else decides she can get out. She isn't going to be quiet or behave. If he comes back, if he hurts her, then so be it, but she is not going to go down without a fight.

'C'mon!' she croaks. 'C'mon! See if you can stand the noise!' The awkward angle of her wrist means she is in pain already, but she doesn't care. She doesn't care when she feels the rough metal score at her skin, or when she slams the heavy padlock onto her finger by accident. Feeling in her very soul that she is fighting for her life, she slams it harder, again and again.

And only stops when the room is flooded with light from above, temporarily blinding Bronagh when she steps back, as if the gate were suddenly electrified.

At the top of the stairs, there are two figures. She can see that much despite the sting in her eyes at suddenly seeing daylight again.

One tall and one short, they stand in shadow for a moment, not speaking. Bronagh can't make out their features but from the build of the taller figure she is pretty sure it is him. The man. And that means the short figure – so small and so slight – can only be one person.

The person who started it all.

'Do you like it down there?' The man's booming voice echoes off the bare walls of the basement. Bronagh opens her mouth to answer, only to be cut off by the sound of a small voice.

'No. No. No.' The boy, Zachary, is crying. His voice is shaking.

'Why don't you like it?' the man asks.

'S'scary,' Zachary says, his voice breaking as he sobs. 'S'dark. I want Mumma.'

'You don't like the dark. Because of the monsters.'

The boy wails, his fear unmissable.

'Stop scaring him!' Bronagh croaks, but she knows her voice is distorted. A croaky half-whisper.

Both figures at the top of the stairs are coming into focus as her eyes start to adapt to the change in the light, and she can see now that Zachary is clinging to the man for dear life, his head against the man's leg.

'Did you hear that?' the man asks, and Bronagh can hear that he is enjoying Zachary's discomfort just as he enjoyed squeezing the life from her. 'Did you hear the witch?'

Zachary whimpers. The man is right though, with her croaky, strangulated voice, she does sound exactly like a witch. It shouldn't surprise her that a man as cruel as her captor would use that to further scare the child, and keep her in her place. He is betting on her not being able to let the child suffer. This is his way of keeping her in line.

'When she is hungry, the witch bangs on the gate for food,' the man continues as Zachary's whimpers turn into howls. 'Would you like to go see her?'

'No. No! NO!'

His cries cut straight through Bronagh's heart. How can she continue to call, or bang, knowing that she is putting this poor child through so much distress?

'If she keeps banging for food, we're going to have to give you to her,' the man says, 'or she will just get louder... and louder...'

Zachary is screaming now and scrambling with the man, trying to get past him and back through the door to safety. His cries are as pitiful as his fear is palpable. Bronagh lets go of the padlock and steps back into the darkness knowing that, for now at least, she is defeated.

'Maybe the witch can learn to keep quiet,' the man says, 'if you're a very good boy.' With that they step back through the door, closing it with a thud and plunging Bronagh back into darkness, coupled with a healthy dose of despair.

What sick, twisted game is this man playing? Scaring a child. Locking her up like an animal. Luring her from her own home and keeping her here. She does not know him. She isn't the kind of person who makes enemies easily. She's just a normal woman living a normal life. She's not worth anything. There is no family wealth – no big ransom ready to be paid out. Her parents might not even know she is missing. She's not sure they'd care much anyway. She can almost hear it now. 'Bronagh, causing a drama again! She'll be off with her friends just to worry us. That one's always seeking attention.'

They were never cruel parents. Not evil. Not like that man and how he has been using Zachary – scaring the child witless – but they were not good parents either. They did what needed to be done but, to Bronagh, it always seemed as if there was an air of begrudgery to it.

She sits, and cries for herself and for Zachary. Both of them are trapped in this nightmare, being controlled by a man who seems to thrive on inflicting pain and fear. And her only way out will involve hurting that little boy even more. There's no way she could live with that on her conscience.

30

MAL

There seems to be some activity outside. Mal has heard a couple of cars pull up and doors open and close. He wants to run outside to see, telling himself foolishly that maybe it is someone bringing Bronagh back.

It's these moments of hope that are the sweetest and yet the most devastating to him. The hope doesn't last long enough as Shelley peeks out the window and informs him it's DCI Bradley and DS King, with a couple of others. Some in uniform, like Constable Morrison, and some in plain clothes.

'The police are swarming,' Shelley says.

'Like flies round shite,' Mal says grimly.

'They are trying to help, Mal. You know that, don't you?'

He shrugs. He knows, of course, they are trying to help. He's not a complete moron but he can't help but feel increasingly angry about all the lost hours. No one has been able to tell him what went wrong yet. All he's had is a half-hearted apology and a promise to investigate with all urgency. It won't make a difference now though. It's not like it will turn the clock back and return those crucial hours to them. Explanations don't mean a damn thing when they don't change the reality of the situation.

God knows what Bronagh was enduring, or where she was being taken during those hours. 'I know,' he says standing up and coming to join her at the window. 'I just wish there were more helping and less standing around the street giving sound bites and looking important.'

'We're only seeing a very small part of the investigation,' she soothes. 'I imagine they are talking to all sorts of people. And sure isn't it important to get her on the news and get her face out there? The more people know who she is, the more likely someone is to spot her.'

Shelley means well; he knows that. But even she is starting to feel like a fly he wants to swat. What if it's not the case that exposure is a good thing? What if it means Bronagh becomes 'too hot to handle' and whoever has her decides to get rid of her?

He sighs and turns away from the window and walks through to the kitchen to put the kettle on for the hundredth time. He doesn't even like tea all that much, but it's what you do, isn't it? In a crisis? Mrs C from next door had arrived earlier with a plate of home-made scones, fresh out of the oven, and some of her home-made jam. She'd said she could only imagine how tough things were right now. She really does have no idea, Mal thinks, but he managed to be gracious about her gesture all the same. There's no point in alienating the neighbours as well.

'And still no one knows who that poor wee boy is? Isn't that very odd? You'd think his mammy or daddy would've seen him. Or an auntie. A wee school friend or someone?' There had been something about her demeanour that made him think she was fishing for information, but he had none to give. He'd just shrugged. It was as strange and maddening to him as it was to her that the child had not been identified. Although he had to concede that the CCTV footage was not of the best quality.

All these thoughts play through his mind as he starts the mindless task of once again making tea for him and for Shelley.

He walks back into the living room with the two mugs in his hands. 'I need to do something today. Get out somewhere.'

'They're not going to let you near the greenway or the fields,' Shelley says, taking the steaming mug of tea from his hands. 'You know that?'

He nods. The police have their own officers combing the area. The last thing they want now is every Tom, Dick and Sally contaminating the crime scene.

'I know. But I need to do something. Go somewhere. A walk even. Or go for a swim. Or, I don't know, something to get me out of here and out of my head for a bit. I think I might go mad sitting in here like we're sitting in a goldfish bowl, waiting to see what they decide to tell us. Worrying if the next time they come through the door there's going to be some sort of bad news.'

As he says this, the doorbell rings, startling both him and Shelley. They look at each other with an expression of fear.

'I'll get it,' Mal says, setting his mug on the coffee table. The splash of tea he spills is an indication of the shake of his hands.

'It will just be an update. A plan of action for the day,' Shelley says, but Mal can't help thinking she is just trying to reassure herself.

When he opens the door he sees DCI Bradley and DS King standing side by side. He desperately tries to read their expressions but they're giving nothing away. He wonders if they teach this stoic manner in Garnerville.

'Mal, good morning. Do you mind if we come in a moment?' King asks.

'Of course not,' he replies. 'Any news?' He isn't in the mood to wait for any preamble to finding out the one thing that really matters. If they're coming to break news of any kind, he wants them to rip that Band-Aid right off.

'Nothing of note,' King replies as she follows him into the kitchen. 'We've had quite a few calls since the appeal took off last night, and our team are sifting through each of those to see if there is anything of merit in them. We're waiting for traffic division to see if they picked up the car anywhere, but without a clear plate to go on it might not be possible. Still, we have put the description out there. There's still no identification on the child but even if it doesn't feel like it, it's early days in the investigation.'

King is right. It doesn't feel like it's early days in the investigation. Or at least it shouldn't be. But if there is no news, it kind of begs the question as to what exactly they are here for.

'Cup of tea?' Mal asks them. 'Kettle's still warm.'

'We're good, thanks,' DCI Bradley says as his phone starts to ring. Mal watches as he looks at the screen, and then to DS King. One eyebrow raised, she seems to be asking him who it is, but he doesn't say anything except 'I need to take this,' and he answers while walking out of the room.

Mal's heart sinks. Could this be the call that brings bad news to his home? Is that what it is going to be like now? Jumping with each knock on the door, each call on the phone? Trying to read the expression of the police, who are supposed to be helping him, for any changes or any signs that his world is about to come crashing in around his ears? How is a person supposed to live like that?

He stands in awkward silence with DS King. He gets the very strong impression that she does not like him and would perceive anything he says as an admission of some sort of culpability. It's better, he thinks, to stay quiet, especially as his head feels so messy right now.

His muscles are tense and his head is pulsing. He doesn't know how long he can endure this, but at the same time he knows that is not his choice to make. He has no control over any of this. That's what scares him most of all.

If Bronagh were here she would tell him that he'd simply have to 'grind it out' – keep his cool and do whatever the hell he had to do to get through it. She'd tell him 'The only way out was through', or some of her other positive affirmations. Her little sound bites did at times annoy him – for a man who works in the creative industry, he likes a logical approach to problem solving.

But now, holding on desperately to the belief that she will come home to him, he reminds himself that she would tell him to take it one hour at a time and, if necessary, one minute at a time. Today, if he has to, he will take it one second a time. And DS King can eye him suspiciously all she wants. He doesn't care about her. He only cares about Bronagh.

It isn't too long before DCI Bradley comes back into the kitchen, glances first at King before looking at Mal.

'Mal, I have some news on your emergency call. Is it okay if we have a chat about it?'

31

INGRID

Debbie has sent her mobile number and I don't waste any time in calling it. The call has barely connected when she answers it with a husky 'Hello. Debbie speaking.'

'Debbie, it's Ingrid Devlin. You just sent me your number. I'm calling about Bronagh Murray and Mal...'

'Yes, yes. I saw that,' Debbie says, sounding as if she is puffing on a cigarette as she talks. 'That poor girl is missing, you know. It's bound to be him. He's a badd'un. Rough, you know. Fond of the drink. Bad news just like his da before him.'

'In what way?' I ask, as I grab a notepad and a pen from my bag, and start to write.

'You don't know the Coopers then? Are you not from round here?'

I explain to her that I'm not entirely sure of where exactly 'round here' is to her, but that I am from this city and have spent all my life here. Yet I still don't know of the Coopers – or at least not of a Cooper family populated by 'badd'uns' as she put it.

'Look, I don't want to speak out of turn,' Debbie says,

sounding all too happy to do so. 'But you need to ask about his da, Frankie. He was fond of using his hands, if you know what I mean. Had his poor wife battered black and blue. Fond of the drink too. Malachy grew up in that house. He grew up where violence was normal and his da treated women like dirt. You don't grow up like that and turn out normal.'

Okay, I think. This is brand-new information. A history of violence in his family. A drink problem in his family. And now, of course, I know he was over the limit on the day of the accident. Had driven drunk on at least one occasion. God knows how many other times. God knows if he's still drinking now. If he has the same fiery temper as his father.

'And how do you know all this?'

'Neighbour,' she says. 'I've lived next door to them in Shantallow since the late nineties. I heard it all. Malachy was just a wee young thing then, of course. But I heard the thuds and the thumps and the sound of that poor woman getting thrown down the stairs more than once.' She takes a deep breath. 'I'd hear him coming home after a night at the pub, falling in the door and shouting abuse. I'd hear the wains crying.'

'And did you call the police? Or intervene? Any of this on the record?'

There's a pause as Debbie clears her throat. 'Well, no, I didn't call the peelers. You didn't do that in those days. Are you mad? It would've started a riot if they'd landed back then.'

She's not wrong, I suppose. Even though the late nineties were a time when great strides were made in the Northern Irish peace process, the police – who were being transitioned from the controversial Royal Ulster Constabulary into the new, more balanced, PSNI – were still seen as the enemy in many republican strongholds. The Catholic population had minimal trust in them.

'I did talk to a few fellahs though,' Debbie cuts through my thoughts. 'They had a word with him. Roughed him up a bit. He'd be quiet for a while but he always went back to bad habits. I tell you this: the day he died there were no tears shed in that house.'

'But that doesn't mean Mal is guilty of treating Bronagh the same way,' I say, wondering if she has anything more than her own conjecture to back up her belief.

'Well he took after his da with the love of the drink,' Debbie said. 'And I heard things too. I heard him raise his voice to his own mother more than once. Whatever he has told you of himself, he's not the clean-cut knight in shining armour he makes himself out to be.'

For a moment I'm stunned, not sure what to say next.

'I've always worried for that wee girl,' Debbie says. 'I could see he was serious about her by how often he brought her round to the house. I'm not saying he doesn't try to be the best kind of person he can be, but when the badness is a part of you, you can't keep it buried for long. See that accident? And him with drink in him? She's lucky she wasn't hurt worse. She's lucky he didn't kill her that day. That's when I had enough and I knew I had to warn her – same wee girl didn't listen though. And now look at how things have worked out. I warned her. I did. I warned her.'

32

BRONAGH

Bronagh's not sure how much time has passed but she knows she's hungry and she once again needs to pee. She has no idea what she is meant to do about that though. If she calls out for help she risks angering the man, and if he gets angry then he may hurt or threaten Zachary again. She can't have that on her conscience. She can't get the image of his innocent little face – clearly absolutely terrified – out of her mind. The way he had clung to the man – someone who clearly held little to no love for the child in return – was pitiful.

It was one thing for Bronagh to be scared. She's a grown-up. She can handle it. But that poor boy is much too young, much too innocent to have to face the things he has.

Quite quickly, Bronagh realises she will have no choice but to use a patch of floor as a makeshift toilet. Somewhere far from the side of the basement where she has been lying. Somewhere near the persistent drip dip drip of water she can hear.

She could never have imagined she would find herself in this position but here she is and if nothing else, it's preferable to trying to get help. The man, she has realised, is not here to help anyone but himself. There's a cruelty in him that she has never seen before and knows she never wants to see again.

It's hard not to let the hopelessness overwhelm her. Especially as she crouches down and pees on the floor – shame warming her cheeks. How can this actually be happening to her? When will it end? *How* will it end?

She'd give anything to have Mal here – or better still to be somewhere else entirely with Mal. Somewhere far away from this new fucked-up reality.

A creak of the door makes her jump. Even though she is in the dark and in the farthest corner of the room – and even though she has already lost all her dignity, the sound of someone at the top of the stairs makes her quickly pull her underwear and joggers back up. She doesn't want the man, or anyone else, to see her degrading herself by squatting in a corner to pee.

'Hello?' A female voice. Maria. Timid and shaky. 'Are you there?'

'Yes,' Bronagh croaks.

'Are you okay?'

It's such a strange question, Bronagh thinks. Is she okay? Well, she's locked in a basement, having been strangled half to death and as far as she knows, no one has a clue where she is, and she has no idea how she will get herself out of this mess.

'Super,' she replies, unable to bite back her sarcasm.

There is another creak on the stairs as Maria moves towards her.

'I know. I'm sorry,' she says. 'Please, come here. I have water for you. And bread. I have to be quick, in case he comes back.'

Even though Maria is still in silhouette, Bronagh can almost see her fear radiating from her.

Overwhelmed by the fact she is putting herself at risk to

help her, Bronagh walks towards the stairs, letting the shaft of light from the door guide her towards it. The thought of cold water on her bruised throat is so very tempting, but how does she know she can trust this woman? This could be another game – another way of lulling her into a false sense of security before pulling the rug, once again, out from under her feet.

'You can trust me,' Maria whispers, and God, Bronagh really wants to. 'Please, take this drink. Take the food. You need to keep your strength up. It will help.'

Maria sounds harassed and harried. Her hand shakes as she reaches between the bars of the gate with a plastic beaker full of water. Bronagh still isn't sure whether or not she should trust her, but the appeal of the water is too much for her to resist. The feeling of it, cold and wet, in her swollen mouth and aching throat is blissful. A moment of blessed relief in this nightmare.

For once the water isn't tepid, but cool and fresh – so soothing that it might as well be the nectar of the gods. Tears of gratitude spring to Bronagh's eyes and she wants to thank the woman, but thanking her would mean stopping drinking and she can't bring herself to do that. Not yet. She can see the fear in the other woman's eyes, her pleas to drink quickly in case he comes back ringing in her ears. She wants to drink as much of it as she can, unsure when she will get more. Or even if she will get more.

'Is he out?' she asks.

The woman nods. 'He has taken Zachary with him. He didn't say where they were going or when they'd be back. Sometimes he goes out for an hour, sometimes it's five minutes. He never tells me how long he'll be.' She holds out a slice of bread for Bronagh, glancing behind her. 'He wants to keep us on our toes. Please,' she says, 'eat this or take it for later. I will need the cup back. He will check. He checks everything.'

'Who is he?' Bronagh asks. 'Why is he doing this?'

Maria simply shakes her head, her expression reading as if she is having some sort of internal battle. 'I suspect he does it...' she says, 'because he can.'

Bronagh takes the bread from the woman and tries to eat it, but her throat is too sore and too swollen. Her stomach too tight. She gags, spits it out and immediately apologises, her hand going to her neck by way of explanation. 'I'm sorry,' she says. 'I can't eat it. My throat...'

'I know what he did to you. I saw through the window. He's a very bad man.' Her voice cracks and Bronagh feels a renewed kinship with her – one she can now see the woman feels in return.

'We can get away,' Bronagh says, her voice urgent.

Maria's panic is immediately palpable – infectious even. Bronagh pushes it back, instead reaching through the bars of the gate to try and take her hand.

She pulls back. 'You have to make peace with this,' Maria says. 'There is no getting out of here. Has he not taught you that lesson already?' She points to Bronagh's neck and even though no one is touching her, Bronagh can almost feel the crush of his meaty hands again, squeezing tighter and tighter. She tries to sip more water, but feels as if her throat is closing in.

'You have to be smart if you don't want him to hurt you more,' Maria says. 'Or poor Zachary. He's only a baby. We have to protect him. Even if the only way to protect him is to sacrifice some of ourselves.'

This entire situation feels hopeless – and despair is gnawing at her stomach just as hunger is. But just like her hunger, there is nothing she can do to tackle her despair. She is in an impossible situation with no way out of the darkness, unless she can convince this stranger – who clearly does have some sort of a conscience after all – to help her.

'We can work together,' she says again. 'If we work together, then maybe we can do it. Both of us. And Zachary too. There has to be a way. We don't have to make peace with staying here.'

'The cup,' Maria says, reaching her shaking hand through the gate once more. 'I need it now. I need to get it back upstairs.'

'Just say you'll think about it? Think about working together?' Bronagh pleads, holding the cup to her chest, realising it is the only bargaining chip she has.

Maria looks behind her, panicked now, as if she expects the shadow of the man to loom over them both at any second. When she turns back to Bronagh, her fear is obvious. 'Please, I've been down here long enough. If he comes back...'

'He can't fight us both.' She holds the red plastic beaker tight, and feels guilt bloom in her stomach as she sees the fear grow in the woman's eyes.

'The cup, please!' Maria says, and even in the half-light Bronagh can see she is now crying. She can hear it in her voice. 'You have to understand. Whatever he does to you... What he did to you... That is nothing.' The desperation in her voice as she speaks is enough to make Bronagh's blood run cold. 'The cup!' the woman sobs.

Bronagh can no longer put her through this fear of being caught. She might not know much about her apart from her name, but she knows she is someone who cares enough to bring her water, and tried to get her some food. She has to take that as a win. She certainly can't risk losing the allyship she's been given – even if it doesn't go as far as she'd hoped.

She reaches out and hands the cup over. Maria pulls it close before turning to scurry back up the stairs and out of the dark hole Bronagh has found herself in.

It's only when she reaches the top of the stairs that she turns and looks back at Bronagh. 'I'll think about it.'

Bronagh is desperate to say more – to argue her case for longer. But before she can say another word, the woman has disappeared back into the main body of the house and the door is being closed, shutting her back in the dark.

This time though, she doesn't descend into the same sense of hopelessness. Maria will think about it. That's a good thing. It might be foolish for it to give Bronagh such a boost, but it's all she has and right now she is happy to cling to it.

For the first time since she woke in this house of horrors, she finds herself smiling. It might only be a small smile. A hint of one, really. But it's something.

33

MAL

Mal wishes DCI Bradley would just get on with it. If there is news about the emergency call, then he wants to know. He wants to know how and why the police did not respond to his report and why he had to go to the station himself to force them to take action.

'I really hope there isn't going to be some sort of cover-up here, DCI Bradley. It isn't good enough.' Mal can hear the shake in his own voice as he talks.

'No, no cover-up. I can assure you of that.' Bradley sits down on the armchair across from Mal, looking deeply uncomfortable. Mal is glad of it. Glad that Bradley is squirming, but also somewhat terrified at what he is about to say.

'Our dispatch team tells me that there have been a number of hoax emergency calls directing services towards this address.' He looks Mal in the eye.

'Yes, but they weren't from this address. It wasn't me. Or Bronagh. And it's been... I don't know, six months since the last one. We don't know who was behind them... but it wasn't us. And this was a genuine emergency.' Mal sees the expression on

Bradley's face. There is something accusatory about it. Does he really think it was Mal and Bronagh who were behind them? Who sent the police, and the ambulance service and even, on one occasion, the fire service to their doors?

'The police at the time said it was probably teenagers. We logged it as harassment and nuisance calls. You should have that on file.'

'Well, yes, we do,' Bradley says. 'And I'm not for one moment suggesting that either you or Bronagh were behind them. However, we think what might've happened on the night Bronagh went missing, was that your call fell down the priority list due to the number of hoaxes in the past.'

Mal can hardly believe his ears.

'It shouldn't have happened,' Bradley says. 'And we are looking into why and how. The division was under incredible operational press—'

'Save it,' Mal says, as a red mist descends. If he hears that the PSNI were under pressure once more, he might just lose it. He's tired of excuses and veiled accusations. He's tired of being eyed as a suspect. They were plagued with hoax calls over a three-month period, not long after Bronagh had recovered from the accident. It had put them on edge, never knowing when the next incident would happen. It hadn't just been the emergency services either – taxis and pizzas arrived at their door. But then it stopped. All of a sudden. Maybe he should've mentioned it before? He just didn't think.

Unable to stand it any longer, he storms from the room into the kitchen where he lifts a mug from the table and hurls it against the wall with a roar.

He's lifting a second mug, not feeling fully satisfied by the breaking of the first, when he feels Shelley grab his arm.

'Mal, this isn't helping,' she says in a hushed whisper,

nodding her head towards the living room. 'Think of how they see you. Losing your temper isn't going to help.'

He spins round to look at her and while a part of him knows she is right – feels it deep in his soul – he is not in the frame of mind to listen. It's not unreasonable for him to be angry now. Why should he have to hide that from the police? It's their fault after all. There would be something wrong with him if he weren't angry. If he were calm and accepting, they'd use that against him too.

'So what is going to help, Shelley?' he counters, his voice loud. 'I'm allowed to be angry! Why does no one see that? Why do I have to watch my every move as if I'm to blame? I'm not to blame. They are!'

Shelley blinks back at him, and he sees her face colour as if she is about to start crying but right now, he doesn't care. He knows that makes him an asshole. He knows he should care. There probably is a part of him, deep down, that does, but right now – Shelley can cry. And the police can see him lose his temper. And the whole damn world can go to hell.

His body is vibrating with anger. His muscles tense with unspent adrenaline. He shakes Shelley off and lifts his hand to smash the damn mug on the floor. And when he's done that, he intends to lift another. And another if need be. Because if he doesn't break something right now, he is scared that it will be him who breaks.

'I'll smash. As many. Bloody mugs. As I want,' he shouts, punctuating his words with the crash of delph hitting the tiles and the kitchen cupboards. He would rip the entire house apart if he could. He might just. Because this is unbearable. It is utterly unbearable.

He doesn't care that Shelley is in the room. Doesn't notice

DS King walk in, and when she grabs his arm, he shakes her off as if her touch burns.

'Mal. You need to calm down,' she says firmly, as if she were his teacher or his mother, and God forgive him but he wants to lash out at her and, to his horror, it takes every ounce of willpower in his system not to take a swing at her.

34

BRONAGH

Bronagh is jolted awake by a loud crash. Her heart thuds as she hears a loud, deep roar. The man is back.

Another crash follows, sounding as if it is directly above where she is now cowering. There is crying – a wailing that makes her blood run ice cold. At first, she is convinced – it is so high-pitched – that it simply must be Zachary.

It's not a cry of sadness, but one of fear – one of pain. Surely he could not be so evil as to hurt that poor child. Scare him, yes, but hurt him? Is that possible?

She wants to put her hands over her ears to try and block out the noise, but a part of her thinks she has an obligation to bear witness to it. If she manages to get out of here – and please God she *will* manage to get out of here – she wants to be able to tell the police, and anyone who will listen, all that has happened. For Maria, and for Zachary.

But it is excruciating to hear the whimpers and cries, punctuated by the low rumble of his angry voice. She can't decipher what he's saying but the threat in his tone is all too clear.

Another crash, followed by a thud and a groan, that makes

Bronagh want to throw up. It is not the groan of a child. The pleading that follows is definitely not the pleading of a child. Maria, Bronagh thinks. Her new ally. The woman who has gone out of her way to bring her water and food.

Is she being punished for offering that help? Is this Bronagh's fault? Her stomach turns at the thought. And what about Zachary – she knows the man is not afraid to scare the child. Maybe he doesn't care about causing him physical pain too.

Bronagh can't allow that to happen. Even if she is limited in what she can actually do to help, she has to do *something*.

Even if all she can do is make some noise, it might distract him from his onslaught. It might give Maria a chance. If Bronagh can draw the man away even for seconds, it might be enough for Maria to run, and Zachary too if he is being hurt.

Quieting the inner voice that tells her she will only be turning his anger towards herself, and that she is fighting a losing battle, she gets to her feet and feels her way in the darkness to the stairs and the metal gate.

All she can think to do is start rattling it as loudly as she can, hoping the noise and the vibrations reach the man's ears and direct his anger away from Maria and Zachary. She'll worry about the possible consequences to herself later.

'Stop!' she shouts, but her voice is still strained, her throat still bruised and battered from his earlier attack. 'Help!' she croaks, shaking the metal gate harder and with more vigour. It rattles and clangs, banging against the lock, the very hinges rattling, and even though her fear is growing with each passing second, Bronagh cannot stop. The crying upstairs is getting louder and, she realises, so is the man's booming voice. He is coming closer. Following the noise she is making. Just as she hoped.

She wills Maria to run. To go straight for the door and run

as fast as she can while the man is making his way down to her to threaten or beat her. Or worse.

Bronagh has no doubt that this man is capable of killing someone. He had not hesitated at all when it came to squeezing her neck so tightly that she was sure her time was up. He didn't look like a man who understood the concept of mercy. No, the only thing that Bronagh had seen in his eyes was cruelty – a stare so cold it chilled her to the bone.

She is trapped on the wrong side of the gate, but Maria and Zachary have a chance and she hopes and prays that they take it.

As the door to the cellar is thrown open, flooding the room with light and temporarily blinding her, Bronagh freezes. Her rattling stops. Her croaking cries are silenced. Her bravado deserts her as his face, dark and angry, comes into view. He has warned her before. He has punished her lack of co-operation – her fight to get away from here. He will do so again.

As he starts to walk down the stairs, his boots heavy on the wood, his fists clenched, the reality of what she is likely to face kicks in. There is nothing she can say that will mollify him.

In the background she can hear the crying continue – more plaintive now but no quieter. There is no hint that anyone is running, or leaving. She wants to shout to Maria to run. She wants to somehow get the message to her that there is no time to sit and cry. This is as serious as it gets. But then again, Maria knows this man better than Bronagh does. She has been here longer. From what little she has said, from the fading bruises on her face and the ever-present fear in her eyes, maybe she knows how pointless any attempt to escape is. But what's the alternative? Give in to him?

'I thought you had learned your lesson,' he booms. 'What is

it with you stupid women? Why can't you listen? Even when I warn you! You have to push and push.'

He is jabbing a key into the lock of the gate, and Bronagh starts to feel panic set in. Her instinct to run has kicked in, but she has nowhere to go. No escape route. She is nothing more than an animal trapped in his cage and being baited by him.

She looks around, hoping against hope that there is something in the room she simply hasn't spotted before but which she can use as a weapon to attack him and give herself a chance.

'There will be consequences,' the man says, opening the gate. 'Did I not warn you?'

She doesn't answer him, her mind whirring as she tries to find a way to escape. If she can get past him. If she can get on the stairs and pull the gate closed. If she can get the key. If. If. If. She tries to see behind him. Tries to see the way out but he is advancing on her too fast. He is too big. Too burly. His outline blocks her line of vision.

'DID I NOT WARN YOU?' he bellows, crossing the room in a few steps. 'ANSWER ME!'

She steps to the side, readying herself to run for the stairs but he simply does the same, blocking her. 'Don't be stupid, Bronagh,' he says, and it's the first time he has used her name. It sounds odd – ugly – on his tongue.

He is in front of her now, close enough that she feels swamped by him. Once again she can smell his acrid breath, his body odour. The tang, she realises, of fresh blood on his skin. It's too much to think it is his own blood and that it is him who has been hurt, and not the woman upstairs, or the boy.

'Did I not warn you?' he asks once more, so close that his presence is suffocating. How can she bring herself to breathe the same air as him? He grabs her by the chin, holding on and pressing his bony fingers into her skin so tightly that she swears she can feel the bruises already starting to bloom. She is too frightened to speak, but he is clearly in no mood to accept her silence.

'Come on, Bronagh. You were shouting the odds a minute ago so I know you can speak. You can answer me now.'

'You did,' she says, knowing he will only grab tighter and hurt her more if she doesn't speak.

'Did what?'

'Warn me,' she says with a whimper.

'But you still want to shout the odds? That's very foolish, Bronagh.'

'I... I heard crying,' she stutters. 'And crashing. I was worried. I wanted to check...'

'Check what?' he asks, his face right in front of hers, much too close for comfort. His thick, hot breath so close that she can almost taste it.

'That everyone is okay,' she says.

'Why would they not be okay?' he asks, raising one eyebrow. He is playing with her and more than that, he is enjoying his game.

'The noise...' she stutters again, her chest tight, her head starting to spin. 'The crying...'

'Why would anyone be crying?'

'The crashes,' she says, 'the thudding. I... heard shouting.'

'Why would anyone be shouting? We do not shout in this house. We follow the rules and no one gets into trouble. You understand that?'

He doesn't wait for her to answer. Instead, still holding her by the chin, he forces her to nod.

'But if someone breaks the rules...' he says, 'then there *are* consequences. You understand that too.'

Again he forces her to nod, and she starts to cry, increasingly aware of where this is going.

And then, unexpectedly, he lets go, pushing her back from him. She stumbles but somehow manages to stay on her feet. She looks at him with eyes filled with fear. She was prepared for his violence. She was not prepared for him to push her away.

'Go upstairs,' he says, his voice calm but no less menacing, as he grabs her arm and pushes her in front of him.

She pauses, blinks, not wanting to go upstairs – scared of what she might see or what she might be forced to do. The crying has silenced. She doesn't think that's a good thing.

A shove to her back forces her towards the steps – steps only an hour ago she'd have given anything to be able to walk up to get out of this pit. Now the thought of them fills her with dread.

He is behind her though – uncomfortably close, close enough that the heat from his body bears down on her with an oppressive edge. 'Keep walking,' he says. Bronagh does as she is told, taking one step at a time and doing her best to go as slowly as possible. She needs time to think. Could she run? Again? Go for the door and make one last attempt at escape? He is behind her, after all, and not waiting for her in the garden like last time. She could turn, maybe, and push him, sending him rocking back on his heels on the narrow wooden steps. Maybe he would lose his balance and fall – maybe that would be enough to give her the time to run.

But could she leave Maria? And Zachary? Yes, she thinks. She could because she would run to get help. Best to go as fast as she can rather than double back to the kitchen to try and take them with her. She doesn't know what state they might be in or what he might have done to them. She doesn't know if they would even be capable of running, but she is. She's tired, and sore, and hungry but she could still run if she needed to. If she gets the chance.

All she has to do first, is turn and push as hard as she can. If she's lucky he may even fall back and land on his head, or break his thick neck. It's not murder if it's self-defence and she has the bruises and the defence wounds to prove her case.

'Keep walking,' he hisses, his spit reaching her ear and making her wince. She takes another step knowing that it is a case of now or never. She has to do it. She has to push. It has to be now.

35

INGRID

So Mal Cooper is not perhaps as innocent as he makes out. A drink problem. A short fuse. Growing up with the trauma of a violent father. Worrying a neighbour so much that she wanted to warn Bronagh. Surely someone like that could make an enemy or two. Or possibly even be guilty of hurting someone. It's not beyond the realm of possibility.

I'm not saying he will have done it on purpose, of course. But when tempers flare, things can happen. A loss of control can have devastating repercussions. I covered a case once where a young girl had been killed – a push in anger. She'd fallen, cracked her head on a stone and that had been that. The killer had tried to cover it up – had been successful for years, as it happens – but the truth always comes out. By that stage the fact that it had been an accident didn't seem to matter any more. It was the covering up that did the damage. Kept a family from justice. Made it difficult to believe his story. I wonder if Mal knows that.

But no, I shake my head, that doesn't explain the child in

the video. I'm pretty certain that Mal can't have had a secret child that no one who knows him wouldn't recognise.

I pinch the bridge of my nose, fighting off a headache that is born of not enough sleep and not enough caffeine. I can't think straight when my head is fuzzy. I'll go and grab a coffee, maybe a bagel or something before hunger gets the better of me and I'll think about what comes next. First though I pop a quick message to my police source to check if they have had any luck accessing Mal's record. Perhaps there is something there – a history of assault or disorder – that might back up what Debbie has told me. Although, again, if there is a history of violence, won't the police be all over that? Won't it have been one of the first things they checked?

As my brain continues to take diversions down numerous dead ends, I decide that the one thing I know for sure and for certain is that sitting here outside a registered childminder's in the rain isn't going to get me anywhere.

I'm just putting my car into reverse when a knock at my window makes me jump. It's Lisa McGinley.

I wind the window down and she stands, one hand shielding her face from the rain. 'Can you come back over to the house? I can't have it on my conscience not to talk to you, just in case it might help.'

I thank the gods of guilty consciences and tell her I'll be right there before switching off the engine and following her back to the house. It's quiet – bizarrely so, given the racket that the children had been making just minutes before.

'I've put a film on for them,' Lisa says by way of explanation. 'Do you want to come into the kitchen and I'll get you a tea or coffee?'

'Coffee would be amazing,' I tell her, my sore head grateful at the promise of a caffeine hit.

'I'm not sure what I can tell you,' Lisa says as she fills the kettle. 'Except that yes, Mal was in the crash and yes, he had been drinking. It's unforgivable, but that being said, he wasn't the worst driver on the road that day. That was Eamonn Patrick, the *bastard*.' She stage-whispered the word *bastard* – no doubt afraid little ears might hear.

There's a pause. 'You don't think Mal really has anything to do with her going missing? The last time I saw him, outside the court, I gave him a piece of my mind. I can assure you he is no friend of mine but that doesn't mean I'd think he'd be the kind to disappear his girlfriend. Then again, you never can tell, can you?' The kettle rattles and fizzes as she reaches for the canister of instant coffee. Not my favourite, but my brain will take whatever caffeine hit it can. I'd inject it directly into my veins if I could.

'So Mal's case definitely went to court then? I couldn't find it online,' I say. At least she might be able to fill this particular blank in for me.

'Oh yes. He went to court all right. I went to see it but got stuck in traffic and was late. I caught the end of the sentencing though. I wish I hadn't bothered – another joke of a judge. A fine and a year-long disqualification. Sure that's no deterrent at all!'

'I can understand why you'd be angry,' I say. 'I imagine the others were too?'

'Do you blame us?' Lisa asks, incredulous. 'He mightn't have been the young one gunning it up the road at ninety miles an hour, but he did take a risk nonetheless and it's only by the grace of God no one else was killed because of his actions. It was bad enough, what we all went through. My poor daddy, getting it worst of all. I won't even tell you what the coroner's report said. It was the stuff of nightmares. I'll never get over it in this lifetime.'

She stops for a moment as if reading the report again in her mind and she shudders.

'The judge had the opportunity that day to take a stand against drink drivers. In my opinion Malachy Cooper should have been made an example of. What message did his sentence give? A year without a licence and a fine? It's an insult.'

I just nod. I can't argue with her. I don't want to argue with her. I have neither tolerance nor sympathy for drink drivers. They deserve whatever is coming to them. Which unfortunately in this case is not at all enough.

Lisa hands me my coffee and nods towards a milk jug on her kitchen island as a roar makes its way to us from the playroom. It sounds as if war has broken out among her charges.

'I'll just pop my head in the door with the wee ones and be right back,' she says, setting her own coffee cup down. When she leaves I look around her beautiful kitchen. It has the look of one that has been recently remodelled and screams 'heart of the home'. Her walls are festooned with pictures of friends and family and there, at the centre, is an A4 photograph of a smiling man, slightly balding with greying hair. I recognise him immediately as her father. It's the same picture that was released to the press. In the picture he is still a youthful-looking man – certainly not one whose life should have been snatched from him.

'All settled again,' Lisa says as she comes back into the room. 'Just a minor falling-out about a blankie.' She rolls her eyes heavenward.

I smile and nod as if I know what it's like to look after children. I'm very happily child-free and likely to stay so, given my age. 'I'm sorry for coming here and taking up your time. And for any distress I might have caused you by bringing up memories of your dad. I'm just trying to get some kind of a lead on where Bronagh might be. She's been through a lot, and now this. For some reason I'm finding it hard to track down the reports from the legal proceedings and the court can't help me – technical difficulties, apparently. Call it a hunch – but I think there might be something relevant in all that paperwork. Even if it's only that maybe this Mal character isn't the loving, devoted boyfriend he paints himself as. I just thought that if there were any extra insight we could give the police to help them along and get her home nice and quickly, it would be worth looking into.'

Lisa sighs. 'I don't know much more than I'm telling you. As I said I didn't get to the court until late. A few of the others went too. You might try asking them – if you can get ahold of them, that is. I don't know where you'd find them though.'

I think of the information I have in my handbag. One in Derry and one near Magherafelt at the other end of the county. 'I found their addresses online after a bit of digging,' I say. 'Maybe I'll go and speak to them.'

'No... I don't know what addresses you have but the others – I don't think they're local any more. Griffen and Ciara moved down the country somewhere to access intense physiotherapy for her. That's where her people are from. Poor woman is unlikely to walk ever again, you know. There's brain damage there too. I'm not sure of the extent of it, but I believe it's bad. And Ella, I heard she moved away too. Went to teach in Thailand or something like that.'

This is not going to be as easy as I'd hoped it would be.

An inevitable scream from the playroom stops any further rumination. 'For the love of God. Those children! I have to go if I want my house to still be standing at the end of the day.'

'I understand,' I say, before taking a few gulps of my coffee. It's unlikely I'll be able to finish the full cup so I just have to be grateful for small mercies. 'I'll leave you in peace, but if you think of anything that might be helpful, can you give me a call?'

I reach into my bag, take out one of my cards and hand it over.

Lisa reads it, furrows her brow and looks up at me. 'There is one thing though... it's probably nothing but... Ella was in hospital too after the crash. Same ward as Bronagh as it happens, though she was only in overnight. I remember her telling me that they'd had a very heated argument where she told him he needed to sort himself out, or clean up his act, or something like that. I don't remember exactly. But I know Ella definitely got the impression it wasn't just a one-off. God only knows how I forgot that...'

I nod and thank her, wishing I could get ahold of Ella to find out more. But even if I don't, I have two different people telling me Mal displays some problematic behaviour.

And that makes me very nervous indeed.

36

BRONAGH

'Don't!' the man says, his reflexes shockingly fast – or maybe it's the case that Bronagh's are shockingly slow. She's tired, exhausted, disorientated from the dark. She'd barely time to turn around before he had grabbed her by the wrists and he is staring directly into her eyes. Her plan to push him backwards down the stairs is over before it has even begun.

His grip is so tight, she is afraid he might snap both her wrists like twigs. 'You can't win,' he spits. 'You know that. Don't be stupid and make it harder for yourself.'

He squeezes tighter, using his thumbs to bend her wrists backwards. She can feel her knees starting to buckle under the pressure of his grasp. Maybe, she thinks, if she falls, she will at least take him down with her. But he loosens his grip just as quickly as he had tightened it.

'Go. Upstairs. Now,' he says, his voice low and menacing. 'This is your last chance.'

Defeated, she turns, knowing that she has to do what she is told. He is too quick. It's as if he already knows her every move. She thinks again of what Maria has told her. How the only way to even try and get through this nightmare is to do exactly what he says. Bide her time and wait for the moment when he isn't watching her like a hawk and make her break for freedom then. But the thought of being here – staying here in close proximity to this man – makes her choke up, tears starting to fall unbidden down her cheeks.

'Why?' she mutters, as she takes another step ahead of him, then another. 'What do you want?' She's annoyed to hear the thickness of tears in her voice as she speaks – hates that she is giving him open access to her distress.

'You know what I want,' he says. 'You've known all along.'

She takes another step. 'No. I don't. Why are you doing this to me? To Zachary? To Maria?'

'You know her name?' he asks, and Bronagh's blood runs cold. 'I knew it. You have just proven to me that she's not to be trusted. You two have been talking, yes? Plotting? Scheming against me?'

Panic unfurls in the very pit of Bronagh's stomach. No. She cannot get Maria into trouble. She cannot be responsible for any harm coming to her. How could she have been so stupid? Maria trusted her with her name. She didn't want to, but she did.

Taking another step upwards, she notices her legs are shaking. She is like a newborn foal, wobbling with each forward motion – but it is fear, not inexperience, that is causing her legs to struggle with the most basic of movements.

She doesn't know how to fix this. Her mind has gone blank, so she opts for the only way to protect Maria that she can think of. 'It was me. Not her. I made her. She didn't want to. She's told me to do as I'm told.' Her voice is punctuated with pauses as she tries to breathe through her rising panic.

'To the kitchen,' the man says, walking so closely behind

her that he almost trips her up as she goes. Bronagh daren't argue – not again – so she complies, allowing him to direct her to the left. She recognises the hallway she is in – recognises the dank feel of it, the dated wallpaper, peeling in the corners, the smell of damp and something sour. Something that smells like the man when he gets too close. This is the hallway she tried to run from earlier – or maybe it was yesterday. Time doesn't seem to have any meaning here. She catches a glimpse of the doorway that leads to the garden to her right and she sees the doorway to the kitchen yawning open in front of her. Still no noise can be heard from the room. Not so much as a whimper.

'I don't know why you didn't just do as you were told,' he mutters, prodding her to keep moving. Her heart is beating so fast, thudding so hard she can feel it in her throat, threatening to choke her. 'It didn't have to be this way.'

Her mind is whirring, desperately trying to find an escape plan she can grab onto and use to her advantage, but with each step she knows that she is running out of time, and options.

Even though she has feared the worst, it is still a shock to see Maria lying on the kitchen floor, curled into the foetal position. Her clothes and hair are dishevelled – her T-shirt having ridden up her back exposing her thin frame, coloured with splodges of purple, green and black as bruises in various stages of healing make for their own macabre artwork. She isn't moving.

Bronagh trembles so violently that she can't discern if there is any rise and fall on Maria's chest. Her whole world feels as if it is shaking – and there's a ringing in her ears that only seems to be getting louder.

She doesn't want to keep looking and yet she can't turn her head away. Taking another step forward towards the woman prone on the floor, she spots two little feet, clad in worn-out trainers, poking out from under the kitchen table.

'Zachary,' she gasps, dropping to her knees so that she can see him better. He too is silent, but sitting, his knees drawn up to his chest, his arms wrapped around them and his head bowed. He does not stir when she calls his name again. His precious toys are scattered around him, discarded.

'Zachary, it's okay,' she says. 'It's okay.' Even as she speaks she knows she is lying. There is nothing about this that is in any way okay, but what else is she supposed to say to him? How is she supposed to make any of this less terrifying for a child who has just witnessed whatever horrors have been inflicted upon Maria, who remains still and unmoving? Bronagh notices spatters of blood on the kitchen cupboards. They still look wet. Fresh.

She dreads to think what this absolute bastard has done.

'I thought she knew better,' the man says, as he crosses the room and crouches down beside Maria. He lifts her arm, checking her wrist for a pulse before dropping it to the floor with an unceremonious thud.

'She's alive,' he says, with no hint of emotion. 'For now, anyway. Stupid woman. She just had to play the game and keep you quiet.'

'She needs help,' Bronagh gasps, ignoring his words. 'She needs an ambulance.'

The man snorts. 'You must know that's not going to happen. An ambulance? No. You can help her.'

'I'm not a doctor!' Bronagh cries. 'I can't help her!'

'Then I suppose no one will,' the man says with a shrug of his shoulders. 'And maybe you will both learn a lesson that you must do what you're told. Don't ever think you can get one over on me. I have eyes everywhere.'

He glances to the table, under which Zachary still cowers. Is he implying that Zachary has been reporting back to him? Sure, the wee lad wasn't even in the house when Maria had brought her the water earlier.

'Help her!' the man growls, and Bronagh scurries to where Maria lies. Just as the man did before, she takes her wrist and checks for a pulse. She doesn't trust the man to tell the truth. Relieved to find one, she rests Maria's arm back on the floor gently and tries to think of all the medical dramas she has watched on TV. Surely there is some idea of what to do that can be pulled from her bank of acquired knowledge, even if it was acquired from watching *Grey's Anatomy*.

Airways, she thinks, and pulls Maria's dark hair back from where it is draped around her face. She is shocked to see a bruise, already vivid purple, across the length of her cheek. It looks as if she has been punched directly in the face. Blood bubbles and trickles from her mouth and Bronagh thinks she might be sick. What if Maria chokes on her own blood?

She knows she can't waste any more time before checking there are no obstructions to the woman's breathing, so placing her head on the floor, she gently opens Maria's mouth and looks to see if there is an obvious cause or source of the bleeding. Not, she realises, that she will know what to look for, or what to do if it *is* something serious. This entire episode feels futile, but she has to try. She needs to try.

With a sense of relief, she sees that the blood is seeping from a series of deep bite marks on Maria's tongue. She can only imagine the force with which this brute of a man struck her to cause so deep a bite.

'Maria,' she says with a shaky voice. 'Maria, can you hear me?' Gently she feels around Maria's head for any sign of further injuries – for any idea of what may have caused the blood spatter. As she reaches the crown of her head, she feels the warm sticky sensation of fresh blood coating Maria's hair. There is a laceration, maybe three inches long.

'I need something,' she says, feeling increasingly desperate, 'a towel, a cloth, something I can put against this wound to try and stem the bleeding.'

The man nods. 'Zachary... get towels.'

The boy scrambles out from under the table, his eyes wide and his face sheet-white. Bronagh can't help but notice the damp patch on the front of his joggers from where he has wet himself. Her heart breaks for him but as much as she wants to run and comfort him – to protect him – she knows that she cannot move. She must do exactly as the man has said, unless she wants to end up on the floor beside Maria.

She watches Zachary run to the kitchen drawers and open the second one from the top. Given the disarray around her, she is surprised to see the drawer is filled with neatly folded, clean tea towels. There is an order to it that she hasn't seen elsewhere. He takes several of them and, after closing the drawer, walks to Bronagh and hands them over. She can feel his tiny frame trembling as his hands touch hers. 'It's okay,' she soothes. 'She will be okay.'

'Mumma,' he says, weakly, tears pooling in his eyes and falling down his face.

'Your mummy will be okay,' she says, immediately feeling guilty for lying to him again. Is she giving him false hope?

'Mumma,' he says again, but this time his finger points to her.

'Good boy, Zachary,' the man says, seeming to take some pleasure in the boy's compliance. 'And he's right. Maria is not Zachary's mother. She's nothing to him.' He is talking about her as if she were no more than trash on the floor. There's no emotion. No feeling. No guilt or regret. Just a correction that Maria is not Zachary's mother, but of course Bronagh knows she is not Zachary's mother either.

As Bronagh presses a towel to Maria's head, the poor creature lets out an almost imperceptible groan. Relief floods through Bronagh. At least if Maria is making noise, there's a chance she is regaining consciousness. That has to be a good thing.

'She needs a doctor,' she says again, hoping against hope that she can get through to the man and convince him to get help – proper help. Not just her – a woman who has no notion of what she is doing, armed with some tea towels in a grotty kitchen somewhere unknown. 'Take us to the hospital. Drop us outside. I'll bring her in and you can leave. I'll keep my mouth shut. I promise. I won't tell anyone what you've done. I'll stay quiet.'

'No!' Zachary sobs. 'Don't go, Mumma!'

Meanwhile the man stares at her unblinkingly for a moment as if he is considering her idea. She wills him to see sense, or to show some compassion at least.

'You don't have to be this person. You can help her. I promise I won't—'

'NO DOCTORS!' he cuts through her before pulling a chair out from under the table and sitting down. 'If you knew what she was doing to you, you wouldn't fight so hard for her,' he says, a hint of a smile on his lips. 'You'd realise how worthless she really is.'

37

MAL

He sees the fear in Shelley's eyes. She knows how close he is to losing it. She is willing him to stop. To calm down. To not make matters worse.

'Mal, I think you need to take a breath,' DS King says as Bradley walks into the kitchen behind her. 'All okay here?'

Mal's eyes dart between the three others, heart thumping in his chest, his rage being replaced by fear and embarrassment at his own stupidity. Dear God, this is the last thing he needs to do – get himself arrested for assaulting a police officer.

'I'm... I'm sorry,' he stutters, his entire self shaking. 'It's just... she's gone. She's gone and we've all let her down and I don't know if I'll get the chance to tell her I'm sorry. And it's not good enough.'

'I appreciate that, Mal,' King says, as Mal tries to steady his breathing. 'And it might be of little comfort, but we are looking into it. All of it. Is there anyone you can think of that would target either of you with hoax calls? Or might want to hurt Bronagh? I need you to think about this very, very carefully.'

He shakes his head. 'We thought it was just stupid teenagers acting the maggot. The hoax calls, that is. And then they stopped so we kind of put it to the back of our minds, but surely it can't be related to this?'

'Everything can be related,' DCI Bradley says. 'That's why we ask you to tell us everything. No matter how small or insignificant it may seem. Sometimes we find the answers in the margins – in the details no one thinks to tell us.'

Mal shakes his head. He's trying to think. Honestly he is, but his head is swimming. His mind racing. Raking over the duration of their relationship for clues, but everything of importance feels out of reach.

'So these prank calls started after the accident?' DS King says. 'Could they have been related to that? Would someone hold a grudge about the accident perhaps?'

'I don't know. Maybe? But the accident wasn't my fault and it definitely was not Bronagh's. I know I'm not blameless but...'

'It was a pretty big accident though. Terrible tragedy. That poor man,' DCI Bradley says.

Mal nods as images of that day replay in vivid colour in his mind. The rain battering on the windscreen so fast that even on their highest setting, the windscreen wipers struggled to cope with the deluge. Headlights of oncoming vehicles sparkled like prisms. Bronagh was in a rubbish mood, sure she was going to miss her flight to Spain and her parents would be angry at her for 'wasting their time and money'. The radio had been playing – 'Creep', by Radiohead. He remembers that. He remembers thinking it's such a cracking song and it has a timeless quality.

Then there was the roar of the engine, the squeal of brakes, water from the road spraying upwards as a car ahead aquaplaned. He pumped the brakes, but not fast enough, not hard enough. The car in front of him obviously had the same idea. He saw the flash of the brake lights, heard the scream of the tyres trying to find purchase. The blare of a horn. The crash of metal as the car in front careered nose first into the side of the aquaplaned vehicle, pushing it further up the road before coming to a standstill. No matter how he tried – and he did try – he couldn't stop his car from careering to the other side of the road before crashing into the wood and wire fence separating it from the lush fields. The car he had been travelling in went into a spin as it tried to negotiate the carnage and slammed into the growing mountain of metal and flesh. Before Mal could get his bearings, before he could register which direction he was facing, or why he could taste blood, or why Bronagh was crying, a final crash shunted their car forward and the windscreen shattered in around them.

A cold sweat breaks on the back of his neck as he thinks of how much the crash changed him, and how much he almost lost. 'But surely you can't really think it could in any way be related to Bronagh's disappearance?' he asks.

'There were a lot of people hurt that day. Not just the poor fellah who died,' Bradley says.

'There were. Bronagh included,' Mal says, remembering the sight of her leg twisted and bent at an unusual angle, and the blood – so much blood – running down her face.

'You managed to walk away relatively unscathed,' Bradley says.

'A few cuts and bruises. I was very lucky,' he says, feeling increasingly uncomfortable.

'You were,' Bradley says. 'Considering you were over the limit.'

'I was. But only just. I would never have got into the car if I'd thought I still was. I accept that I was still in the wrong, and I have my driving ban to show for it, but I don't see—'

'Well, there are a couple of things we need to talk about,'

Bradley says. 'I accept your evidential blood alcohol test did come in just over the legal limit. But there had been a delay in taking the test due to the chaos at the crash site. I'd say you got an extra couple of hours' grace and if you'd been tested at the time of the crash, you would've got a much higher reading.'

Mal nods. He's aware that, being honest with himself, he probably had known he was over the limit but was arrogant enough to think he would get away with it. He had been foolish and cocky. Convinced his driving wouldn't be impaired. He could hold his drink. And those limits shouldn't really apply to everyone. There are some people who are tipsy after half a glass of wine, whereas he could down a full bottle and not feel the effects.

Besides, he had promised Bronagh he'd take her to the airport and he didn't want to let her down. 'Yeah, I messed up,' he says. 'I never should've gotten in the car. I wish I hadn't. I wish I could turn back time but then even your own officers said there's nothing I could've done differently during the crash. My driving was not under question. I'm not saying I didn't deserve to get a ban, or that I'm proud of myself. I haven't touched a drop of alcohol since, as it happens. I've done the work. I realise what I could have lost but I don't see how it could relate to Bronagh's disappearance.'

'How were things between you and Bronagh at the time of the accident?' Bradley asks, and Mal notices King sit a little taller. This is a line of inquiry she isn't prepared for, he thinks. It must be related to whatever phone call Bradley just took.

'We were fine,' he says. 'Normal.'

'No tension or arguments?' Bradley asks.

'Not more than any other couple,' he says, but he is lying.

38

BRONAGH

She doesn't ask him what he means. What Maria was 'doing to her'. It doesn't seem to matter too much anyway. The only thing that matters is keeping Maria alive. If only she knew how.

Ignoring the man and his jibes, she presses the tea towel tighter to Maria's head. 'I can try and stop the bleeding from her head, but I don't know what other injuries she might have. She's very bruised. There might be broken ribs, or internal bleeding...'

She desperately wants to get through to him that this is serious. It's not about whether or not she can get away. It's not about anything except not letting this woman – who has tried to help her – die.

'Please. We need help. Proper help. I'm afraid she might die,' Bronagh says, fear squeezing her chest tight and making it hard to breathe.

Zachary lets out a small wail before he scurries back to his hiding place under the table. When Bronagh glances at him, he has his hands pinned tight over his ears.

'Zachary is scared. Can't you see that? Please, you can't just leave her like this.' Surely even the most hateful of men have an ounce of humanity somewhere inside them.

The man looks at her, and to Maria on the floor. For a moment she thinks she might be getting through to him. Please God, let that be true. But he shakes his head and stands up, starts pacing up and down the grotty kitchen while Zachary's crying becomes louder and louder.

'She was going to leave you here!' the man says, loud and angry.

Blood starts to soak through the tea towel she is holding to Maria's head and she swears her breathing is more shallow. Bronagh blinks at him, unsure of what he means but also not caring what he means. Her focus right now is helping Maria. Suddenly she can't hold back her rage any longer. 'For fuck's sake! Call for help! She's a human being and she's injured. She needs help.'

She has barely finished speaking when she feels herself being hauled to her feet by the hair on her head. On tiptoes, her head bent backwards, she tries to keep her balance but the man is much too strong for her to contend with.

'She. Was. Going. To. Leave. You,' he spits. 'You were her replacement. If she broke you in, made you compliant, she was going to get to leave. She was leaving you here. That was the deal. Do you still want to save her? Do you still care?'

His words hit hard. Is that why Maria had begged her to do what she was told? It wasn't about self-preservation – it was about escape. She'd have gone and left Bronagh to her fate. But even if that is true, Bronagh thinks, Maria does not deserve this ending. She doesn't deserve to die on sticky linoleum in some filthy kitchen God knows where.

'Zachary!' the man shouts, and Bronagh can hear the scuffle

of the boy's feet as he pushes himself farther under the table and out of the way of the man's grasp.

'Now, Zachary!' the man calls and the boy whimpers.

'It's okay, Zachary,' Bronagh says, trying to provide what little comfort she can to him. Immediately she worries she might have done the wrong thing. What if she coaxes him out and the man hurts him? She will never forgive herself.

But it's too late for that. Hearing her voice, Zachary eases his way out from under the table. Still grasping Bronagh by the hair, the man bends so he can grab the boy by the arm.

'Both of you,' he hisses, dragging them from the room and to the top of the cellar steps. 'Get down those stairs. I can't think straight with you yapping in my ears. Get the fuck down there.'

Bronagh takes Zachary's hand, squeezing it tightly and trying to offer him what little reassurance she can as she leads him down the stairs, his body vibrating with fear as he goes. Of course, he thinks the cellar is populated by monsters and witches. She wants to tell him the real monster is the man who is forcing them down here.

39

INGRID

Lisa McGinley directs me to Ella's Facebook page before I leave. I message her asking her to get in touch with me, desperate to see if she remembers any more details about the argument between Bronagh and Mal at the hospital.

Had she issued him an ultimatum and, if so, had it related to his drinking? Or to violent behaviour? Had Bronagh been covering for him all this time? Hiding a darker side?

I scratch the plan to get in touch with the other couple who were in the crash. They have moved away and it really does seem like they have more than enough worries on their plate. They are unlikely to have spent any time with either Mal or Bronagh so I might be upsetting them for the sake of nothing.

God, I am getting soft in my old age.

While I wait to see if Ella comes back to me, I decide to return to Springbrooke Avenue. Hopefully DCI Bradley will be there and I can have another one of his preferred 'off-the-record' chats. Tell him about Debbie Young, and about the argument in the hospital too.

As I drive over, my source – a rather cocky response cop

named Tony – calls me. 'Conviction for drink driving. Banned. Ban still in force. Apart from that it's a clear record,' he says.

'I don't suppose you could do a similar search on his dad? Now deceased? I've heard he was a bad character.'

There's a sigh. 'Ingrid, I was pushing my luck as it was. I'm not going in sniffing around the files of dead men. I'd be asking for trouble.'

'Not even as a special favour to your favourite journalist?' I ask. There was a time once when this kind of flirting worked wonders.

'Not even for you,' Tony says. 'Not for anyone. Too many questions being asked about police procedure. Especially at the moment. This call-out situation with your missing woman has us all on edge. Sorry, Scoop. You're on your own.'

With that he is gone and I have to settle myself. Some stories are harder to chase down than others. It's frustrating but it's the way of the world.

As I pull into Springbrooke Avenue, my phone rings again and even though I don't recognise the number that flashes on the screen, I answer it anyway.

'Ingrid Devlin,' I say.

'Ah, Ingrid. Hello, it's… Lisa McGinley here. You were with me a wee while ago. Asking about the crash?'

Now this I had not been expecting.

'That's right. What can I do for you, Lisa?'

'Well, I just remembered something else. Sorry my head is such a sieve at the minute. Menopause, I think, and trying to keep focused on all those wains running about. It would wither a person.'

I pull my car off to the side of the road and switch the engine off. 'I can imagine you've barely a moment to yourself.'

'That's the truth. Look, I remembered – I was talking to you about Ella, and about Griffen and Ciara and I said they'd moved from Magherafelt to down the country somewhere for intense therapy for Ciara.'

'That's right,' I say.

'Well, I remembered it was only Ciara who moved. Down by her parents. As far as I know, Griffen is still in the north, although I don't think he's at the same house. That all kind of fell down round their ears after the accident. I can't think where it was I'd heard he'd moved to, but I imagine he'll be well enough known. He'll have the wee boy with him. Dote of a wain, he is. Autistic or something though. Quite delayed in his speech and that. As if they didn't have enough on their plates. Hard to think of a mother leaving her child, but I suppose she's not fit to care for him any more.'

Something lights up in my mind and I wonder if my journalistic instinct isn't that much on the blink after all.

'Lisa, what age is this wee boy?'

'God, now you're asking. I'd think maybe six? Five or six maybe? I'm sorry – head like a sieve like I said.'

My heart is thudding, and that surge of adrenaline that comes with getting close to a story is starting to kick in.

'Have you seen the footage from the doorbell camera of Bronagh just before she went missing?' I ask.

'No. God, I've not had a chance to watch the TV. I just saw a few people talking about it on Facebook. I know. I'm awful, should have watched. Why?'

'Can you go and watch it, like right away? You'll get it on the BBC news site, or on *The Chronicle* site, or from *The Derry Journal*.'

'Hang on a wee minute,' Lisa says, and I wonder if it could really be this easy. Surely not. Surely someone would have known this wee boy before? But if Griffen and Ciara kept themselves to themselves...

Looking through my car windscreen, I see DCI Bradley and DS King come out of Mal's house and start to head towards their car. I want to thump on the horn to tell them to stop because I really think I might have something here. I really do.

'Right,' I hear Lisa on the other end of the line. 'I'm watching.'

40

BRONAGH

Zachary cried so hard she had been afraid he wouldn't be able to catch his breath. He could not speak, could only wail and cling onto her and she did her best to soothe him, but he must've been able to sense her own fear.

He must've felt her body trembling too. She was scared she too might lose the ability to catch her breath. Maria is up there in the worst of conditions and they are down in this dark hole, and God only knows what that man is doing.

Now Zachary has managed to cry himself to sleep, his sobs slowly tapering off into hiccupping gulps of air. Bronagh is under no illusion that he simply exhausted himself. When he wakes, she imagines his distress will come back just as strongly.

But for now, she has to make the most of the quiet. She listens for any signs of movement from upstairs, but all is silent. Anxiety sets her stomach churning. She'd give anything for a faint hint of Maria's voice, or the sound of ambulance sirens. Even the thudding of boots through the hallways. Paramedics on call. But then again, she knows deep down the man will never risk that.

How could he explain Maria's injuries? They are clearly not accidental. Anyone with an ounce of sense will be able to tell from the very outset that they were not caused by banging her head off a cupboard door, or taking a tumble down the stairs. The blood spatter alone would ring alarm bells and there is no way the man can take the chance of anyone seeing who he truly is. That thought chills her to the bone.

Poor Maria, she realises, is going to need a miracle to get through this. Guilt swamps her that she has not been able to do more to help her. How useless was she, using a couple of tea towels to stem the blood from her head wound. That won't make a difference. Not enough of one anyway. At least, she thinks, her airway was clear and she was just about in the recovery position. There might be half a chance that will help her if Bronagh can just get away, or get a message to the outside.

In this moment, in the dark cellar, she doesn't care if Maria was going to leave her there. It doesn't seem to matter any more. Not when it all seems so utterly hopeless.

With each moment that passes, each new assault on her senses or her freedom, she is starting to accept that the chance of getting out of here is slim. Chances are, she realises, she will simply end up like Maria, eventually – bleeding out on the floor.

And she might never know why. She may never know the name of the man who will likely end up her killer. She'd cry if she weren't so exhausted – the tiredness having a numbing effect. For now – and she can only allow herself to focus on the here and now – she is okay. She is breathing. She is not the one lying on the kitchen floor. While she is still breathing and still has her wits about her, she has a chance.

Shivering, she pulls a sleeping Zachary closer to her. He

will be cold too. His joggers are still wet and he only has a light T-shirt on his top half. This poor boy.

Without thinking, she drops a kiss on his head – her heart breaking at the stale smell of his soft hair. This is not a childhood anyone should endure. She is gently rocking him when she hears a thud, and a low dragging noise. The kind of noise she imagines a body would make as it is pulled across the floor.

She longs to hear a noise from Maria. Even a cry or a scream. A sign of life. But there is nothing. Just the dragging, and then a whistling as the man gets on with the work of cleaning up his mess.

Stuffing her fist in her mouth to stop herself from screaming, she rocks, back and forth, back and forth.

41

MAL

Things had not been good between Mal and Bronagh at the time of the accident. In fact that was an understatement. And Mal knows it was entirely because of him. He was on a mission to self-destruct. Even though he had been happy with Bronagh, he had been feeling the pressure of work, and of the aftermath of his father's death.

He had started to drink more and more. He'd joke about self-medicating, hoping that if he got the jokes out first, Bronagh might well believe he had it under control. It wasn't anything serious. He was able to joke about it after all.

He should've known the warning signs. He'd grown up watching the same cycle of binge, destruct and dry out repeat itself time and time again. Each time the binges became bigger, longer, more severe. The destruction more violent. The dry-out periods shorter and shorter. He knew that, genetically speaking, he was likely to deal with addiction problems.

But he kept telling himself, in the way addicts do, that he could handle it. He was not like his father. He could never be like that man.

Until the day he started to drive his girlfriend to the airport knowing full well he was over the limit. In fact he realised he had probably driven over the limit more times than under it in recent weeks. Just short trips. Keeping his speed down. He was fine. He was in control.

He had promised Bronagh he would not drink on the day of her trip. Sworn he was sober and more than able to drive her to the airport. He'd lied. And he'd been caught out.

It was only by the grace of God that things were not much, much worse.

Bronagh had been so very angry, but more than that she had been disappointed. He could see it in her eyes and he would do anything in his power never to have to see that same look again. He'd promised her he would do whatever it took to earn her trust again. She had shouted, told him he needed to get his act together. That she could not, and would not, watch him blow his life up or throw it away like his father had done.

He'd vowed to change. He'd started, only recently, to believe he had won his battle. But now? Now he's not so sure. There it is, you see, just under the surface, the urge to drink. The ability to lose his temper. To throw away the life he'd just worked so hard to rebuild. That cycle of repair and destroy all over again.

The realisation hits him like a tonne of bricks and he can't bring himself to focus on what is being said around him. Or how Shelley is trying to soothe him and reassure him that everything will be okay. He is lost in a pit of self-loathing.

'I think we might have a lead,' DS King calls, walking back into Mal and Bronagh's house without knocking or ringing the doorbell.

'Did she just say they have a lead?' Shelley asks, looking towards the door, ready to see King walk in and fill them in. Mal is frozen on the spot, afraid to hope, afraid if the lead is a bad one – one that leads to some sort of tragic ending. He realises in this moment that while the waiting is horrendous, there's a safety to it. While they are waiting, there are no definites. There is still hope. There is no moment where an officer will sit him down and tell him that they are very sorry, but they have bad news. It is a purgatory to exist in, but at least it is not hell. He can't bring himself to speak. He can hardly bring himself to breathe. Shelley, however, is on her feet and heading towards the door as if the act of her walking fast across the room will speed King's arrival.

He doesn't want to say he's scared, because he's a grown man. A protector. An adult. But he is scared. He's more scared in this moment than when he realised he had no choice but to let his car career into the fence at the side of the Glenshane Pass. He's more scared than when Bronagh issued him the ultimatum.

And this might just be a 'lead', but he is scared to hope. But even more scared to contemplate the fact this might all end very badly. For all he knows it might have already ended in its own way.

'Okay,' King says walking into the room. 'We've literally just had a lead come in. Potentially a very strong lead.'

Mal still can't speak. He's afraid to ask any questions. He doesn't dare hope.

'About where she is?' Shelley asks. 'Or where she might be? If she's okay?' He can hear the emotion in Shelley's voice. He can see how she is animated – the exhaustion of the last couple of hours gone.

'Okay,' King says. 'We have a possible ID on the child.'

'Who is it?' Mal asks, and his voice sounds strange. Not like his own voice.

'We don't have it verified yet. We're going to try and do that as quickly as possible, but it would mark a significant step forward in the investigation.'

'A child didn't kidnap her,' Mal says, feeling like he should keep everyone's expectations measured.

'That much is true,' King says, and he thinks she can't understand why he isn't jumping for joy and thanking her for her hard work. But hadn't the same woman said they had lots of leads, most of them meaningless, getting called in since the appeal went live? How can they be so sure of this one if it 'literally just came in'? Why are they telling him about it now, when they haven't told him about all the other leads they had received? Surely if she has only just found out about it, in the less than fifteen minutes since she last left this house, she can't possibly say it's a strong lead yet.

'But it's who the child is connected to that is of interest to us. If the child has been identified correctly, of course,' King says, and she is starting to look a little flustered. Mal should maybe feel bad about this, but he doesn't. He has seen the same CCTV footage everyone else has. It's grainy, distorted by the rain on the lens, and only catches the child from the side with his hood up and from behind as they walked away. There is no way he is getting excited about this.

'Look, I can understand why you don't want to get your hopes up, but this really could be a very positive development.'

'Could be,' Mal says. 'That's the problem.'

'Mal,' Shelley says, in a tone he recognises as a warning to calm down, and he realises how poor a light he's presenting himself in, in front of DS King who quite clearly has a low opinion of him anyway.

He takes a deep breath and sits down, his legs and hands shaking. 'I know,' he says. 'I'm sorry. DS King, I'm sorry. I just... this is just...'

'I understand, Mal,' King says. 'It's a tough time. A really tough time. You are living through a nightmare and your mind, and your moods, must be all over the place.'

He closes his eyes, breathes in again and can't help but feel everyone is waiting for him to lose his cool and prove all their worst fears to be justified. Maybe all this talk of a lead is a way of dragging a response out of him that confirms he's an angry man, an argumentative man, and one who could possibly be a danger to women. He thought he'd moved beyond all that. Had moved beyond the shame that came with last year, but here it is haunting him even now.

He feels Shelley sit down beside him and wrap her arm around his shoulders.

'We'll get her back, Mal. We will. I feel it in my bones. Besides, this is Bronagh. She's kick-ass.' *God love Shelley*, he thinks. *She's doing her very best to sound brave.*

DS King's phone buzzes into life and she answers it, not leaving the room like Bradley did before. He can't hear who she is talking to or what they are saying, but she keeps glancing to him and Shelley before turning her back.

'Okay. I'll be right there,' she says eventually. She ends the call and turns to face them.

'Positive news,' she says. 'One of your neighbours has found more footage of the boy on their doorbell camera. He's not with Bronagh in it, it's just him walking down the street but it might be enough to confirm our earlier lead.'

Mal sees it then, the smallest trace of excitement on King's face. He allows himself to believe, even if for a second, that this might work out. That's before the crushing reality that identifying a child on camera doesn't actually bring Bronagh home. There are so many more hurdles to cross.

'That's great news,' Shelley says, her grip on him a little tighter. 'See! I told you. We're going to get her back!'

42

INGRID

'Oh my dear Jesus,' Lisa McGinley had said as she watched the clip from the news. I'd heard her gasp over the phone. 'That's him. I'm sure of it. Wee Oisin. I mean, it's not the clearest, but it definitely looks like him. What is he doing with Bronagh? And this is to do with her going missing? No. No. I don't believe that.'

'But you think it is him?' I'd asked her, my heart thudding so loudly I'm surprised she didn't hear it too. I wanted her to tell me more. I wanted to tease more out of her but Bradley and King were outside of the car now and looking like they were just about to get in.

'I think it is,' Lisa had said. 'I really think it could be.'

I'd ended the call very quickly, no doubt leaving Lisa's head spinning, but I'd no time to waste. I was out of my car and running down the street within seconds of hanging up, shouting, 'DCI Bradley! Hang on! Hang on!' I realise in this moment I am putting the safety of Bronagh Murray before my career. I have been all along. I am not the journalist I was before and I do not care. I care about doing the right thing. I've seen enough women hurt. Enough bullies win. I can hardly hold the police to high standards about their attitude to crimes against women if I am not prepared to do the right thing myself.

Needless to say the sight of a woman in her late thirties pelting down a street screaming to the police attracted his attention, and that of almost everyone else standing around. By the speed with which Constable Morrison turned towards me and reached for his gun, it was clear that they may have been perceiving me as a threat.

I raised my hands in mock surrender. 'Please, I have information. I might have very important information.'

I'd stood right here on this street, where I am still standing now, and told them all about Lisa McGinley, how she thinks the child in the video might be the son of Ciara Breslin who was very badly injured in the crash.

'Ciara was paralysed from the waist down, was she not?' Bradley had asked me, and I'd nodded.

'I believe so.'

'So how could she be involved in some sort of kidnap plot?' He absolutely did not believe me or take me seriously in that moment. I can't really blame him given that he didn't know the full story.

'Her partner, Griffen, didn't sustain any long-term injuries,' I'd told him. 'And according to Lisa McGinley they are no longer together, and Griffen, along with their son Oisin, are still in the north.'

David Bradley usually plays it very cool but even he couldn't hide the excitement from his face. I'd given him Lisa's details while DS King had run into Mal's house to brief him on what had happened. She was no sooner gone than we were approached by one of his minions regarding some new doorbell footage.

Lucky old me, I had been right there to hear it all first-hand and now I'm sitting with Mal and Shelley and it seems DS King didn't tell them the full story.

'So, she thinks it's Ciara Breslin's son, Oisin.'

'Ciara and Griffen's son. Yes.'

Mal's brow furrows, adding more wrinkles to a face that already looks as if it has aged a decade over the course of the last twenty-four hours.

'But why? Why Bronagh? That doesn't make sense...' Mal says.

I don't want to tell him what I suspect. My initial instincts were right. That it's not actually Bronagh who is the target here. It's him.

43

BRONAGH

Even though she is tired down to her very bones, Bronagh finds it impossible to sleep. It's cold in the basement, and damp. The chill of the stone floor is spreading through her body and making her very core ache. She is lying on the floor, her body the big spoon to Zachary's pathetically small little spoon. She hopes if she is curled around him she might feed some of her warmth into his emaciated frame.

It has gone quiet again upstairs. Deathly quiet. No footsteps, muffled voices or ominous dragging sounds. If Bronagh had been hoping to hear Maria's voice again it was in vain. There hasn't been so much as a moan, or a whisper.

It's so silent, in fact, that she wonders if the man is even in the house. It's too much to hope he might be off somewhere accessing help for Maria. Bronagh can't allow her mind to wander to what he may actually be doing with the woman she hoped would walk out of here with her.

It is clear though that the man does not care – not one ounce – about anyone else but himself. Any hope Bronagh had that he might even care for Zachary had been dashed when he had ordered them both into the cellar – knowing full well how terrified the boy would be.

She wonders how long they will be down here. Her stomach is already sore with hunger, and her throat parched. It has surprised her that Zachary hasn't cried out for food before, but then again she has no idea when he last ate and, the brutal reality is, the poor boy is so very thin that she imagines it has been a long time since he has eaten a good meal.

There's no point in using up what little energy she has to get out though – the gate is closed and locked, but even if it weren't, she knows she cannot risk running or trying to escape again – not with Zachary to consider.

She has seen the man's brutality enough times to know it will end badly. As she adjusts herself in the vain hope of getting more comfortable, she starts to feel despair seeping into her bones in much the same way the cold and the damp are. Soon enough, she thinks, she will be nothing *but* a human form of cold and despair. She will adopt the same haunted look as Maria, and the same gaunt expression as Zachary. Worst of all, she might not ever know why the man is doing this, or what his endgame might be. Does he just take woman after woman, using them until they are spent and broken before moving on to the next? How many 'mummas' has Zachary had? she wonders. Did he ever really know the woman who gave birth to him?

When exhaustion finally grows bigger than her discomfort, she drifts off to sleep, to dream of faceless women, each of them bloodied, lying all over the floor while Zachary picks his way among them, becoming more and more of a ghost himself with each step.

It is Zachary crying out that wakes her. When she opens her

eyes, she realises he is no longer beside her but in the darkness, she cannot see him.

'Zachary!' she calls, but not too loudly. The last thing she wants to do is attract the attention of the man.

'Mumma!' she hears him cry out.

'I'm here, sweetheart,' she says, not feeling as if she can be so cruel as to remind him she is not his mother and is instead a virtual stranger to him.

'Mumma!' he calls again. He can't be too far from her, so she follows the sound of his voice, crawling on her hands and knees and reaching out in front of her. She has her bearings enough to realise that he must be close to the stairs and the gate.

A loud rattle of metal confirms this to be true. It's only as Bronagh gets closer that she registers another sound. It's a voice. Or, more accurately, voices. There are at least two of them. All she can make out is muffled murmurs – made even more difficult to decipher because of Zachary's wailing.

Zachary rattles the gate again and, panic washing over her, she fights the urge to tell him to stop. She knows that is fuelled by her own fear but if there is someone else in the house, then surely she should use every part of her to make as much noise as possible and be heard. She doesn't know who the other voice belongs to. It could be someone who will help. It might be a paramedic, or even a police officer. They have to take the chance, because she's not sure how many more chances they will get.

Her heart thumping, she joins in, encouraging him to rattle the gate harder as he starts calling out 'MUMMA!' at the top of his lungs. He's sobbing now, every ounce a little boy desperate for the attention he clearly deserves.

'Help!' she screams as loud as her still-sore throat will allow. 'Help us!' She can taste blood in her mouth, the capillaries weakened by the man's attempt to choke the life out of her now bursting from the effort of her screams.

As the panic grows further, she has to bite back her fear and the desire to change her mind and silence them both. This is a gamble and it might pay off but, if it doesn't, it will bring his anger down on them both, and she has seen this morning that he does not care about who he hurts or how. But at the same time, she doesn't want to frighten Zachary any more than he is already. She doesn't want to let him see her fear, nor does she want to silence his plaintive cries for help.

'Mumma!' Zachary screams now – his shrill voice cutting through her. When the door opens at the top of the stairs, she joins in with the screaming, using this opportunity of an open door to make sure the others in the house have no choice but to hear them.

The now-familiar bulk of the man appearing in shadow in the doorway instils a sense of terror in her, but the thought of just quietly giving in to whatever he wants scares her more.

'I said keep QUIET!' he says, roaring the final word as he takes one, then two heavy steps down towards them. Bronagh stands just behind Zachary, determined to protect him. She whispers in his ear to be brave. This man – this monster at the top of the stairs – has no heart. He has no sense of compassion or empathy – not even towards the child – but she is determined to make sure he doesn't win.

The boy doesn't stop crying. He continues calling for his mother, and rattling the gate. As the man gets closer, she tries to unfurl the boy's fingers from around the metal bars so she can pull him to safety, but he hangs on tightly with much more strength in his little body than she would've anticipated.

'Zachary,' she pleads. 'Come with me. Come back a bit.' Still he persists, shouting over the cacophonous banging of metal on metal. He is still gripping on tightly when Bronagh feels the man's shovel-like hand reach through the bars and clamp down on hers.

At this sight Zachary immediately falls silent and steps back, almost missing the stair behind him and tumbling. Bronagh is able to steady him – just – and she leads him down to the bottom of the stairs while the man swings the gate open and steps towards them. As soon as he reaches the bottom, Zachary runs to him and clings to his legs.

'What's all the fuss?' the man asks, not shouting this time but instead talking in a gentle voice. It is almost more alarming than when he was bellowing at them. This Jekyll and Hyde approach unnerves her.

Zachary sniffs and clings even tighter to the man's trouser leg. Bronagh can't help but feel the trauma bond between them must be exceptionally strong if the little boy can have witnessed whatever horrors occurred in the kitchen before and still run to cling to this man.

'Did this bad lady hurt you?' the man asks, his face sneering in her direction.

'I did not touch—'

'I wasn't talking to you! I was talking to the boy.'

She blinks at him. She wants to defend herself, to argue her innocence but soon realises he isn't interested in the truth of the matter. He wants to scare her. No, maybe scare isn't the right word. He wants to control her. He wants to show her how he can control everything in his little world – so much so he can even change the truth.

'Zachary,' he asks again, 'did this bad lady hurt you?'

Shuddering in the shadows, she knows it's impossible to predict what Zachary will say. If he will tell the truth, or if he will do whatever it takes to please his captor. Her breath catches in her throat as she waits for him to answer. He doesn't speak, instead just looking back at her, blinking back big tears from eyes that are way too sad to belong to a child. Inwardly she pleads for him to save her. To make it known she didn't hurt him. She couldn't hurt him. She doesn't have it in her to hurt anyone. Desperation is paralysing her, making it impossible to shift breath in or out of her body.

Slowly, Zachary looks up at the man – and shakes his head. 'No.'

Bronagh feels weak with relief, sagging as her legs turn to jelly under her.

'Are you sure?' the man asks.

Keep quiet, Bronagh wills herself. *Don't speak. Don't defend yourself. Don't do anything to anger him. Stay safe. Stay alive. Behave. Be a good girl.*

The boy nods.

The man looks back at her, slowly taking her in from the very top of her head to the very ends of her toes. Even the way he scans her body is enough to make her want to puke.

'Is he telling the truth or is he protecting you?' the man asks her.

'He's telling the truth,' Bronagh says in a shaky voice, no longer able to fake any bravado. She has seen how this man can turn in a second, and how he can inflict pain and suffering without blinking.

There's a pause while he examines her again, his eyes taking in her every curve. Despite being fully dressed, she resists the urge to cover herself up, knowing that if she crosses her arms over her chest she will only draw more attention to her unease and he will feed off it.

'Very well,' he says, 'both of you come up. I need you to meet someone.'

It's only then that she realises he has just extinguished all hope of escape. And she doesn't want to go upstairs and meet anyone. If whoever is up there is an ally, there is no way the man would be bringing them up to meet him. He is not the kind of man who gives in easily.

No, this cellar might be cold and damp, and as dark as the night, but there is safety of sorts here and she feels a longing to stay.

She dares not resist or hesitate though. She knows if she does she will pay for it, or worse perhaps, the boy will. This brute of a man has her exactly where he wants her. It has only taken a couple of days to break her spirit. His cruelty is unmatched. Silent, with her head bowed, she does exactly what she is told and starts to climb the stairs, while the man and Zachary follow behind her.

44

BRONAGH

Reaching the top of the staircase, she waits for him to tell her where to go. 'Kitchen,' he says. It's a one-word bark that directs her towards the now-hushed kitchen. As she walks, she wonders if Maria will still be there. Perhaps back from the doctor's or hospital, head wound in crisp, white bandages. She wonders about this, even though she knows in her heart of hearts that Maria is gone and will most likely never come back.

The blood spatter, she imagines, will still be there – a stark reminder of what can happen when you cross the wrong person. The old Bronagh may have tried to find some space in her heart to understand what is going on with this man. She believes a person is not born intrinsically evil and yet this is what he is showing her. He is showing her that people can be cruel – even to a child. At first it had seemed like he wanted her to nurture Zachary – to act like a mother to him. But now? How can any man say he wants to protect his child and force him to witness violence, and force him down into a dark room against his will? After feeling the air being squeezed from her own lungs, she no longer feels that all people are born good and that it's life that colours them. She saw the darkness in his eyes. She has seen how he treats people – as if they are disposable property and not worthy of love and freedom. It is truly terrifying to see that up close.

Following his instructions and walking down the hall, she startles when she feels the warmth of a small hand slip into hers. Turning her head she sees that Zachary, sucking on a cheap lollipop, is walking at her side – tears dried. He squeezes her hand tightly, a simple gesture that gives her a moment of light in this darkness. Zachary trusts her. She knows that. And with that trust comes the responsibility of doing whatever she can to get him out of there as well as herself.

She walks on, keeping her head down, afraid to see what and who is in the kitchen. She's afraid to look at the spot where Maria was lying before – and she doesn't know what would scare her most. To find Maria gone, or to find her still there, still bleeding, or no longer breathing.

With her head low, she spots a pair of denim-clad legs, leading to a pair of scuffed trainers. She doesn't see any other feet, but knows there may well be someone behind her that she cannot see and she dares not turn around. Zachary lets go of her hand and run towards the man in the trainers, clearly not afraid of him. She watches as Zach is lifted off his feet and swung around. 'Zachy boy! How are you today?' he says in a local accent and Bronagh forces herself to raise her head and look at them.

The man in the trainers is grinning at Zachary, who is clinging on tightly and laughing, his head thrown back in delight. It is, Bronagh realises, the first time she has heard the child laugh. Even amid all this horror, it is a beautiful sound.

She freezes when the man holding Zachary stops swinging him and looks her directly in the eye. 'Jesus, lad. What have you got yourself caught up in now?' He looks genuinely horrified and Bronagh can only imagine what she looks like. Dirty clothes, bruised, matted hair and blood streaked on her arms from trying to help Maria.

She blinks and turns her head quickly to the side, desperate to see if the other woman is still there, but there is no sign of her and to her surprise, there is no sign of the blood that was left spattered on the cupboard doors. It's as if Maria had never even been here to begin with – but she was here. Bronagh knows that. This is not some fever dream. It is all very real.

Her eyes flick to the man to see his response and for the first time she notices that while he is still the same, angry, brooding creature he was before, there is something else there now in his demeanour.

If she's not mistaken, it's fear. 'I fucked up, Christy,' he says. 'This isn't how it was supposed to go. I need to clean up this mess. I need your help, pal.' And with that he looks her directly in the eye, pauses for a moment and starts advancing directly towards her. All she can see are those same sharp blue – yet soulless – eyes.

45

MAL

Mal is shaking. How is he supposed to react? What is he supposed to think? It seems so insane that this might actually be connected to the crash. He can't wrap his head around that being true. All he keeps asking himself is: why Bronagh?

'I don't know if I buy it,' he says, jolting Shelley out of her thoughts. They've been having variations of this conversation for the last half hour. He has gone online and done his very best to search for Ciara Breslin, her son Oisin, and her partner, Griffen Amin.

Their names come up in relation to the crash and he is able to uncover numerous social media profiles under the name of Ciara Breslin, but he has no idea what she looks like and so has no idea which one is her. Or if she even uses social media.

He doesn't know if Oisin uses his mum's or his dad's surname, so he tries searching both. It's a bust. There are too many hits and not enough concrete information.

Griffen Amin is also an enigma, it seems. He's only mentioned in relation to the crash, and there are no pictures. There is a mention from an article last year that says he and

Ciara live outside the County Derry town of Magherafelt, but that again would be like searching for a needle in a haystack and what's he going to do anyway? He can hardly get in the car and drive down there to conduct a one-man search of the area. It's not like any of his searches are likely to bring up an online map to where he might have taken Bronagh.

This information isn't really any use to him at all, but he has to hope it will be useful to the police. He has no choice but to put his faith in them now. Ingrid's been in the kitchen on the phone constantly. She says she's trying to check in with as many of her relevant contacts as possible, hopeful that one or more of them will be able to direct her towards Ciara's family or Griffen's contacts.

Ciara should be a little easier to track – or at least her family should be, Ingrid has said. Yes, Breslin is a common name but people on this island love a good sad story. There will be information somewhere about a poor mother who was injured horribly in a car accident. Ingrid says she's sure of it. With Griffen, on the other hand – while his might be the more unusual name – there is no guarantee he is even still in the country. He may well have gone home to his native Turkey, taking Oisin with him.

Mal doesn't know what to think. His mind just keeps going back to the big why. Why would Griffen Amin take Bronagh? What has she ever done wrong in her life to hurt anyone? It's not how she operates. It's not how her heart works.

Shelley looks at him and shrugs. 'Things don't always have to make sense in this world, Mal,' she says.

He thought having some more information would make all this feel a little better – perhaps feed him some hope. A few hours ago he would have given anything for a lead and now they have one, it just feels so incredibly frustrating and he can't shake the tension in his body. His shoulders are in knots; his head feels like someone has fixed a rubber band around it and is squeezing it for all his worth.

As Ingrid walks back into the room he gets to his feet. 'What can I do, Ingrid?' he asks. 'There has to be some way I can help here, because sitting doing nothing is making me lose my mind. Should I go on TV and make an appeal? Ask this Griffen or Ciara to come forward?'

'I think an appeal might help,' she says, 'but loath as I am to say it, don't mention any names unless the police give you the green light to do so. You don't want to risk the investigation, and you definitely don't want to do anything that could put Bronagh in any further danger.'

Mal wonders how it is possible she could be in any further danger. She has already been stolen from her life – but he also knows Ingrid would not be telling him to keep the names quiet without good reason. If she doesn't want the scoop of naming suspects, it has to be serious.

'I can probably get you on the early evening news though,' she says. 'Just say the word. I'll get the police press officer to brief you on what information they want you to put out there. My phone's been bombarded by so many news organisations it won't be a problem. BBC are keen to have you on and if I were you, I'd go with them.'

'Then let's do that,' he says, feeling positive that he is at least doing *something*. He looks at the clock. It's after two so there's hopefully plenty of leeway to hit the teatime bulletin, and hopefully he'll get it online even sooner.

'I'll arrange it,' Ingrid says as her phone rings and she turns to answer it, walking back into the kitchen and talking animatedly as she goes.

'Are you sure you want to go on TV?' Shelley asks. 'You

could be opening yourself up to all kinds of judgement. You know how people study those things and come up with all sorts of weird and wonderful conspiracies.'

'Let them. Shelley, I don't give two hoots about what people think,' he says, even though that is clearly a lie, but there are more important things at play than his reputation. 'We have to keep the pressure on, and we have to hope she sees it, and that she'll know we're looking for her. Can you imagine if she thinks no one is bothering?'

Shelley shakes her head. 'Wise up, Mal. She's not going to think that. She knows she's loved. She knows we'll be going clean out of our minds looking for her.'

46

INGRID

'Right, I have a name and a number for you,' Erin Hutcheon – one of my former journalism colleagues – tells me. 'It took a bit of poking about but I've found the Breslin family in Monaghan. There was a GoFundMe campaign last year done in the town for their daughter who was involved in an awful car crash. It made mention of her being a mother to a wee boy and that she had been planning her wedding. It didn't have the name of her fellah or her boy – I'm told the family are incredibly private – but it's too much of a coincidence to be anyone else, isn't it?'

'I tried searching for any fundraisers and came up blank,' I tell her and it's true. Not a word of a fundraiser for Ciara Breslin could be found anywhere.

'You would have. As I said the family are very private and I'm told by my source, who is fairly reliable, that there was a bit of a furore over the fundraiser. The family didn't like to be seen to take charity was the official line, but my source tells me there was some gossip at the time too – about the fellah. Apparently, he's a bit of a bad shite.'

Erin, I think, has such a way with words. I do miss her

straight-talking from our days in the newsroom. She gets just as excited as I do when a story starts to come together, and I can hear that excitement in her voice now.

'A bad shite in what way?' I ask, thinking that if he has the wee boy with him, he surely can't be that bad.

'A bit fond of slapping Ciara around, I'm told,' Erin says. 'Pity it wasn't him who was left injured after the crash. If only he could've lost the power of his hands or something.'

If only, I think. But in my experience, the bad shites seem to get away with far too much.

'Anyway, the family had the fundraiser scrubbed.'

'And is Ciara with them now in Monaghan?' I ask.

There's a pause. 'Now here's the thing I heard – and it might be a load of nonsense – but I think given our friend's handsy past, there might be truth in it.'

I'm intrigued.

'She's not there. They don't talk about wherever she is. They won't talk about her at all. Any time they're asked how she's getting on they change the subject or ignore the question.'

She has me curious. What could possibly be going on there?

'Very interesting,' I say, although this doesn't necessarily bode well for me getting in touch with them and getting any kind of useful information out of them.

I take the details from Erin, tell her I owe her a couple of pints the next time we meet.

'It's a date,' she says. 'And keep me posted. Sounds like a juicy one.'

It most certainly does.

Standing in Mal's kitchen I tap the number Erin has given me into the phone and wait until it connects. It rings three times before a woman answers with a cheery hello.

I tell her who I am and that I'm looking to speak with her about Ciara, or more precisely her former partner and her son.

The call is cut off before I can finish my sentence.

Taking a deep breath, I call the number again, not terribly optimistic that it will be answered but it is, by the same woman with a slightly less cheery voice this time. I know that this is the last chance I will have to get through to her. It's a miracle she even answered again. There is no chance she will answer a third time. So I have to go straight for the kill.

'Look, I think there is a woman in very serious danger and I think that Griffen Amin might be involved, and I know you all want to be left alone but if you can help...'

There's a long silence. So long and so silent in fact that I wonder if she has hung up, but I look at my phone and see the call is still connected.

'That man is an animal,' the woman says. 'Who is he hurting now? Did you know he took our boy from us? He wasn't driving the day of the crash, but he's no less guilty than the man who was.'

47

BRONAGH

'What the hell are you caught up in this time?' the man in the scruffy trainers says. 'This doesn't look good, lad.' He plasters on a smile again for Zachary and puts him back on the ground.

'Look, you have to help me here,' her captor says and, for the first time, Bronagh sees she was right. He *is* scared. He's not quite the same big man now that he was. 'You owe me.'

'There's owing someone and there's *owing* someone. Who is she? I need you to tell me what is going on.'

'Does it matter who she is? I needed someone to help with Zachary. The boy needs a mother.'

'Of course it matters who she is.' The man in the scruffy trainers takes a cigarette pack out of his pocket and pulls one out, lighting it and dragging the warm smoke into his lungs. She can see his hands are shaking. He narrows his eyes and looks at her again as if trying to place her.

Bronagh used to smoke. A long time ago. A foolish habit she got into in her late teenage years in a bid to look cool. She must be off the cigs about ten years, but the smell of smoke is so enticing, and she longs to ask for one. To take a long drag herself to settle her nerves. It's impossible to ascertain if this man is friend or foe – but she very much fears it's the latter.

'All you need to know is that this is justice. Or I thought it was justice. Now, I don't know. She is causing me too many problems.'

The man in the scruffy trainers examines her – no doubt wondering how this bruised and battered woman could be causing problems. Bronagh stays quiet. She wants to see how this plays out.

'You wanted a mother for Zachary here? So, what, you just took one? Jesus Christ!' He laughs. 'You've some balls on you, Griff. But this is proper madman territory. What happened to your woman? That new girlfriend of yours? Maria, was it?'

Bronagh is trying to take this all in. The man's laugh. That he knew about Maria and, what, thought she was a girlfriend? How could anyone have looked at the state Maria was in and think she was a girlfriend?

It's then the name registers. Griff. She knows that name. She blinks and looks up at him again. The pieces start falling into place while he prattles on about Maria being too mouthy and too much trouble. Bronagh thinks of the meek, cowed woman she has known over the last few days. Of the fear that was all over her face. Of her pleas to do what was asked of her or face awful consequences and she can't imagine her as 'too much trouble' for anyone. And she thinks of this man – this monster – and his talk of justice and all of a sudden, she knows who he is. She knows what he is. And all of a sudden she has had enough of his threats, his bullying and his violence. If this is going to end badly for her, she will go down fighting.

'Griffen,' she mutters, and he turns to look at her, his eyes blazing with fury.

'I didn't give you permission to speak.'

'You're Griffen Amin,' she says, absolutely stunned by the realisation. 'From the crash. You're Ciara's boyfriend.'

Griffen's face contorts with anger. 'Shut up!' he screams, his face now impossibly close to hers. 'Shut the fuck up!'

'Steady on, lad,' she hears the man in the trainers say. 'She has the measure of you. Calm yourself.' He sounds nervous, as if he is well aware of exactly what type of man he is dealing with.

Meanwhile Bronagh's mind is racing. Ciara – poor Ciara who was injured so severely in the accident she will never walk again. And, yes, of course, they had a little boy, didn't they? But she's pretty sure his name wasn't Zachary. It was something else. Odhran or Oisin... yes, Oisin. That was it.

'Oisin,' she says out loud and looks to where Zachary is sitting under the table. At the mention of his name he scrambles forward, a smile on his face as if delighted to hear that name again. Fuck, she thinks. Fuck. Her head spins.

Until she feels the weight of Griff's palms pushing hard and fast against her shoulder blades sending her falling backwards, until she lands with a thud on the floor, her hands sliding in the pool of blood left by Maria as she tries to gain purchase.

'His name is Zachary,' Griff says as Bronagh tries to catch her breath.

'Oisin,' she hears a small voice say from across the room. 'Oisin,' Zachary says again and again.

As Griff turns his attention to his son, Bronagh tries to scramble to her feet, determined if nothing else not to let this man hurt the child. Not any more than he already has.

'Griff, how does she know Ciara? And the wee man?' the man in the scruffy trainers asks as Griff tries to quiet Zachary, telling him to be a good boy and play with his toys and remember Oisin is a bad name now. For bad people.

'I was in the crash,' Bronagh blurts. 'I was hurt too.' She pulls up the leg of her joggers revealing the six-inch scar, along her right leg. 'I've no idea why he's come for me.' Her voice cracks as she struggles to understand what game this Griff is playing at. Has he targeted her because she was in the crash? Because his child needed a mother? This is madness. She knows she is risking Griff's wrath but she also senses this is her last chance – her only chance – to get away. This Christy seems as shocked by Griff's behaviour as she is.

'What the fuck, Griff?' the man in the scruffy trainers asks. 'Come on, mate! This is insane! I don't want a bar of it. I don't know why you brought me here. I'm not into playing sick games.'

'It is not a sick game. It is justice!' Griff says. 'Her man was drunk. He was drunk and in the crash. The crash that took Ciara from me. That took her from her boy.'

'Mal wasn't responsible for the crash!' Bronagh says. 'I'm so sorry for what happened and I don't know what has gone on since with you and Ciara, but it was not Mal's fault and it isn't my fault.'

'That crash took the boy's mother and left me with him. With a boy who cries for her all the time. Who never gives me a moment's peace. She raised him to be too soft. A pathetic little mummy's boy. What am I supposed to do with him?'

Griff glares at his son who has crawled back under the table and is once again sitting with his knees drawn up to his chest. When Bronagh looks in his direction, he is staring wide-eyed at her, as if pleading her to help him. Her heart hurts. This boy just wants to be a little boy who is loved and cherished.

'This Mal, he owes me. An eye for an eye,' Griff says. 'He

drinks. He gets into a car and there is an accident. He doesn't care about you. You could've died. You could have been left useless to him, like Ciara is to me.'

She winces at the harshness of his words. How can he talk about his child that way? And about his partner? As if neither of them is anything more than a possession for him to play with and discard once he has broken them. Ciara is better off away from this madman. 'So I will take you where I can protect you... and you can protect my boy in return,' he says.

'You're off your head, Mal,' the man in the scruffy trainers says, 'and I don't want anything to do with this sick fuckery. Why the hell have you brought me here?'

'You owe me, Christy. And I need help because this bitch, this bitch who I was going to protect, is all over the news. With my boy. So I need to get away from here. I need you to help us get away.'

Something deep inside Bronagh snaps and she can't hold in the sharp laugh that rises from her chest. 'You were going to *protect* me? *This* is protecting me?' She lifts her hair exposing the livid bruising around her neck before bowing her head and showing the bloody matted mess caused by the blow to the head during the kidnapping. 'And what about Maria? Did you protect her too? When you beat her to a pulp on the floor? Don't believe him when he says she was too mouthy,' she says, staring straight at Christy. 'Ask him where is she now. Ask him if she's still alive because it very much looked like she was dying the last time I saw her. When your friend here wouldn't get help.'

She doesn't know where she is finding this inner bravery from. She suspects it is just born of anger.

'Griff, I'm not here for this,' Christy says. 'I'm not about hurting people, or making people disappear. You know that.

Any stolen goods you need fenced, or supplies you need shipped in, then I'm your man. But I'm not going to be a part of this shitshow.' He is shaking his head. 'You're not right in the head, lad.'

Griff stands frozen, staring at each of them in turn as if trying to work out his next move. But Bronagh isn't done talking. Now that she has started, she doesn't want to stop.

'And your boy? You don't deserve that child, and he sure as fuck doesn't deserve a monster like you!' She is shouting, but she doesn't care. This whole situation is so absurd, and anger is flooding through her veins. This man – this big scary man – who can't manage to look after his own child without beating a woman into submission first. Who has to call in reinforcements for every silly little task. Reinforcements like Christy, who may well be shaken but who clearly hasn't any respect for the man in front of him. Griffen Amin is nothing more than a dirty, rotten coward. It would be laughable, if she weren't sure Maria was either dead or close to it somewhere. If there weren't a little boy reliant on this man to raise him and provide him with moral and emotional guidance. And where is Ciara? Does she know the kind of man her precious boy is with?

Just who does this brute of a man think he really is? She wants to tell him he's as stupid as he is ugly. That she didn't do anything to deserve this and nor did Mal.

She is not the kind of person to make enemies. She lives a small life. Goes about her day like anyone else. Inoffensively getting on with things. Like most other people she gets up each morning wishing for an extra five minutes' sleep, goes to work and does her best – most of the time – until it's time to get back in her car and drive home. She makes dinner for her and Mal. Sometimes he cooks. Sometimes they order in a pizza or go out. Most nights, especially during the week, they spend their evenings watching TV together, or she takes a long soak in the bath listening to her latest audiobook.

She hurts no one. And yes, Mal had made a mistake and he was lucky that his crime did not make a horrific accident even worse. But he faced his demons. He went to court. He went to AA, and he still does. Every single week. He doesn't drink any more. He works hard on himself and they are just a couple who have settled into their own little lives and get on with things. He has made her more proud in the last year than she could ever have hoped for, she realises. She knows she trusts him. More than ever. Unlike this complete bastard who hurts women and terrifies children and is shouting about justice.

What about justice for Maria? He'd left her on the floor, the lifeblood literally running out of her, not caring if Zachary was watching, not caring that Bronagh was pleading with him to get help, telling him it was beyond her capability. He'd refused to call an ambulance.

She thinks of how he ushered her and Zachary, his own son, into the darkness of the cellar even though the boy was clearly terrified. What this child has seen and been complicit in is nothing short of child abuse – what about *his* justice? Where is that?

There is no justice in him standing over her like this, eyes blazing, threatening... what? More violence? He says he wants a mother for his child – but what of Ciara? And Maria? How many mothers does this man want, or need, or will he just keep tearing his way through women for as long as he can get away with it?

Griff is glaring at her and while she is scared, and her body is vibrating with fear, she refuses to bow down to his bully-boy tactics.

'What are you going to do?' she asks. 'Are you going to tell me to shut up again?'

She's aware of Christy staring at her, gawping, but sidestepping towards the door. She suspects he's as big of a coward as the bully standing over her. She knows Zachary, or Oisin, or whatever his name is, is watching too but she cannot back down. She pulls herself to standing. If he is to answer her, he can do it to her face.

She pauses, takes a breath to steady herself. 'I asked you a question: what are you going to do?'

Bracing herself for the impact of a fist, or a boot, she feels her body tense. No blow comes. He is still looking at her, incredulous that she has dared to speak, startled by her bravado and her ballsiness.

'What am I going to do?' he asks her. She doesn't speak. Griff takes another step towards her. Using every ounce of strength in her body, she resists the urge to flinch or break eye contact.

'That's a very brave question for someone who has so little power,' he says, another step closer. Griff is rattled. Bronagh can see it even though he's doing a very good job of trying to hide it.

And even though she is terrified, she refuses to show it. She will stand up to him. No matter the cost.

So she focuses only on looking him directly in the eye and keeping her breath slow and rhythmic. Her hands hurt with the pain of trying to hide the tremor in them. Her chest is tight. 'What. Are. You. Going. To. Do?' she asks again. A little louder this time.

He doesn't speak. He just stares and anger rises in her further, prompting her to ask again, louder still, 'What are you going to do... with me?'

He steps closer.

'The same thing you did to Maria? Punch me and kick me into submission? Throttle me again?'

He is in front of her, close enough that she can feel the moisture in his sour breath, smell the stench of him – body odour mixed with the metallic tang of blood – blood she is pretty sure isn't his. Maria's face comes back into her mind again. 'I'll do whatever the fuck I want to do,' he hisses and she waits, again, for the sting of his slap, or his fingers probing, his tongue licking, his boot stomping into her bare feet, crushing her bones. When none comes, her anger morphs into the realisation that there is no way she is going to get out of this. Christy is so close to the door it's only a matter of time before he bolts and then, without a witness to curb the worst of his rage, she will face Griff's full fury. So she is going to say what needs to be said and not give in to her fate passively.

He might break her body, but he will not break her spirit.

'You're nothing but a bully and a coward,' she spits. 'And a stupid one at that.'

The first hit comes then. Sharp and swift. She feels the air shift in front of her face before the sting of his open palm lands on her cheek, whipping her head violently to the side. She stays on her feet, rights herself and looks at him again. She does not cry out, or beg him to stop. She just looks him dead in the eye knowing that he will be reading her thoughts and seeing her resistance. It will be driving him mad.

With a crack, he slaps her again. The same hand on the same cheek. This time she hears, and feels, something crack and pop. She stays standing, although the pain in her cheek is blinding and she can taste blood in her mouth.

'Do you want to repeat that?' he asks.

She blinks, feeling her left eye swelling already. He isn't going to win that easily.

'You are nothing but a bully and a coward,' she says, blood trickling from her mouth.

Hearing the whistle of the air as his hand swoops towards her face, she waits for the next crack, the next busted blood vessel, the breaking of skin, the breaking of bone... She must not flinch.

48

MAL

Mal is horrified by what Ingrid has just told him. Completely horrified. And terrified. If he's not mistaken, Ingrid is shaken by it too. Ingrid who must've heard so much and seen so much through her career, but who is shaken by this. Shelley is in tears while he sits, trying to push the grotesque images that are haunting him out of his mind.

Lily Breslin had just outlined the most horrific abuse of her daughter to Ingrid and had confirmed that Ciara is receiving specialist care in a private health facility but that no, she is not prepared to reveal her location. Not to anyone. There are some risks that are not worth taking.

She revealed that Ciara had tried to get away from Griffen several times, but he always managed to drag her back in – a toxic mixture of love-bombing and threats against her and their child kept her in line.

Lily told Ingrid that Griffen had what he described as 'very traditional values' and treated her daughter as little more than a slave. She had lost one pregnancy due to his violence and was terrified that Griffen would hurt Oisin too. Plans had been made for her to leave – and were at an advanced stage – when they were involved in the accident on the Glenshane Pass. At the time, Ciara's injuries were described as extensive but her daughter had later told her that a significant number of them were fresh and inflicted by the man who was supposed to love her, shortly before they got into the car that day.

'He's an absolute animal,' Lily had sobbed down the phone as she had revealed that he had taken the boy against his mother's wishes when it was clear she would not be returning to him. The pair had simply disappeared off the face of the planet and no amount of tracking them down had been successful.

Both Ciara and Lily maintain he did not take Oisin out of any love for the child or desire to parent him but more out of a desire to cause as much pain as possible to the woman who finally had had enough of his abuse. 'He said it was justice,' Lily had sobbed down the phone as Ingrid promised to do whatever she could to help real justice be served.

Mal can hardly breathe with fear for Bronagh. Even when Bradley and King describe the new information as a huge step forward. It provides no comfort. Because he'll never consider it a step forward until she is home. No one knows where she is, and she is in the worst danger he can think of.

49

BRONAGH

Time seems to slow down, as if informing Bronagh that this is it. She had survived the initial blow that day on the greenway, and she had survived the kidnap. She had survived his strangulation attempt. She had escaped the worst of his temper when he had beaten Maria to a pulp. She doesn't think she will survive this.

His hand is raised. Sound falls away until she can only hear her own breath entering and leaving her body. His face is distorted with rage – almost demonic, she thinks, as she looks into his deep blue eyes again, takes in the pockmarks in his skin, the wrinkles and scars carved deep into his weather-worn face. The way his slicked hair frames his face, and the halo of pathetic light from the forty-watt bulb hanging bare from the ceiling, feed her feeling that she is looking at evil.

A flash of fear – real, deep and just short of heart-stopping in intensity – almost forces her to look away from him and from the open palm that is coming for her. She will not blink. She will not cower. She will let him see exactly what he does but she will not give him the satisfaction of playing the victim any more.

But just as she feels the energy shift in the air close to her face, and just as she anticipates the sharp sting of his skin against hers, she is stunned to see his raised hand stop in mid-air and start to move away from her. Back and back, as if he is staggering. The look of anger on Griff's face changes to something she could swear is shock. His eyes widen, and the noise of the room comes rushing back in. But there is a groan, swearing, a thudding of feet no longer able to stand firm on the floor followed by a howl of fear and of pain.

Her eyes fall to Griff's arm as it reaches around to his back. He bends, folding with pain and she sees he is clutching at something, blood pulsing through his splayed fingertips. It is a vision of horror but she can't look away.

Nor can she move from where she is standing as she tries to process what exactly she is seeing. It's then that it becomes clear. There is a knife's long black handle protruding from the wound in his back. His hand is grasping at it as blood drips from his fingers.

She looks up, expecting to see Christy. Wondering if she misjudged him and instead of fleeing the scene, he was instead ready to come to her defence. She is looking around the room when she feels a hand grab her wrist.

It's Griff and he appears to be as shocked as she is, as if he can't quite wrap his head around it.

'What... what did... you... d-do?' he stutters as his knees buckle under him.

'I... I didn't do anything,' she replies as she remains frozen to the spot. 'How could I? I don't... know...'

Griff looks at his hand, covered in warm, plum-red blood, then again to Bronagh.

'Help me,' he says, pleading in the way he should've done when Maria needed help.

She knows she has a choice. She could try and help him, for whatever it will achieve. As she has already told him, she is not a doctor. She no more knows how to help him than she knew how to help Maria.

She is still frozen to the spot, unable to look away, and she swears she can see the colour draining from him along with his blood. As he starts to buckle, she knows he is in serious trouble. He reaches back once more to grab the knife handle, wrapping his hand around it and wincing, the vibrations of his own touch clearly sending fresh shock waves of pain through him.

She doesn't know much but she knows he shouldn't pull the blade from his wound. It could cause more catastrophic bleeding. 'Leave it where it is,' she urges. She can't think what else to do. Where the fuck is Christy? Gone now he has stuck the knife into this man? Not helping her at all but leaving her with an even bigger mess to clean up? Another impossible situation to manage.

'Please!' Griff begs, his big bad attitude having completely deserted him and been replaced with cowardice and a pathetic pleading quality. 'Zachary... the towels. Get them,' he splutters.

It's only then that Bronagh turns her head towards the table to look for the boy. He might have witnessed unspeakable violence before, but her heart is sore for what he is watching now. She expects to see him still sitting beneath the table, beside his toys, but the space is empty and her fear grips her.

Frantic with worry, she looks around the room and when she spots him, everything stops for a second. He is curled up on his side, his back to her, with his hands over his face. There is blood. On his hands, his clothes, in his hair. Immediately, she moves towards him and drops to her knees. She won't help that bastard who is screaming for her but she sure as hell will not ignore the boy. What kind of a monster would hurt a child? Her eyes darting around the room, assessing the danger that must surely still exist, she calls his name softly – trying her very best to be tender with her words. *Please God*, she thinks, *let him be okay*. She couldn't bear it if he were hurt. He's only a child.

50

MAL

Mal stands outside his front door, a radio mic attached to his jacket while a man in a suit – whom he recognises from the nightly bulletins – asks him to describe his girlfriend for the viewers.

'Bronagh is the best person I know,' he says, taking a deep breath to stop his voice from breaking. 'Anyone who knows her will tell you she's bubbly, friendly and the kind of person who will help anyone she can. I've no idea if she was trying to help the wee boy in the videoclip or what, but I know she wouldn't just disappear like this of her own free will.' Shelley nods beside him, tears sliding down her face. He hears her sniff.

'And do you have a message for her if she happens to be watching? Or for any potential captor?'

He feels a lead weight on his chest. He has been thinking about this ever since Ingrid said she would send a reporter over, but advised him not to mention the link with Griffen Amin. He wants to call him out. He wants to ask why. He wants to tell Griffen to come for him instead – if this is about the crash. He wants to say sorry to Bronagh. On the off chance she might see it. He wants to tell her he loves her. But he knows he has to play it safe. He has to play the game exactly how Ingrid and the police have told him to play it.

They have said this man – this Griffen Amin – is a dangerous character. That Ciara Breslin called the police to their home on numerous occasions for domestic violence but all too often subsequently withdrew her statement.

'He's a brute,' DS King had said as Constable Morrison sat stony-faced beside her. 'He's a very dangerous man. He took the child despite being denied custody and the Garda believe that he may be using the boy as a sort of human shield – a distraction while he gets up to whatever the hell he wants. The footage of him on the Ring Doorbell camera would suggest that is true.'

Mal's heart had plummeted, and just when he had thought it couldn't possibly fall much farther, DS King had landed another body blow. 'Although no official connection has been made, the Guards are looking into the possibility that he may have been involved in the abduction of a woman from Emyvale. A nursery worker, by all accounts, who had cared for Oisin before Griffen snatched him.'

With all this information weighing very heavy on his heart, Mal is scared of letting his fear and his anger escape. But he knows he has to play by the rules. DS King told him to treat this appeal a little like a hostage negotiation. 'It's vitally important not to alienate the abductor,' she'd said. 'I understand your anger but if he feels attacked, that could push him to action.'

He didn't need her to explain exactly what she meant by action. The message got through loud and clear.

'The important thing is,' DS King had said, 'this is now a cross-border operation. So the eyes of the PSNI and the Guards are on the case. Every police officer on the island of Ireland will be looking for her. It's important we don't give up hope. She will be relying on us to not give up hope.'

Clearing his throat, as the first drops of icy cold rain land on his face, he speaks. 'Bronagh, if you can see this – if you are in control of where you are – please let us know you're okay. Call the police, or Shelley, or your parents. Call me. We want you to be safe and home with us. We are all very worried about you. You are so loved.' This time he can't hide the crack in his voice, and it feels as if his heart is cracking open with it. 'If you are someone out there, keeping Bronagh from us, then I beg you to just let her go. She doesn't deserve this. She is the kind of person who would never so much as hurt a fly. We need her home. *I* need her home.'

Off camera, the reporter, Sean Doyle, signals to him with a thumbs-up that he has said enough. The sound bite has been received loud and clear.

It only takes a minute before the whole operation is being packed up and Sean is telling him he has to run to make sure he can get it on air.

'Good luck, Mal,' Sean says as he helps him unclip his radio mic. 'I hope she's home safe and sound as soon as possible. I can't imagine the worry.'

'Thanks. And thanks for doing this.'

Sean gives a small smile – one laced with compassion. 'No worries. Besides, I owe Ingrid a favour or two. You're lucky to have her on your side. She's like a dog with a bone when it comes to digging for a good story. Keep the faith.'

Walking back into their home, which is still much too quiet for his liking, Mal tells himself that he has to do exactly what Sean Doyle suggested – he has to keep the faith.

But as darkness starts to set in once again, and he thinks of

Bronagh out there, perhaps reliant on this 'very dangerous man', he feels his faith being very sorely tested indeed.

Still, he decides to do something he hasn't done in a very long time, and he walks through to their small back garden, takes a deep breath and starts to pray.

51

INGRID

I'm pretty sure I have contacts in every county in Ireland. Where I don't have other journalists I know I can call on, I will have a choice between business people, police officers and even the odd hardened criminal.

It took me a couple of years to really learn that. I needed to move on from the sense of moral superiority that tends to come with either youth or old age. Now I exist in a middle ground – as a journalist who is trusted to listen and not judge.

The key to gaining and maintaining a good network of sources is to treat everyone equally and give them a fair hearing. Even those who do not act fairly themselves – like the criminals, the crooked businessmen and the right-wing nutcases. I listen to them all and I allow them to tell their stories. I don't twist what they say, and I don't push them to say things they don't want to. And that tends to mean they remember me, and when I come knocking on their doors again for a wee favour here and there, most of them are amenable to talking to me.

Perhaps I should leave the Guards and the PSNI to it, but

I'm too invested in this story. I'm too determined to make sure that not only does Bronagh Murray get back without a hair harmed on her head, but hopefully the little boy, and the second missing woman – Maria Fulton – do too.

My fear, which I would never voice to Mal but which I am sure the police share, is that Griffen Amin may feel the net closing in on him. And like most rats, when he is forced into a corner, he will likely come out fighting. And men like Griffen Amin don't fight fair. They take everyone in their sights with them. Not a family annihilation case as such – although Oisin is his son – but an annihilation all the same. It wouldn't surprise me if he took them all out before ending his own life too – a cowardly way of dodging justice himself.

Lily Breslin had told me that Ciara lives in fear of hearing that her boy is gone. That her former partner has decided she needs to be punished some more for her disability by stripping her entirely of the one thing she is living for.

I can understand her fear. So there is no way I can simply do nothing and just watch this from the sidelines.

I'm sitting in my car farther up the street from Mal and Bronagh's and scrolling through as many contacts as I can find in the Magherafelt area, desperate to identify someone who might know the couple from their time there, or their little boy. There has to be someone who knows something about Griffen. Who knows if there is somewhere he would go. Someone who would help him. There is always a trail. No one is good enough that they don't leave breadcrumbs and in my experience, there is no one as arrogant as an abusive man – who believes beyond all reasonable doubt that he will never get caught. And if he does, he will lie and manipulate his way out of it – as he has done in the past. I've met far too many of them over the years in both my professional and personal life.

I've made so many calls that I can see my phone battery is dangerously low, so I go to plug it in to charge off the car battery when I notice the charging cable is gone. That's when I remember I put it in my bag the other day by accident and took it into my flat. Of course it's still in that bag and I lifted a different one this morning when I came out.

Maybe, I think, maybe I still have a power bank I could use. I usually keep one in the glovebox and sure enough when I have a look, there is the glorious little lump of plastic. But when I plug in my phone, which is now in 'battery save mode', nothing happens because of course I've not charged it either.

Fuck.

I know it shouldn't be a big deal, but it feels like it is. I don't want to leave this street. I want to sit here and keep calling people and get to the bottom of this. Maybe it's once again my journalistic instinct telling me that time is absolutely of the utmost importance.

I dial another number, get another voicemail response and garble a quick rundown of what I need before hanging up. Maybe if I drive to the Tesco Express they might have a charging lead for sale there. It's only a few minutes away. I can be back making calls asap. Seeing that I have no choice, I put my car into gear and start to make a three-point turn.

My phone buzzes to life once again with an incoming call and I see the name of a community worker from Magherafelt flash up on the screen. He's a fairly sound man, if I ignore the rumours of his rampant criminality and extortion of local businesses. He's not the kind of man you want to get on the wrong side of, but he can be an invaluable resource in matters such as these. The man hears more secrets than a priest in the confessional.

Reversing back into my spot, and hoping he doesn't ring off, I grab the phone and answer.

'How's it going? Did you get my message?'

'I did. Just now. I called straight away.'

'Well, do you know anything that might help here?'

There is a deep intake of breath. 'Yeah. Look, you didn't hear it from me. I want nothing to do with any of this. But I've... I've seen him about. The wee boy too. And yes, he's back up here. Holed up in a house that is falling to pieces round his ears.'

'The house he was renovating with Ciara?' I ask, pen poised to write down whatever details he can share with me.

'No. No – it's one about half a mile over. No one has lived in that place for at least twenty years. Probate dispute or something.'

'Do you have an address?'

'I do, yeah. It's one hund—'

And it's then, of course, that my phone dies.

52

BRONAGH

'Zachary, are you okay?' she says, trying to keep her voice soft so as not to scare him but wanting to scream at him. She wants a reaction. She wants – needs – to know he is still alive.

'Don't fucking worry about him!' Griff roars. 'The wee bastard!'

Bronagh pays no heed to Griff, instead resting her hand on Zachary's torso, desperate to feel the rise and fall of his ribcage. It's there, she thinks, but her hands are shaking so much she might be imagining it.

Tears prick her eyes, and she moves her hand to Zachary's face, brushing back his overlong hair from his cheeks and seeing blood streak his pale skin. His eyes are closed tight. 'Where are you hurt?' she asks, trying to examine him. 'Oh God, we need help. He needs help.' Should she run and look for Christy? Or would that be walking directly towards even more danger? Griff wouldn't be fit to chase her though. There would be a chance, wouldn't there? But she has no idea where Christy is. Her head is spinning.

'Leave him be!' Griff says. 'I need help more than him.' He

has sat down, leaning forward, the knife protruding from his back, on a rickety wooden chair that looks older than Bronagh. He cuts a pathetic figure wincing in pain, colour draining from his face. Blood is pooling on the floor at his feet, spreading in a slow, deep, crimson tide.

He's wrong if he thinks there is any chance she will prioritise him over Zachary. He doesn't deserve her help, or her pity.

Turning her head away from him and back to the boy, Bronagh tries to peel one hand away from his face, but it's clear that not only is Zachary alive, he is absolutely terrified.

'Are you okay?'

With the smallest shake of his head, he mouths the word 'No'.

A tidal wave of relief washes over her that at least, in this moment, this boy is alive and if not well, at least able to speak.

'Where are you hurt?' she repeats.

She can hear the sound of Griff's breathing becoming more and more laboured behind her, expects to feel someone grab, or hit, or pull her away but she has to continue doing what she can, while she can. Zachary doesn't speak, but he lets out the smallest of whimpers and she pulls him to her, to assure him that everything in his messed-up life is going to be fine. He is going to be fine. He clings on tightly.

'I told you! Leave the boy. Get here or so help me—'

'So help you what?' she shouts, tears choking her. She looks at him for a second before her eyes are back scanning Zachary to try and find the source of his bleeding. 'What are you going to do? You're bleeding out! Don't think for one second that I'm going to help you, of all people.'

She gives Zachary a little shake and his eyes open wide and stare at her. This poor boy. So haunted. 'Where are you hurt?' she asks again.

'Have you not worked it out? He's not hurt!' Griff shouts back. '*He* stabbed *me*!'

Zachary doesn't break her gaze, but he gives a small nod and his face crumples. Her own eyes widen in response. 'He was going to hurt you,' she hears the boy say quietly. 'He hurt Mumma and he was going to hurt you.' He curls his body tighter, turning his eyes away from Bronagh and, she realises, shielding himself, expecting a volley of body blows to come his way.

Heartsore, she turns to look at Griff – now a deathly white – and sees that his hand has slipped off the handle of the knife and is hanging by his side. 'You have to help me,' he mutters, his voice all but gone. His fear is taking over. She feels Zachary grip tighter. He doesn't want to let her go. He is trembling so violently. In shock, no doubt. He's just a baby. He shouldn't have to see this. He shouldn't have to endure this.

But she can't ignore the anguish on Griff's face either – even though in this moment she wants to leave him to his fate. It shocks her to realise how much she wants to let him fade away into nothing, or worse still, how much she wants to drive the knife deeper into his body. For her. For Maria. For Zachary too. Or Oisin. The child not even permitted to use his own name.

She leans close to Zachary's ear and whispers to him that everything will be okay, before she turns and stands up. Spotting the drawer where Zachary had retrieved the clean tea towels earlier, she heads for it and lifts what remains from inside before making her way back to Griff.

He is not talking any more and his eyelids are fluttering. There is blood – so much blood – everywhere. She tries to press a towel to the wound, knowing already it is too late for him. It's hard to imagine anyone could lose this amount of blood and survive. Not even with the best doctor in the world by their side. He doesn't even flinch as she presses as hard as she can.

'Maria,' she says. 'Where is she?'

His mouth opens and closes but he does not speak.

'Please,' she says. 'Tell me where she is. I will help you and then I will help her.' She says this, aware it's likely to be too late for both of them. Still, she has to ask. She can't bear to think of walking away from this place not knowing where Maria is. She can't just leave her wherever this animal has dumped her.

His eyes flutter open and he looks directly at her. She can see the mirror image of Zachary's wide, innocent eyes staring back at her and it makes her heart ache. For while he is an animal now, he was a wee boy once who played with cars and planes and wanted to be loved just as Zachary does. People aren't born bad.

But then she feels the pulse of pain still in her neck and head, and remembers what it felt like to be suffocated while his hands squeezed her neck. She thinks of how he refused to help Maria and she does the only thing she can think of to do. She drops the tea towel to the floor and steps away from him, leaving him to endure his last breath alone.

Her focus now is Zachary. It has to be Zachary. She does not even look back.

She does not know where Christy is. She does not know if he is friend or foe. She just knows she has to get away from this house and get help. Lifting the boy to her hip, she walks to the front door, her focus solely on getting out of here.

She knows Griff is gone and she will not shed a single tear for him.

'Come on, baby,' she says to Zachary who is clutching one of his precious toys in his hands. 'Let's go.'

Opening the door, she steps out into the murky evening.

The light is all but gone and in the isolation of this house, wherever it is, there is no further illumination. In a matter of minutes it will be pitch-black here and she will struggle to see the pathway beneath her feet. Yet there is not one part of her that wants to go back inside that house of horrors. She'll just keep walking, even if she has to take it one slow, measured step at a time.

This time there is no one to grab her as she makes her way down the garden path. There is no one at all and no noise. As she walks through the wooden gate out on onto a dirt road, the ground wet and gritty beneath her feet, she thinks that Christy must have hightailed it out of here already. Or at least she hopes he has.

'It's just you and me, Oisin,' she says to the boy in her arms, keeping her voice as light and sing-song as possible. Although he has seen so many horrors, she does not want to frighten the child any more.

She has not gone very far down the dusty road when she hears the catch of an engine turning over and the path in front of her is illuminated by the much too bright headlights of a car.

53

MAL

Mal is finding it hard to breathe. Shelley is rattling through the kitchen drawers looking for a charging cable, while Ingrid is swearing at her phone.

Once again, his kitchen has become the centre of operations as Eve King speaks on the phone, briefing her colleagues that she may have a location for Bronagh Murray and they should be on standby. And yes, it's the Magherafelt area. She's ordering them to get the police helicopter up and start surveillance. And yes, call in backup from Belfast too.

'We need to consider this man as very dangerous,' she is saying. 'He is known to be violent. The child is likely also there so please take precautions. We have intel from An Garda Síochána that this man is not above using the boy as some kind of human shield.'

Mal sits at the table, wondering if he will ever feel able to breathe freely again. He has never felt so scared in his entire life and he simply can't stop worrying about how he will cope if she doesn't come home safely.

Shelley swears as another charging lead doesn't seem to work and he can sense the frustration coming off Ingrid in waves. 'My stupid bloody phone,' she rants. 'Battery life of a... of a... oh I don't know. It has a shite battery life. He was on the phone and he said he'd seen Griffen about – and that's when the bastard dies on me.'

'And he said he was with Bronagh too?' Constable Morrison asks. If Mal's not mistaken, the younger officer is absolutely thrilled with all the excitement that is unfolding. Probably still too wet behind the ears to realise that unless it's on the TV, drama can have real and lasting consequences. Devastating consequences.

'I need air,' Mal gasps, getting up and going back outside into the damp night. It takes all his effort to haul breath into his body and hold it there long enough for his blood to oxygenate. He does not want to hyperventilate or give in to panic.

Just breathe, he thinks. It's what Bronagh would tell him. It's exactly what she would say. What she has said in the past when he has felt as if the world were spinning away from under him. She has held his hand and counted his breaths in and out for him, while telling him she loves him and she believes in him. He tries to conjure her voice in his ears. He wishes that wherever she is, he could tell her how much he loves her. That he believes in her. That he is so sorry for endangering her. That if she will have him, he wants to marry her and spend the rest of his days making sure no one ever hurts her again. He doesn't deserve her love, but he wants it more than anything. He wants *her* more than anything.

He looks up into the night sky. Despite the damp evening and the grey of the cloud clover about him, he can still see stars fighting their way through the mist to be seen. They are still there. He has to believe Bronagh is too. She is still here and she will be back with him soon. There is no other acceptable outcome.

54

BRONAGH

Bronagh freezes for a moment in front of the blinding lights from the car. Zachary raises one arm to cover his eyes while she tries to process what is happening. Christy. It has to be Christy. Not that she plans to wait around to find out. No, she is going to run. She's going to run as fast as her legs can carry her and she doesn't care if she is tired, or if she can't see what is underfoot. She doesn't care if her feet tear and bleed. She doesn't care if she falls – she will simply get back up again and keep going.

She has not come through all of this only to fail at this stage. No way. Not now, and certainly not with Zachary to protect.

'Hold on as tight as you can,' she says. 'And don't let go. It's going to get a little bumpy, okay?'

She feels him nod his head.

'But it's going to be okay. We're going to be okay.'

He nods again and she turns on her heel and starts to run. She knows better than to stick to a straight route. It would be far too easy for a car to follow her down a dirt road. He'd over-take her in seconds and stop in front of her. She has to get off the road as quickly as possible. That means running towards the hedgerow and ignoring the bite of stones and pine cones, twigs and nettles beneath her feet. It means ignoring the tearing of her skin by the branches. She doesn't have time to think about pain now. She doesn't even have time to feel it.

The roar of the engine is in her ears, as well as Zachary's breath and the shudder of his quiet cries. Her heart is thumping, her brain only concentrating on the next step and the safest route. She has no idea where she is. What part of the country she's in. She doesn't know if the field she finds herself in leads to more road, or more fields. If the man in the car knows the patchwork of fertile land like the back of his hand.

She could be running towards a river, or a clifftop for all she knows. But she has no choice; she has to keep moving and hope that she meets someone who can help. That she finds a house, or a village, or a passing car. And if she can't find any of those, that she finds a suitable hiding spot where she and Zachary will be safe until morning. She will use her body to keep him warm. With her lungs burning as she runs, she thinks that she let Maria down and there is no way she would forgive herself if she let Zachary down too. His mother – his real mother – must be worried for him somewhere. Bronagh knows Ciara was badly hurt in the accident, that she suffered a traumatic brain injury, but it's not severe enough that she wouldn't know her child is missing and that must be the hardest pain of all to carry.

Her legs aching, desperate for her to stop and rest, and her arms heavy from carrying Zachary, she wants to fall to the ground but she can't give up. She has to keep going.

As she runs, the enormity of what has happened – what she has been through – hits her in waves and she desperately tries to push down the sobs that threaten to overcome her.

In the quiet of the night she swears she can hear someone call her name. A man's voice. The sweep of a torch in the hedgerow opposite her instils a whole new level of panic, as does the sound of a helicopter overhead, casting its own light from above.

Exhausted and not knowing what is help and what is a trap, she feels her fight start to dim and slide away and she falls to her knees, unable to take another step.

She has done what she can. Her body can't keep going. She is worn out. All she is able to do now is hold Zachary to her chest and rock him gently, providing a little comfort. She's aware of a person approaching, of the beam of a torch moving ever closer.

'Bronagh,' a voice says, and a torch shines directly on her. 'It's okay. It's okay.'

She looks up, hoping against the bitter experience of the last few days to see a friendly face – a police officer – only to see Christy staring down at her, and she visibly shudders.

'Don't hurt him. He's only a baby really. He didn't mean it. He was scared. He didn't mean it.' She knows she is rambling now, falling over her words, but she cannot stand the thought of what will become of this child. He has already been hurt so much.

'I'm not going to harm you,' he says. 'Or the boy.'

She doesn't know whether or not to believe him. She is afraid if she does – if she trusts him – he will only cause her more pain. That this nightmare will continue. That it will get worse. She shudders, pulling herself away from him.

'See that helicopter?' he says, pointing upwards. 'I'd put money on that being the cops. They are on their way to get you and the boy. People have been looking for you. I don't know what that sick bastard was at, but no one deserves whatever the hell it was he was doing.'

He waves his flashlight in the air, desperate to grab the attention of the police above. The sound of police sirens in the background tell her help – proper help – is on its way but she's not sure whether or not she can believe in it.

She can't speak. It's as if she has forgotten how. She just rocks back and forth, holding Zachary to her, worrying about him and what will become of him. He was just a child who has seen too much but who, even at his tender age, had more courage than the man currently trying to protect her, or the police circling overhead.

He has more courage than she has, she thinks as her body begins to shake. It's her turn for the shock to land, to take hold of her muscles and her bones. Shaking so violently she is afraid she might hurt Zachary, she tries to still her breathing while Christy takes off his jacket and wraps it around her shoulders.

'I'm so sorry,' he says. 'I'm so, so sorry. You're safe now though. I didn't know what he was at. I didn't know how bad it was for Maria. I'd have done something before. I swear,' he says as he steps back and she sees paramedics and police running across the field towards them. 'You're safe now.'

EPILOGUE

Bronagh and Mal sit together on their sofa in their living room on Springbrooke Avenue. Mal fixes a blanket across Bronagh's knees and she tells him off for fussing, but it's a gentle telling-off. One born of love and sheer delight that she is being pampered. Mal has barely let her out of his sight since she came home from hospital after being assessed for her injuries. Yes, she was dehydrated, but apart from that she has gotten away with a smattering of bruises and lacerations. Some are pretty hardcore, but none, thankfully, are life-threatening. 'Still,' she says and smiles, 'I won't be taking any selfies soon.'

Ingrid Devlin, who is sitting opposite the couple, smiles back. 'Arnica,' she says. 'Take some arnica. It will help with the bruising.'

'Already on it,' Mal says, pointing to the small tube of cream among the lotions, potions and pills on the side table.

'Great,' Ingrid says. 'So, I suppose... Why don't you tell me what happened, in your own words...'

Bronagh glances to Mal, acutely aware that this is his story too, and he nods. She takes a deep breath, closes her eyes and starts to recount the madness of those few days from the moment she had found Zachary on her doorstep.

'He was only a child and he was so very distressed. He looked terrified, the poor pet. I couldn't have left him there, or ignored him. I think I just did what every decent person would do.'

Bronagh wells up every time she thinks of the boy and what he has seen and endured. Now once again going by his birth name of Oisin, he has been returned to the care of his granny and grandad Breslin – and is rebuilding a relationship with Ciara who is making progress with her own rehabilitation.

He has a very long road ahead of him – a lot of therapy to help him come to terms with what he's been through, but also what he did to protect her and himself in the end. She hopes he is surrounded with as much love as he deserves, and has enough toy cars, and planes and trains to keep him happy for hours.

As much as she would like to see him again, when she is feeling stronger, she totally understands that doing so might re-traumatise him. And he deserves to find what remnants of childhood he can without reminders of their horrific shared experiences. It would be selfish of her to push to maintain some kind of relationship with him but she thinks she will probably send cards. Maybe gifts on his birthday and Christmas. She doesn't have to sign them. She'd just like to know he has good things in his life. He deserves the same good things that other children have. He deserves to have the same carefree childhood that Shelley's twins enjoy. Of course, Bronagh knows that what he has experienced will always haunt him on some level, but he is young enough, she hopes, to have enough good experiences to overcome the bad.

At least he has a chance at recovery. The same can't be said for Maria. Just as Bronagh had feared, she had succumbed to her injuries. When police had raided the house she had been held in, they had found Maria's body in an outbuilding. He hadn't even had the decency to cover her up. Maria had been missing from her home in Emyvale for just over a month. She was only twenty-eight. A shy girl who kept herself to herself. It seems that Griff had taken a shine to her as he watched her interact with Oisin in the playground. He had simply decided to take what he thought he deserved to own, but perhaps, as he had told Christy, she was just too much trouble. Too mouthy. Bronagh would've loved to have known her in her mouthier days before she had been beaten and starved into submission. She doesn't know if Griff was telling the truth when he said Bronagh was taken to be her replacement, and that all along Maria had been plotting her own escape – at Bronagh's expense. Right now, it doesn't actually seem to matter. This was not a normal situation. Maria can't be judged for having the desperate need to escape.

It's also impossible to know if it was always Griff's plan to keep a mother figure for Oisin. Or if he was just a sadist. She suspects both might be true. To men like Griffen Amin, people were mere trinkets to collect, pieces to move on a chessboard.

Bronagh hopes, desperately, that she will be able to get a good night's sleep soon where she doesn't wake terrified that she will find him standing over her.

'I'm really glad you're back home,' Ingrid tells her as they finish the interview.

'You and me both,' Bronagh says with a smile. 'And I know you played a significant role in that. I don't know how to thank you.'

'There's no need,' Ingrid says, shaking her head. 'Some stories just hit a little harder.'

'I don't know what I would've done if I'd not bumped into you outside the police station that morning,' Mal says. 'The fates must've aligned or something.'

'Kismet,' Ingrid says, packing up her belongings.

'You never did say why you were there?' Mal said.

'Meeting with David Bradley. To discuss the PSNI's approach to tackling violence against women as it happens.' She smiles.

'Definitely kismet then,' Bronagh says, her lower lip trembling. She can't bear to think what could have happened had things been different.

'So, this Christy fella,' Mal asks. 'What is his part?'

'He's like Teflon,' Ingrid says. 'Nothing sticks to him and he actually didn't do anything wrong bar knowing the wrong people. I've spoken to him a few times over the years, you know. He's a bit of a Jack the Lad – always up to something, but I really don't think he knew what Griff was at. I don't think he would have called me to tell me where you were if he had been deeply involved.'

Bronagh keeps it to herself that he had admitted to fencing stolen goods and shifting drugs. She has no desire to get him into any kind of trouble. He might not be squeaky clean, and he might have run out rather than help her and Zachary as Griff turned violent, but he did get help.

Tiredness threatens to overwhelm her, and she knows she needs to rest. She and Mal have rescheduled their holiday for a fortnight's time. They will have something to celebrate when they are away. He popped the big question as he had hugged her to him in the hospital, determined he never wanted to leave her again. It was such a stark contrast to the night of the accident when she had told him he had one last chance to clean up his act.

The sparkler on her left hand reminds her that better days are coming.

'You two look after each other,' Ingrid says as she stands up. 'And I'll keep you posted about the article and my documentary pitch. You are both still okay to come on board?'

They nod. 'Least we can do,' Mal says as he sees her to the door.

'I'm going to keep pressure on the police as well,' she says. 'About the call. That's not going to go away for them.' Mal nods in gratitude and offers her a quick hug. It feels like the right thing to do.

They say their goodbyes, but as Ingrid walks down the path to her car she hears a voice calling out. 'Excuse me! Hello! Excuse me!'

She looks around to see Mrs Cosgrove, now walking with a colourful cane to help her bad hip, hobbling down the neighbouring path. 'You're the journalist, aren't you?' she asks.

Ingrid nods.

'Well if you need any more stories about these two, I'm your woman. I see everything that goes on here,' Mrs Cosgrove says, looking absolutely delighted with herself.

MORE FROM CLAIRE ALLAN

The next pulse-pounding psychological thriller from Claire Allan, is available to order now here:

https://mybook.to/NewClaireAllanBackAd

ACKNOWLEDGEMENTS

I have promised myself I will not overshare in these acknowledgements so I will keep this short and sweet to protect the guilty!

Thanks to Rachel Faulkner-Willcocks, an editor with incredible insight, endless patience and a good dollop of empathy.

And to all the team at Boldwood Books especially, but not exclusively, Jenna, Megan, Ben, Nia and the tour de force that is Amanda Ridout.

Thanks to Helena Newton for impressive copyediting skills. I will never use the word 'now' again! And to Christina de Caix-Curtis for bravery in the face of several hundred 'justs'.

To my agent, Ger Nichol, who has represented me and my scribblings for almost twenty years and who has never waivered in her support, encouragement and generosity.

To my family – and most especially to my amazing children who are the reason I get up every morning and the reason I never sleep soundly at night. I have never been more proud of you than I have been in this past year.

To my parents, my siblings, my in-laws and my nieces and nephews – words cannot express my gratitude and love for your support.

To my friends – just thank you. Especially Fionnuala, Fiona, Vicki, Julie-Anne, Marie-Louise, Lesley, Amanda, Emma

Heatherington, and the Journal girls. You know why your friendship means more to me than ever.

To the booksellers and the book readers – thank you. To Libraries NI and the members of book clubs everywhere, but especially the Bridge Books Book Club for constant warm welcomes and great questions.

And finally to everyone in the world who does their best to remind us that at its heart, this is still a good place to be.

ABOUT THE AUTHOR

Claire Allan is the internationally bestselling author of several psychological thrillers, including *Her Name Was Rose*. Boldwood publish her women's fiction under the name Freya Kennedy and will continue to publish her thrillers.

Download your exclusive bonus content from Claire Allan here:

Visit Claire's website: www.claireallan.com

Follow Claire on social media:

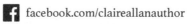

facebook.com/claireallanauthor

x.com/claireallan

instagram.com/claireallan_author

bookbub.com/authors/claire-allan

ALSO BY CLAIRE ALLAN

THE *Murder* LIST

THE MURDER LIST IS A NEWSLETTER DEDICATED TO SPINE-CHILLING FICTION AND GRIPPING PAGE-TURNERS!

SIGN UP TO MAKE SURE YOU'RE ON OUR HIT LIST FOR EXCLUSIVE DEALS, AUTHOR CONTENT, AND COMPETITIONS.

SIGN UP TO OUR NEWSLETTER

BIT.LY/THEMURDERLISTNEWS

Boldwood

Boldwood Books is an award-winning fiction publishing company seeking out the best stories from around the world.

Find out more at www.boldwoodbooks.com

Join our reader community for brilliant books, competitions and offers!

Follow us
@BoldwoodBooks
@TheBoldBookClub

Sign up to our weekly deals newsletter

https://bit.ly/BoldwoodBNewsletter